KILLER SMILE

—

Marilyn Pappano

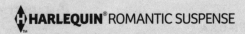

HARLEQUIN® ROMANTIC SUSPENSE

Recycling programs
for this product may
not exist in your area.

ISBN-13: 978-1-335-45664-9

Killer Smile

Copyright © 2018 by Marilyn Pappano

Oklahoma, dogs, beaches, books, family and friends: these are a few of **Marilyn Pappano**'s favorite things. She lives in imaginary worlds where she reigns supreme (at least, she does when the characters cooperate) and no matter how wrong things go, she can always set them right. It's her husband's job to keep her grounded in the real world, which makes him her very favorite thing.

Books by Marilyn Pappano

Harlequin Romantic Suspense

Killer Smile
Killer Secrets
Detective Defender
Nights with a Thief
Bayou Hero
Undercover in Copper Lake
Copper Lake Encounter
Copper Lake Confidential
Christmas Confidential
"Holiday Protector"
In the Enemy's Arms
Copper Lake Secrets

Visit the Author Profile page at Harlequin.com for more titles.

W

"There was a prowler at my house last night, Tash," Daniel said quietly.

"Also, we have a witness who says he's seen a guy watching you."

Natasha's muscles froze, leaving her unable to breathe or process his words. She didn't feel the trembling in her hands until she saw rings spreading across the surface of her coffee. Daniel's right hand took her left, and she reflexively grasped it, squeezing tightly, focusing all her energy on maintaining contact with the one person who'd always, always made her feel safe.

"You went out there by yourself? Knowing that RememberMe wants to—" She finished with a gesture of her left hand, unable to put it into words. The mere thought of the danger she'd brought into Daniel's life could break her heart and her spirit.

"I wasn't alone. I had my weapon." He laid his free hand on the pistol snugged on his belt. "You know I never leave home without it."

The small smile that touched his mouth was reassuring, but Natasha couldn't stop the ominous words in her head. Her stalker was here in Cedar Creek, and he knew where Daniel lived, and he wanted him dead...

* * *

Dear Reader,

I read somewhere that the song "Every Breath You Take" by The Police is widely considered by women to be one of the great love songs. In fact, quite a few of my female friends agree. While I like the song, I also think it's very, very creepy. The composer himself, Sting, called it "sinister" and says it's about "surveillance and control" in an interview with *The Independent* in 1993.

Just goes to show how different perceptions can be.

A woman meets a man in a social situation. She smiles and says, "Nice to meet you." He hears, "I've waited all my life for you."

She shakes his hand. He feels the promise of forever.

She pleads, "Leave me alone." He understands, "Please don't ever leave me alone."

Perceptions.

It had been a while since I'd done a stalker story, and I've always wanted to write my own runaway bride, too. I already knew Detective Daniel Harper, from *Killer Secrets*, was going to be the hero, so I added one commitmentphobic heroine (Daniel was third on Natasha's list of jilted fiancés) and one freaky psychopath and set them on a course that would alter, threaten or even end their lives. And I had a lovely time doing it.

I hope you have a lovely time reading it.

Marilyn Pappano

Chapter 1

When Daniel Harper was a kid, he had decided on two career options for the future: he would become the President of the United States, and in his first term, with his great wisdom, foresight and people-pleasing skills, he would solve the country's problems once and forevermore.

Or he would become a doctor—not the medical kind; he had an aversion to sick people and preferred to avoid their spores when at all possible—and by the time he was thirty, he would discover a little known gene that, with slight manipulation, would cure all of humanity's ills.

Instead, he became a cop.

In Cedar Creek, Oklahoma, with a population of twenty-five thousand—comprised of farmers, ranchers, cattle people and horse people; country folk and city folk; sports fans, foodies and good ol' boys; stubborn men, stubborner women and pretty young things; cowboys, Indians, oil people and church people; winemakers, meth makers and troublemakers.

And beset by the most diverse weather he'd ever experienced, everything from drought to flood to blistering heat and subzero freezes, windstorms, hailstorms, ice storms, tornados and, lately, earthquakes that made his home state of California look like a slacker.

Life in Los Angeles hadn't prepared him for this.

A snort ahead of him drew his attention to his fellow detective, Ben Little Bear, standing on the first of the six broad steps that led into the Cedar Creek Police Department. "You gonna stand there and soak up a little more water? Isn't stepping in the puddle enough for one day?"

Daniel scowled at Ben, then at the water that had collected in the low spot in front of the steps from the downpour that didn't appear to plan on stopping anytime soon. He knew the low spot was there. Knew it filled with water with the lightest sprinkle. Knew because he'd worked there five years, and because he'd stepped in it on the way out two hours ago. The water had finally drained from his shoes and his feet had stopped squelching with every step, and now…

Still scowling, he climbed the first step, shook the excess water from his shoes and his trouser legs, pulled his raincoat closer and swore mildly. His father cussed like the proverbial sailor and had made him cringe more than a few times as an impressionable kid. Now, at thirty-one, he rarely said anything harsher than *damn* himself.

This rain deserved more than a *damn*.

Finished shaking, he trotted up the remaining steps and followed Ben inside the station. It had been a post office back in the day and was as stately a building as any he'd ever been inside. The floor was marble, and so were the panels that went four feet up the walls. Here in the lobby, the ceiling was fourteen feet high, with the original chandelier still in operation. Sound echoed out here, but as soon as he walked behind the tall counter and into the station proper, with its lower ceilings and ugly industrial rugs, the echoes faded.

A row of brass hooks mounted on a gleaming oak plank hung on the wall just inside the doorway. He hung his soppy coat there and picked up the towel he'd left earlier, making half an attempt to dry his face and hair.

"Dan'l, you had a visitor," Cheryl called from her desk. She was the chief's secretary, but she pretty much handled the entire office. Though taking messages and making notes on comings and goings wasn't technically her job, what was the use of working for the police chief, she declared, if she didn't get to poke her nose into everyone's business?

"Daniel," he muttered under his breath.

She looked over her glasses at him. "I thought you'd given up trying to correct me years ago."

He had. The best way to deal with annoying people, his dad had taught him, was to ignore them. Once they saw that their actions were no longer annoying, they stopped.

The best way to deal with annoying people, his father had disagreed, was to knock the crap out of them every time they annoyed you. Eventually they learned to leave you alone.

Both of his fathers were right. Ignoring people worked fine sometimes. Body-slamming them to the ground was sometimes the better option. But Cheryl was on their side, more or less, and Chief Douglas wouldn't take kindly to Daniel body-slamming her.

"Who was it?" he asked, hanging the towel back on its hook so it could dry.

"She didn't say."

Hmm. He knew an awful lot of *she*s, though most of them wouldn't just drop in on him at work. "What did she want?"

"She didn't say." Cheryl slurped the last of her coffee from a giant mug that proclaimed her Queen of the World, and then wheeled her chair off the mat behind her desk and across the floor to what she called the beverage center. It was only fifteen feet. She could have walked with less effort.

"Was it about a case?"

"She didn't say."

He ground his teeth as he watched her fix her coffee. Wishing that someone else, even one of the inmates in the jail in the back, had talked to this visitor, he gritted out, "What did she look like?"

"She didn't— Oh. She was pretty if you like size twos who look like they just strolled in off the beach, and what man doesn't? I'm pretty sure she was wearing tinted contacts because I don't believe anyone has eyes that shade naturally. Oh, and she was wearing the cutest dress, sleeveless, scooped neck, with a fitted bodice and a drop waist with a little pleating that gave it really nice movement when she walked. And her shoes! OMG."

Bewilderment joined Daniel's annoyance. All this

talking, and had she actually said anything? He didn't know what size two meant in women's clothing. Small, he presumed. He would also presume the unnatural eye color was blue, green or some shade of purple. But scooped neck? Fitted bodice? Drop waist?

"So, she was a small woman in a cute dress?"

Cheryl scowled at him. "Isn't that what I just said?"

From his desk in the back, Ben snorted again. Daniel was glad he provided entertainment for the guy. That could be his new purpose in life. Or he could just go ahead and strangle Cheryl like he'd wanted to since fifteen minutes after meeting her. He would even write up the inventory of his own personal possessions, take his own fingerprints and lock himself in the holding cell. No jury who'd ever met Cheryl would find him guilty.

"Next time someone comes in, get a name, would you?" he groused, heading past her desk to his own in the back.

"I asked, but—"

Everyone else in the room—three detectives, five uniformed officers preparing for shift change and two dispatchers in their alcove to the left—all chimed in together, "She didn't say."

Sometimes he hated this place.

No one in the department had a private office besides the chief and the assistant chief, who was out of town for training. The detectives had desks clustered in the rear of the large room and conducted interviews in the conference room off to the right. Normally, he was okay with that, but there were days when a person needed a little privacy and right now, as he kicked off his wet shoes and peeled away his dripping socks, was one of those times.

"She makes LA look better every day," Ben said from his desk a few feet away.

"I thought you'd never been to LA."

"I haven't, but I don't need to see it to know it beats working with Cheryl."

Wringing first one sock, then the other, over the trash can, Daniel scowled at him. "She *likes* you."

"No, she just has more fun with you."

Ben turned back to his computer, where he was making one of his infamous lists. He had one for everything, probably even sex, and reviewed them regularly. It was the way he worked. Daniel preferred keeping information in his head and staring into space while letting his subconscious brain piece it together. It was the way *he* worked.

Though in his lifetime there had been no shortage of people pointing out that his way looked an awful lot like daydreaming. He didn't care. He produced results. That was what mattered.

Footsteps echoed in the lobby, but he didn't turn to look at the newcomer. They had a desk sergeant for that—and, of course, Cheryl. Plus Morwenna, one of the dispatchers, was nearly as nosy as the secretary, just in a much more pleasant manner.

Ben's chair creaked as he swiveled to face Daniel. "Do you want to interview the suspect or the victim in the morning?"

"Victim." It was an easy choice. Ben was more comfortable with suspects, and he'd handled far more domestic assault cases. Daniel had too much experience with bullies and related far better to the victims. It was odd that empathy was one of his better traits as a detective when most people thought he came down on the lacking side of the emotional scale.

"Deal. So...you don't know any pretty size-two blondes with a fondness for black dresses with fitted bodices?"

"What do you know about fitted bodices?" Then Daniel stopped typing mid-word, and he looked up at Ben. "Cheryl didn't say the dress was black."

"That's some good detecting there, son." Ben nodded toward the front counter.

As Daniel slowly swiveled his chair, he realized the room had gone quiet and everyone was waiting expectantly, their gazes shifting from him to the counter and back again. When his own gaze got there, he saw why. There was the blonde, tall, pretty, not small—just a couple inches shorter than him—but slim and curvy and definitely looking like a California beach girl. Her hair was super short—last time he'd seen her, it was long enough to wrap his hands in—and to anyone who didn't know her, she looked like a ray of sunshine on a dreary day.

But he knew her.

He'd been engaged to marry her.

Until she'd dumped him in front of every single friend and relative they'd had.

What in hell was she doing here?

Natasha Spencer would bet there wasn't a person in the room who had any idea how much it was killing her to stand there and let them—let Daniel—stare at her. She used to have a lot of nerve—more then than now. Back then, she would have dared them to look their longest and hardest. She even would have done a few model-on-the-runway turns so they could form their impressions, back and front. Now she just stood, half a smile frozen on her face, and wished for a sudden case of amnesia. People always stared, but if she didn't know why, she couldn't care.

She'd hoped Daniel would come to the counter, maybe walk off to a distant corner or even outside with her. There was an overhang out there that provided protection from the rain. But he showed no inclination to even rise from his chair. He was leaving it to her.

She took a few more steps, until the counter blocked her way, and tried for a better smile. "Hello, Daniel. I was wondering if we could talk."

Her words echoed off the high ceiling, followed immediately by the swivel of eight or ten heads to look at him. His silence was going to be even more booming and echoey, the kind they could get lost in and never find their way out of, and the hell of it was, he was entitled.

"We could always talk. Our problem was communicating."

Funny. The words were in what she considered his usual tone of voice: even, cool, rational, calm. Growing up the way she did, she'd always loved even, cool, rational and calm. It had soothed her every time he'd said something as benign as, *Do you want seafood or Thai for dinner?*

But there was an edge to his voice that she'd heard so seldom she rarely remembered it, a sharp edge that passed for angry in his cool, calm world. It made her gut tighten. She lived with guilt all the time, and she hated it. Almost as much as she hated coming here.

She couldn't think of anything to say to that, especially nothing she wanted to say in front of his co-workers. She didn't turn and slink out, though. Unless he'd changed tremendously in the past few years, he wouldn't shut her out. He was too courteous to leave any conversation hanging like that and too curious to leave this one hanging. No matter what he felt, there was one question he would have to ask: *Why the hell are you here?*

Yeah, this was a curse-inducing moment if he'd ever had one.

Water was pooling around her shoes, and the air-conditioning gave her chills where her dress was damp from blowing rain. She'd left an umbrella next to the door, but it hadn't proven much help when the wind brought the rain in sideways. She thought longingly of returning to the room she'd rented, taking a warm bath, having a bottle or two of wine and coming up with a new plan, because apparently this one wasn't working.

Then, with a heavy sigh, Daniel stood and walked toward the counter. His feet were bare, she realized, cute with his dark gray suit, white dress shirt and black tie. He looked more approachable barefooted...though that was just fantasy. Sometimes he was an easy man for mushiness and sentimentality. Other times, he was logic and pragmatism personified.

He stopped with ten feet still between them. "What?"

She caught a whiff of the cologne he'd worn since he was sixteen, when he'd filched a bottle from his dad's bathroom. She never remembered the name, but she knew the bottle. She'd bought it often enough for him in their time together.

"Archer and Jeffrey send their love."

His only response was a twitch in his jaw. He must have already figured out she'd located him with his fathers' help. It wasn't as if he and she still had any friends in common. With another man, she might have pleaded for him to not be angry with Archer and Jeffrey, but Daniel's relationship with them was such that he would never blame them for giving him up to her.

No, he would save his blame for her.

"There's a diner across the street from the courthouse. Could we go there for a cup of coffee?"

He glanced over his shoulder, but she couldn't tell what he was looking at: his desk, the clock on the wall back there or the big dark-haired detective whose desk was nearest his. Asking for permission to go or an excuse not to?

After a moment, he said an ungracious, "All right," and started to come around the counter. Halfway he turned back, went to his desk, pulled a pair of running shoes with socks stuffed inside from a drawer and tugged them both on. Running shoes with a suit. She would definitely have to tell Jeffrey about that.

Finally he met her in the lobby, shrugging into his raincoat, while she picked up her umbrella. She waited until she was outside, beneath that little overhang, to shake the water away and then open it. Without speaking, she offered to share it with him. Without speaking, he moved far enough away to make his answer clear.

She supposed the space between the police station and the courthouse qualified as a town square. A gazebo stood in pride of place, a grassy area around it, and a parking lot on the east side. She'd never heard of Cedar Creek until Archer had told her the name, and she hadn't seen nearly enough, but it seemed a sweet town, with an old, well-preserved downtown, lots of stone and brick, a lovely mix of commercial and residential spreading about a mile along First Street.

Natasha couldn't think of anything she wanted to say that he might want to hear, so she grabbed the anxious, antsy Tasha in her brain around the throat and kept her quiet. Soon enough, she would have to talk, and she wouldn't get a sympathetic reception, and it was going to be hard enough without Tasha running her mouth.

Her legs were wet when they reached Judge Judie's Diner. The woman who owned the hotel down the street had referred her there for lunch, and the coffee had been unusually good.

She and Daniel reached for the door at the same time. He backed off before their hands touched. She'd forgotten he liked doing little courtesies like that. She pulled the door open, closed her umbrella and set it in a galvanized bucket for that purpose just inside.

"Sit wherever you like, hon." The waitress gave Daniel a warmer smile. "Good afternoon, Detective Harper."

She chose the last booth along the wall and started to slide onto the back bench. Daniel shucked his coat, draped it over a chair at the next table and shooed her to the opposite side, so he faced the waitress, though she doubted that was his sole intent. These days she was more comfortable sitting where she could see the door and who came through it. According to popular legend, so were most police officers.

The flirty waitress came. Natasha ordered coffee. Daniel asked for pop and a piece of pecan pie. When the woman was back behind the counter, he folded his hands together in his lap and said, "Well?"

Something sad settled in her stomach. She'd thought he might give her a break. Five years had passed. He'd moved on, moved up. He'd had other relationships. He'd probably even fallen in love again. She'd thought, for old times' sake, he might bury the hatchet, and not in her.

"How are you?" she asked hopefully.

Irritation flared in his dark eyes. "You want chit-chat? I'm fine. I like Cedar Creek. I like my job. I like it so much that I suggested my fathers consider moving here when they retire. How are you? Why are you here? Just making rounds of the people-I've-screwed-over club? Are you going in order? Kyle, Eric, then me? Did I miss anyone?"

Heat warmed her face. The fact that it was well deserved didn't make it any less embarrassing. And he did miss one. It was Kyle, Eric, Daniel and Zach. Opera had its Four Tenors, her mother teased, while Natasha had her Four Fiancés. Her older sister referred to Daniel as *Runaway Bride, Third Edition*.

The waitress returned, giving them curious looks as she set down drinks and a dish of pie that looked incredible. "Can I get you anything else, Daniel?"

He turned his attention to the waitress, and a sort of smile twitched into place. "No, thank you, Taryn." The smile disappeared as soon as she walked away. He took a bite of pie and washed it down before scowling at Natasha. "Look, I have a body found in a burned-out car, an attempted murder where the victim's still touch-and-go and a woman to interview in the morning whose husband just broke her jaw for the second time in two years, plus her arm and her shoulder and her eye socket and might have done enough damage to leave her blind, to say nothing about the rest of the cases piled on my desk, *and* it's the second Thursday of the month. First responders' league at the bowling alley, and the chief gets annoyed when his detectives don't show up. Just say what you want to say, Natasha, then do your disappearing act again. Preferably for good this time."

This had been a stupid idea. There were a dozen different better ways to do what she needed, ways that didn't involve laying eyes on Daniel or having to feel his bitterness and know she was wholly responsible for it. She dug ten dollars from her purse, laid it on the table and slid to her feet. "I'm sorry. I'll find another way."

He didn't try to stop her. He didn't even watch her walk all the way to the door; she felt the instant his attention shifted elsewhere. When she stepped outside and turned to the right, toward her hotel down the block, she glanced back at the last possible second and saw Taryn sliding into the seat she'd vacated.

Though she had no right to care, somewhere deep inside, it hurt.

By the time Daniel returned to the station, the shift change was over and Cheryl had gone home. Thank God for small miracles. He was surprised she hadn't hung around to ask questions about Natasha—important ones like, *Where did she get that cute dress?* and *OMG, don't you love those shoes?* A person would think, working in a police station, Cheryl understood the concept of

You have the right to remain silent, but it didn't register with her.

He'd slid into his chair and started shutting down his laptop when Morwenna popped out of the dispatcher's shack and zeroed in on him. She was a few years younger than him, had come to Oklahoma from a small village in Cornwall long enough ago that her British accent was hit or miss, and she had a rather unique fashion sense. She was the least annoying person in the office besides Ben and the chief, and she and Daniel had actually considered going out on a few occasions before deciding neither appealed to the other in the right way.

She nudged one of his shoes before perching on the edge of his desk. "That's some fashion statement you're making, Detective."

"Don't tell my dad. He'd be mortified." When Natasha had seen his running shoes, she'd looked like telling Jeffrey was exactly what she had in mind. Of course, Jeffrey's mortification would be feigned. It was the reaction people expected from a man in his business.

"Eh, my mum's mortified all the time by my clothes. She says I'm trying to embarrass her into an early grave."

"Yeah, didn't I see your mum out on her twelve-mile run this morning in the rain? She didn't look like she might drop dead anytime soon."

"Not unless it's from exhaustion. She says she can't skip her training just because of the weather. She's got an ultramarathon coming up next month."

"I don't even know what that is."

"Something extreme and excessive." Morwenna stretched out one leg, flexing her muscles inside the pink tights, and sighed. "Do you know what's it like when your mum has a better body than you do?"

Daniel frowned at her. "Remember Jeffrey? Been a model since before I was born?" A few of the people he worked with knew his fathers were gay, but only Morwenna knew much about them. She liked things that made people different. People who weren't different, she sighed, were so much the same.

"Ooh, yes, I forgot. I saw that last ad he did for Migliora cologne. Whew. If I didn't know… Yeah, I can see how you'd feel second-best compared to him."

"I didn't say I felt second-best," Daniel protested. "He's…"

"Something to aspire to." She slid to her feet and started back across the room.

"Hey. I thought you were going to ask about…"

"Natasha? I'll get to it, all in good time."

"How do you know— I never told you her name."

She smiled smugly. "That's some good detecting there, Daniel. Bet a clue never gets past you, does it?"

Daniel scowled at her until she was out of sight, then began packing up his desk. If somebody offered him a nickel, he'd go home and to bed. But like he'd told Natasha, the chief didn't like it when they skipped bowling night. With all his refined tastes, why couldn't Jeffrey have insisted on teaching him to play polo or ride dressage or something like that?

He made it out of the station without talking to anyone else, slogged his way through puddles and streams and reached the car with his feet soaked again.

It was only a few blocks to the duplex he rented in one of Cedar Creek's older neighborhoods. It was a nice house, built of deep-red brick and topped with green-clay roof tiles. The place had been built with a main entrance on the street it faced and a servants' entrance on the street that sided its corner lot. Fifty-some years ago, the owner, with two spinster daughters, had made the servants' entrance identical to the main one and divvied up the interior into two halves of a whole.

Sad to think all that exacting work was easier than finding husbands for the daughters.

He didn't have to be at Thunder Lanes Bowling Alley until 6:30 p.m., so he showered, then sprawled on the couch to watch the news before heading out. When his cell phone signaled a text, he frowned. His parents had told Natasha where to find him. Had they also given her his cell phone number?

It wasn't her. That was relief he was feeling. He was pretty sure, even if it felt kind of strange. It was Jeffrey.

Are you still speaking to us?

Of course.

Did you speak to her?

No more than I had to.

I hope you weren't rude. Even if she deserved it.

Daniel scrubbed his face. Sometimes he had trouble telling the difference between plain speaking and rudeness. He'd often been accused of the latter when he simply wasn't mincing words. Had he been rude to Natasha? Yeah, the people-you've-screwed-over bit had probably crossed the line. He certainly could have phrased it better.

Though he also could have phrased it the way Archer would have, with a few alphabets' worth of f-words.

I might have been. A little.

Your father said we should ask you first, but it seemed really important to her.

Daniel responded with one of the lessons Archer had taught him that Jeffrey had always tried to unteach: *it's easier to apologize later than to ask permission first.*
His dad prefaced his answer with a frowny face.

Are you okay?

He considered it. Yeah, he was feeling a little cranky, but he was always cranky. He leaned toward the serious-dour-cynical side on the best of days, and this day had already gone down the toilet before Natasha showed up.

I'm good. I get to go bowl tonight.

Hope you get nothing but strikes. Love you.

Daniel typed the same, then tossed the phone aside. What excuse had Natasha given Jeffrey and Archer to get his whereabouts from them? What could possibly be important about talking to him now, five years after she returned his engagement ring via her sister? The time for saying, *Gee, Daniel, I'm having some doubts*, was long past.

Or, *Sorry I broke your heart.*

Even, *Sorry I didn't have the nerve to humiliate you in person.*

Funny that she'd come all this way to talk and, after they left the police station, she'd said a total of nine words to him. *How are you? I'm sorry. I'll find another way.*

To do what? Clear her conscience? If she felt guilty about the way she'd ended their relationship, that was fine, but he had no absolution to offer. It was over and done with. He'd even learned something in the process: to not believe for a second that he could be the one to change her. She'd told him on their second date that she'd run out on two previous fiancés, but he'd been stupid enough to think this time would be different. *He* would be different. He would be the one who made her want to stay.

Over and done with.

He'd believed that for a long time, since he'd reached the point where he went entire weeks without thinking about her. Missing her. Wondering what he hadn't given that made it so easy for her to leave. He'd believed it when he finally started dating again, when he'd thought he was falling in love again. It hadn't happened—the falling in love—but he liked to think it would have if they had been at different stages in their lives.

But if it was over and done with, why was he so darn irate?

The Prairie Sun Hotel, located a few doors from Judge Judie's, was a three-story building with a sand-

stone facade and leaded-glass double doors leading
into the lobby. It had begun life as a mercantile, later
became a JCPenney, then an indoor antiques mall and
now was a boutique hotel. It had been an easy choice
for Natasha after seeing the cookie-cutter motels on
the highways leading to Tulsa. Parking in the tiny lot
out back was the only downside, but she could live
with that.

She could live with it easier if she wasn't convinced
both she and her car were going to sprout mushrooms
if the rain didn't stop soon.

Her room was on the second floor at the front and
had wood floors and tall ceilings and a claw-foot tub
in the bath. Instead of a closet, there was a scarred
oak armoire, standing across from the vintage tubular
steel bed. It was all so lovely that the only thing she
would even think of changing was the line of small
iron birds that danced along the top bar of both the
headboard and the footboard. Not only were they just
too much, as Jeffrey said about excessive decorations,
their sharp beaks and wing tips looked a little dangerous for someone wandering to or from the bathroom
in the middle of the night.

She sat at the small oak table that served as a desk,
her tablet and keyboard in front of her. She intended
to spend the rest of the evening the way she usually
did—a few games of *Candy Crush*, then a few chapters
of whichever book caught her fancy. Fantasy tonight,
she thought, with dragons and knights and self-rescuing
princesses. Something that would take her out of Cedar
Creek and far, far away from Daniel's dislike.

"You dumped him," she muttered aloud. "Did you
really expect him to be happy to see you?"

No. She'd never thought he would be happy. He took things so seriously. Sometimes she'd wondered how someone raised by two majorly passionate people could be so cool and unemotional. Maybe he was just a version of her: coming from such a chaotic family, she'd craved quiet and calm. Maybe he'd craved rationale and reason.

But he felt things. Felt them deeply. He'd trusted until he'd learned better. He'd been fiercely loyal until she'd showed him disloyalty. He would have done anything for her until she'd done everything to him. He was done with her. She understood that. Respected it. Accepted it.

But it still stung.

With the email icon on the tablet screen showing new mail, she raised one hand to swipe across it, then hesitated. The tiny hairs bristling on the back of her neck told her there would be an email from *him*. The reason she had made this trip. The reason she'd had to face Daniel. She wanted to indulge in childlike games: if she didn't open the program, she wouldn't see the email, and if she didn't see the email, it didn't exist. *He* didn't exist.

But he did, and all the pretending in the world couldn't change that.

She had the usual spam in her inbox, a funny message from her sister, Stacia, and a sweet how-did-it-go note from Archer. He was the gruffer, blunter of the two Harper men, but he had a soft spot for her, and she for him.

And yes, there was also an email from *him*.

RememberMe.

The sight of his screen name made her skin crawl

and her hand tremble when she tapped on it. Her cell phone had been blissfully silent today, but Monday he'd texted her multiple times.

You're late for work, Nat. Why?

Your office said you didn't call in. Are you sick? I should call Stacia to find out.

Where are you, Nat?

   On Tuesday, he'd opened with…

There's no family emergency or Stacia would be gone, too. Where are you? What are you doing? Why are you making me worry?

Are you too sick to answer your phone? Should I ask the dispatcher for a welfare check?

Is this about Kyle's accident?

Answer me, damn it.

   His final text that night had made her shiver and hunker deeper into the covers of a cheap motel somewhere in Texas, along Interstate 40.

I went by your apartment tonight, and your car was gone. What are you up to, Nat? Why are you doing this to me?

What he was doing to her apparently counted for nothing, and what he'd done to Kyle…

Goose bumps everywhere, she finally focused on the tablet screen.

You shouldn't have done this, Nat. But it's okay. I'm not mad. I was, but I'm not anymore because I know I'll find you. The connection between us is so deep and strong that I'll always find you, and when I do— after all, Cedar Creek's not that big—you'll never want to leave me again.

Damn it, he knew where she was. Deep inside, though, she wasn't surprised. Coming here had been on the spur of the moment; on Sunday night she'd called Archer and gotten Daniel's information, told Stacia she was leaving, packed her bags and slipped out of the apartment before dawn Monday morning. But she'd known RememberMe would figure it out. He knew everything she did.

Swallowing hard, she pressed her hands together to stop their trembling. He made her feel so damn vulnerable. There had been times when his messages were almost sporadic, a few weeks when she hadn't heard from him at all. She'd readjusted to life quickly, neglecting to be wary when she was out, to look over her shoulder or to search for familiar faces in unfamiliar places. Then, when she'd thought he'd moved on, that some other woman had caught his fancy, another email had found its way into her inbox, or a text to her cell phone, or a card to her mailbox.

RememberMe. When the first emails had come, she'd thought the name was cute, a friendly question without the question remark. *Hey, remember me?* After what had happened to Kyle, she knew there was nothing cute or friendly about him.

And she didn't have a clue in hell who he was or what he wanted besides frightening her. She didn't know why he was fixated on her, how he'd gotten her email address or her cell number or her home address. She didn't know how he tracked her down every time she changed jobs, where he watched her from, what he wanted from her.

What was the point of his sick game?

Right now it didn't matter. All she had to do was warn Daniel. Have that conversation he so clearly didn't want to have. Give him one more reason to hate her. She would do the same with her other two exes—she was still searching for them—and then she would find herself a hiding place so far away that RememberMe would never find her.

She closed her email and stared at the screen a long time before opening the browser. Cedar Creek was a pretty little town, but she needed to put it in the rearview mirror as soon as possible. Vulnerable wasn't a pleasant way to feel, and she wanted it done.

It wasn't likely that a town the size of this one had more than one bowling alley, and a search showed that was true. She'd discarded her wet shoes when she came in from the diner and hadn't brought another pair that went so well with the dress, so she changed into jeans and a button-down, put on chunky-soled boots that should keep out the worst of the water, grabbed a raspberry-colored slicker and her bag, and left the room.

Claire Baylor, proprietor, manager and housekeeper of the Prairie Sun, was sitting behind the grand oak counter, a book propped open on the desk. When she closed it, Natasha caught a view of the cover. *The Unlucky Ones*.

"I've heard that book will give you nightmares," she commented.

Claire came to stand in front of her. "It makes me unbearably sad."

"I haven't read it. These days, if it doesn't make me laugh or give me the thrill of adventure, I don't read it."

"It's disturbing but hopeful. She survived horrible things and went on to live a good life." Claire glanced past her to the wet street outside. "Are you heading out?"

"Yeah. I was wondering where to find Highway 97."

"Main Street, a couple blocks west, becomes 97 when it leaves town. Anyplace in particular?"

"The bowling alley."

The woman winced. "I had to take a physical education class in college, and I chose bowling because… well, let's face it. I'm not a physical sort." She patted her rounded hips. "Luckily, the instructor graded on effort, because I don't think I threw a single ball all semester that didn't go into someone else's lane."

"I've never tried the game. I just can't see the point of heaving a twelve-pound ball at a bunch of pins that far away. Of course, I never got the point of golf or tennis, either. Hockey—that makes sense to me. Pounding people who get in your way."

Claire's laugh was hearty and easy, as if it was second nature. "I'm with you, sister. Anyway, just go up to Main, turn right and it's a couple miles north on the right side of the road. Have fun."

Claire left the desk and walked with Natasha to the

rear door, where the hour and the weather kept the lot dimly lit. "Feel free to park on the street out front when you come back. Your key unlocks both front and back doors, and after talking about that book, the front's just less creepy."

"Thanks." Natasha jogged to her car and locked the doors as soon as she was inside. There'd been a time when that had instantly made her feel safer. Not any longer. Even a thorough look around the vehicle didn't inspire confidence. She didn't know what skills RememberMe possessed. He'd found her new email address every time she'd changed it; within twenty-four hours of her changing her cell number, he was calling again. She'd moved from an apartment in her own name to one in her cousin's name, and flowers had arrived at her doorstep the next morning. Was tampering with her car beyond him? Was *anything* beyond him?

The tears that had put a quaver into Kyle's mother's voice last weekend answered that question effectively.

But the car started fine, and when she turned on the heat to dispel the chill, nothing noxious poured from vents. This was one of the problems of a stalker: he frequently made her lose sight between reason and paranoia. At the moment, she wasn't convinced there *was* a difference.

The gutters along First Street were overflowing, spreading into the street and sometimes bubbling onto the sidewalks. With no oncoming traffic, she drove, straddling the dividing line to stay out of the deepest water. It wasn't seven thirty yet, but it seemed hours past her bedtime. The clouds, the constant flow and splash, the damp and the chill all combined to convince her winter was on its way in a place where it mattered. Not the mild few months they got at home but real cold, real snow, real ice.

Thunder Lanes couldn't be missed. It sat in a mix of industrial and residential structures, the only business open now, its blacktop parking lot full. Natasha was lucky to find a space near the front as another car backed out. She swooped in, sat there gripping the steering wheel for a while and then forced herself to let go. Open the door. Take off her seat belt. Get out. Close the door. Walk to the main entrance and…and…

She actually decided to leave but got caught in the shuffle when two customers left and four more came in at the same time. Before she got untangled, she was on the other side of the doors, with escape behind her and loud music and loud voices ahead.

She wasn't intending to talk to Daniel tonight. She would just walk inside, keep her distance from his group. How hard could it be to avoid a bunch of cops, deputies and firefighters? She would get a snack and find an out-of-the-way place to watch him for a bit. See how he interacted with the others. See if he was still angry.

See if he'd brought that girl, Taryn.

The lanes were busy. The food counters weren't. She got a beer and a corn dog, a glob of mustard and napkins and scoped out the best place to go unnoticed. The arcade was mostly empty, and only a couple of kids played in the enclosed toddler playground next to it. A narrow counter and chairs lined one side of it so parents could keep watch.

Only one woman sat there, dark-haired, pretty, the messy remains of hot dogs and pop to one side, along with a mountain-sized pile of dirty napkins. She caught Natasha's look and smiled drily. "Silly me. I thought it would be hard to create disaster with a bun, a wiener and a spurt of ketchup. Who knew?"

Natasha left two seats between them and sat to the woman's left, where she would have an excuse for looking toward the first responders at their side-by-side lanes at the far end. "Your kids?"

"Oh, no. Samwell is my husband's cousin's child. He's spoiled rotten, throws temper tantrums at least once an hour and thinks he will absolutely 'diiiieeee' if he doesn't get his way every single time. The girl who ignores him and plays so politely is the daughter of one of the firefighters over there."

"You don't bowl?"

"I only come for the popcorn. Who are you with?"

Natasha's face flushed. "I only came for the corn dog and the beer. I'll have to try the popcorn next."

Briefly taking her gaze from Samwell, the woman smiled. "I'm Mila."

"Natasha." She dipped the entire end of her corn dog in mustard and was taking a big bite when Mila made an interested sound.

"Are you *the* Natasha?"

Mustard went down her throat the wrong way, and bits of breading tried to work their way up and out her nose. She covered her face with a handful of napkins, spitting and wheezing at the vinegary burn, so lost in her little fit that she barely heard Mila say, "I'll take that as a yes."

Followed by, "Ooh, I'll take that as an even bigger yes."

Natasha swiped the tears from her eyes and wiped

her face clean before looking toward the lanes where all the good-looking guys were. Had been. One was weaving his way around benches and bowlers toward them.

And he didn't look happy.

Chapter 2

"What the hell are you doing here?" Daniel saw Mila arch one eyebrow, then heard his choice of word too late. Too bad. *Heck* just didn't get the emotion over.

Natasha coughed to clear her throat. "I heard the popcorn here is the best around."

His gaze flickered at the corn dog on its paper sleeve. The popcorn was good. The corn dogs were like every other corn dog found in the freezer case at the market. "Why are you following me?"

"Judging by all the writing on your screen over there, you've been here a while. I just came…" A tiny hesitation, an offer of a smile. A sure indication she was about to lie. "For the food."

"You need to leave." His voice wobbled before he got it under control. "You need to leave the bowling alley, the hotel, the town and the entire damn state, and you need to go now."

Mila was keeping an eye on the kids while discreetly following the conversation, and Daniel knew without turning that they had an audience back on the lanes. He didn't often give them anything to talk about, other than how often he got hit on by the females he came across on the job. He didn't want them talking about this, either, not even if he had to bodily eject Natasha from the bowling alley.

Which he had zero grounds for doing, especially with more than half of the county's law enforcement officers looking on.

Natasha's discomfort was palpable as she pushed back her chair. "Talk to me—*listen* to me—and then I'll go."

He clenched his jaw, though he managed to keep his hands flat and loose at his sides. He hated being outmanipulated, outwitted or outgunned. It wasn't anything his fathers had drummed into him, though they both had competitive streaks a mile wide. It was just something he expected of himself. And he especially hated being undone by Natasha. Mila, Morwenna, Taryn— they were okay. Cheryl and Lois, the first-ever and still-serving female officer in Cedar Creek—it was a given they could undo him without even trying.

But Natasha? The idea made his stomach turn sour.

He glanced at Mila, whose attention was still on the kids, but a faint smile touched her face. She was his boss Sam's wife, survivor of several assaults and murder attempts a year ago. In the beginning, he hadn't cared a thing about her other than her ties to the case, but since then, they'd become…distant friends, maybe, or close acquaintances. He liked her, respected her, and when she gave him a tiny nod, he struggled not to grouse.

If listening to Natasha was the only way to get rid of her, he would listen.

"Fine." He directed the response to Mila—he didn't want to see the triumph on Natasha's face—then pivoted and returned to the lane to change into his boots and get his slicker.

"Jeez, he even gets hit on twelve lanes away by the prettiest woman in the place," Cullen Simpson muttered, then shot a look at Sam. "No offense, Chief."

"None taken," Sam said before pointing his beer at Simpson. "If I thought you were spending your time thinking about how pretty my wife is, I'd have to pound you into the ground." Before Simpson could stumble over a denial that could only get him in hot water, Sam turned to Daniel. "I'm guessing you won't be back."

"Probably not."

"You're awful damn close to a perfect game."

"I've had plenty of perfect games."

Ben clapped him on the shoulder, practically knocking him off balance. "You gotta love the boy's modesty, don't you?"

"Just stating a fact. I'll see you in the morning." As he stalked back toward the play area, Daniel pulled on his slicker, making sure to cover his pistol and badge, then waited in the broad corridor for Natasha to dump her corn dog and beer in the trash.

She walked toward him with the long, fluid strides that had always seemed more than just a form of locomotion to him. Her jeans clung snugly to her thighs, and her shirt did the same with her upper body. She had gained a few pounds since he'd last seen her. They gave her body a softer, more womanly look.

Not that he cared. He was just appreciating a fine form. Jeffrey had always encouraged him to appreciate beauty.

Archer had taught him that sometimes it could be deadly.

When they reached the vestibule, they both stopped. He supposed it was best to decide their destination before stepping out into the deluge. There were plenty of places open, just none that he wanted to go to with Natasha. Her hotel was out of the question, and so was his house. There was no way he could let her in there.

"There's a McDonald's on South Main," he said shortly. The micro-change in her expression showed that she remembered he wasn't a McDonald's fan—all those kids and all their oblivious parents with their cell phones. Better to go someplace other than usual, right?

"I'll follow you."

His car was parked in the row nearest the highway. Hers was twenty feet from the door. He jogged to his vehicle, the hood of his slicker down, cold rain running down his neck. By the time he got inside and started the engine, Natasha was waiting near the exit.

There wasn't any traffic to speak of, nothing to delay the moment they would reach the restaurant. As he crossed the street that would lead to his house, he sent a mournful look that way but continued south.

Daniel waited for her in the parking lot—it was the polite thing to do—and held the door for her. They both ordered black coffees, each paying for their own, and carried them silently to the table farthest from other customers. It was a bench, actually, with stools for chairs. He felt like he was hunkered at the kids' table, like his knees might bump his chin.

Natasha looked as if she perched on the most elegant chair ever imagined.

She sweetened her coffee, stirred it, then gazed out of the streaky window at a scene so saturated with water that everything overflowed: the street, the gutters, the sky itself. "Is the weather often like this?"

Irritation flared at the pointlessness of her comment. "No. Sometimes it rains really hard."

Her gaze jerked back to him, her lips turning up in a startled smile before it faded beneath his scowl. "Sometimes I forget you have a sense of humor."

Her comment gave him the same fleeting startle. Sometimes he forgot, too. He hadn't laughed at anything lately. There was nothing lighthearted about his job. Usually the grimness of cases rolled off him—he'd learned coping mechanisms when he was a little Harper—but the past few days, they'd seemed a little harder to shake.

Maybe a portent of the shake-up to come.

Man, was he shaken.

"What do you want?" he asked before that admission had time to unsettle him even more.

She opened her mouth, closed it and wrapped her fingers tightly around her coffee. Her nails were polished pale pink with tiny flecks of hot-pink glitter. She'd always been such a girly-girl, no matter what she wore. Even in one of his dress shirts and nothing else, she'd looked like a princess ready for the ball. Now, when he felt like a drained rat, she was beautiful.

After a minute, she eased her grip on the cup and

raised her gaze to him. "I'm sorry about the way things went."

For a moment, he thought that was just a start, that she would go on with some crappy explanation, but when she didn't, he stared at her. "That's it? That's what you came all this way to say?"

"No. I came to tell you…"

He knew how to conduct interviews, how to get a reluctant person to talk, how to sort through everything a talkative person said to get to the important details, how to get his instincts at work on determining truth versus lies versus obfuscation. He knew the best action was to be silent and still; soon enough, she would talk just to fill the void.

He knew all that and ignored it. Instead he stood up, reached into his pocket and slapped a business card down on the table. "There's my office number and my email address. If you ever decide to actually say what you came to say, you can leave a message. Once that's taken care of, I assume you'll be getting the hell out because that's what you do, isn't it?"

He hadn't managed a single step when she spoke. "I think you might be in danger, Daniel."

Saying the words out loud was hard. Hadn't she already provided enough upheaval in his life? But she couldn't have not said them, not if she wanted to live with herself. She felt so bad about what had happened to Kyle, and she'd had no advance warning. Finding out that one of the others had been injured or even killed when she'd made no effort to stop it would have been too much to bear.

The incredulous look he was giving her wasn't easy

to bear, either. It made her face hot, made her want to squirm on the ridiculous stool where she loomed like a giant over a doll's table. Slowly, he sank back onto his own stool, his hands gripping the table in front of him, his fingers pressing tightly like he was imagining them around her throat. He squeezed his eyes shut for a moment, then pinched the bridge of his nose. Those were his first outward symptoms of frustration, a habit she'd rarely seen directed her way but was still familiar with. Did he know he'd picked it up from Jeffrey? Except Jeffrey didn't pinch. He just pressed two knuckles to that spot between his eyes.

When Daniel spoke, his voice would seem calm to most people, but she heard the stress, the tight control. "Would you say that again?"

She thought about repeating it verbatim, just to tweak his frustration a little tighter, because she knew he didn't want a repeat. He wanted an explanation.

Deserved an explanation.

After drawing a deep breath, she exhaled, hoping to blow out some of her own stress, but it didn't work. "I have a stalker," she said flatly. "I got him about a year ago, right around Halloween." That was Stacia's birthday. Her sister had even joked about how bad her luck was: *her* birthday, and Natasha got a secret admirer. "Last weekend, he sent me a message that he had enjoyed his visit with Kyle on Saturday. You remember—"

Daniel growled. Of course he remembered her first fiancé.

"I still run into Kyle occasionally, so I called to see what he could tell me about this guy, and... I talked to his mother. He had a bad accident that day. He fell down the stairs at his house. He's in a coma, and they don't know whether he'll survive." She closed her eyes briefly, and an image of her first fiancé came to mind: boyish, auburn-haired, bearing a strong resemblance to Britain's Prince Harry. The idea that he might die broke her heart.

"RememberMe said—"

"What?" Daniel interrupted, still looking flummoxed.

"RememberMe. It's his email address. It's the only name I have for him."

"You don't know who he is?"

"If I knew, I would call him by name." She mimicked his dry, stating-the-obvious tone almost perfectly. "I have no idea. Stacia and I considered every guy I ever met and came up with nothing." It was hard, looking critically at people she'd been friends with, had dated, kissed or more, and wondering if they could be dangerous. Could one of them be the one so determined to terrorize her? Was anyone she knew actually capable of that?

Dear God, she hoped not.

"What *do* you know?"

The memory of her first contact with the man was clearer now than the day it happened. At the time, it had been no big deal, just one more email from a stranger in an inbox that got plenty of those every day. His was friendly, lighthearted. It had made her smile, and she'd needed the smile, and she truly hadn't found anything intrusive about it. She'd always had the option of deleting the email and, in that case, would likely never hear from him again.

Instead, she'd chosen to answer. What would have happened if she hadn't?

"He sent me an email, just a short note. It had been a gray and dreary day, and he said it reminded him of the day we'd met. He said, of course, I probably didn't remember because I had been surrounded by admirers. He said—" She broke off, pulled out her cell and scrolled through her email. She hadn't known in the beginning why she kept his messages. It certainly wasn't foreboding, and she hadn't had any idea that they might be important someday. Maybe she'd just liked the picture attached to the first one, or the cartoon embedded in the second, or the link to a funny video in the third one. But she had kept them. Every one.

She offered the phone to Daniel, and he took it. It was big enough that there was no chance of an accidental touch. His touch had always been simple. No-nonsense. Comforting. It had made her feel safe and protected and loved and aroused and so very lucky. And afraid. She'd wanted to love him and adore him and never, ever hurt him, and she'd done it all—the loving, the adoring and the hurting.

He wouldn't let her hurt him again. She knew that. He wouldn't let anything the least bit sweet enter into his thoughts or his actions, because he had to protect himself from her, and that hurt her.

Daniel read the note, then gave the photo a cursory glance, unimpressed by it. It had taken her breath away the first time: sunset that very day over the ocean, the sun's rays bursting out of dark clouds to form a halo of gold and deep pink and dark blue and luscious purples. She'd thought about having it enlarged, printed and framed to hang on her wall, and Daniel gave it just a look. *Huh. A sunset.*

He went on to read the second mail, the third, on down the list. After four minutes, according to the bank sign across the street, he looked up. "These aren't exactly what comes to mind when I think 'stalker.'"

"I didn't think of him that way, either. I honestly thought it was someone I knew who was being coy. Seeing how long it would take me to figure out who it was. That was before."

"Before what?"

"Before the number of emails passed five hundred in the first four months. Now it's around two thousand. Plus he's sent me nine hundred plus texts, twenty-eight cards, a half dozen flower deliveries and four personal deliveries. The ones you've read, he was still being charming and fun and not creepy."

He stared at her a long time, his dark gaze steady. He could make a person squirm with that gaze, in both good ways and bad. She could easily imagine him in an interrogation room with a suspect across the table, getting a confession without saying a word. That look just compelled a person to talk.

"Did you contact the police?"

"Yes. Apparently, stalkers aren't a big deal these days. Just about everyone in Los Angeles has one." Then she sighed. "I talked to a detective, asked for advice. She looked into it and agreed it was probably just someone I knew playing games. He hadn't actually *done* anything. She suggested I change my email address and my cell number. I'd already done both a half dozen times. She said moving couldn't hurt. I'd already done that. She said let her know if he escalated.

"I called again after Kyle's accident. She looked into it again. He was home alone. He was carrying some boxes down the stairs and apparently misjudged a step. His parents believed it was an accident. His girlfriend believed it. No one had a reason to hurt him."

Her conversations with the detective had all sounded so logical over the phone in her tightly secured apartment or sitting at the woman's desk in a building filled with armed people. She was overreacting. Hypersensitive. Reading more into the emails than was there.

But there'd been one small issue that prevented Natasha from taking the detective at her word.

"Who did you talk to?" Daniel asked.

"Felicia Martin."

His face tightened. He'd gone through the academy with Felicia. They'd called her Flea because she was nearly a foot shorter than most of them, wiry and compact, constantly in motion and tough as hell to get rid of. He and Flea had liked and respected each other. It had seemed only natural to Natasha that, after the way she'd ended their engagement, Flea neither liked nor respected her.

"She's a good cop."

Natasha didn't respond. Cops were also people, and people were influenced by a lot of things. Was Felicia a good cop? Probably. Would she have taken more interest in Natasha's complaint if they were strangers? Maybe. But that wouldn't have changed the bottom line: that Natasha was being haunted by a phantom who didn't leave the slightest trace and Felicia didn't have the resources to discover who he was.

Daniel set her phone carefully on the table between

them. "So, how did you make the leap from Kyle falling down the stairs to thinking that I'm in danger?"

"The same message where he mentioned Kyle. He said he was looking forward to meeting with you, Eric and—" Her mouth froze, and it took her a moment to get it working again. "And Zach. He said he hoped the visits would be as satisfying."

"Zach." Daniel's voice was hollow, his mouth quirking in a sardonic twist, his gaze rolling skyward in a grimace of distaste. "There's four of us now? Is that all, or did RememberMe miss one?"

"That's all." She barely managed a whisper. Four men. Four loves. Five broken hearts. And all the blame lay on her.

He was silent a moment longer, until a gust of wind rattled the window beside them. Rain hit it so hard that it sounded like pebbles hitting the glass. She knew the sound, because once when she'd teased that no boyfriend had ever tossed pebbles at her bedroom window when she was growing up, Daniel had done just that the next night with a handful of aquarium gravel.

"Have you talked to Eric and Zach?"

She shook her head. "I'm looking for them."

His shoulders straightened, his expression going blank, as he gathered the empty sugar and creamer packets he'd used. "Okay, so now I know. There wasn't any need to come here. You could have called. You could have just given the message to my parents and let them pass it on. But I appreciate the heads-up. Don't feel like you need to stick around any longer."

With that, he stood and walked away. Natasha turned to watch him throw his coffee and litter into the trash, then go out the door and into the rain. He didn't look over his shoulder until he was inside his car and then only to check traffic before backing out of the parking space.

A lump rose in her throat as he drove away. It had gone better than she'd had any right to expect, she told herself as she threw her own coffee away, then exited the restaurant. He was probably right. She should have just told Jeffrey and Archer and let them handle it. But she'd needed to get out of LA, and she'd found it hard enough talking to him. She didn't think she could have borne the anger that his fathers surely would have felt finding out that he was in danger because of her.

"And you wanted to see Daniel," Tasha whispered, filling all the corners of her brain with malicious glee.

All right. Yes, somewhere deep, deep inside, she'd wanted to see Daniel.

Stumbling to a stop in the drive-through lane, Natasha tilted her face to the sky and let the rain wash over her. It ran down her cheeks, caught on her eyelashes and dripped from her chin. It didn't make her feel better, didn't wash away her hurts or regrets.

But if a tear or two happened to seep from her eyes, no one would suspect. *It's just rain*, she could say.

She could even pretend she believed it.

The rain had stopped sometime during the night, giving the waterlogged city a chance to drain and catch its breath. Daniel needed to catch his breath, but it was going to take a lot more than a break in the clouds to do that. He didn't even have a chance until he knew for sure that Natasha had left Cedar Creek and Oklahoma far behind. He figured he would be able to feel it in his bones when it happened.

The police station was quiet and dimly lit. He'd dressed down today—black tactical pants, a gray polo shirt embroidered with the department's badge and boots—only very slightly in deference to the fact that it was Friday and everyone else always dressed down on Friday. Mostly it was because of the weather and his desire to keep his feet dry but also because of the trouble he'd had with his tie this morning. The agitation that hummed through his nerves all night long would have made self-strangulation far too tempting if he'd had to give the silk noose one more effort.

He checked the time and grimaced. It was a little after six, so shortly after 4:00 a.m. in Los Angeles. Flea would kill him if he called now. He wondered if Natasha had shared her danger theory and Flea had found it without merit. She obviously hadn't felt the urge to pass on the information to Daniel. But if she wasn't taking the stalking seriously, why would she take the stalker's remark as a threat?

He was tired from a night of restless sleep, he had a headache and when he'd tried to drink a cup of coffee while getting dressed, it had gone down so poorly that he'd thought he might throw up. Thank God the weekend was here. Maybe he would retreat into his bedroom until Monday morning, or maybe Morwenna still wanted a weekend trip to Eureka Springs. Surely her company, the Arkansas town, the tourists and the hundred and fifty miles' distance would allow him to get his mental balance back.

"Why are you in so early?"

Blearily Daniel glanced up as Ben dumped a half dozen spiral notebooks on his desk. They were wrapped in a plastic trash bag to keep them from getting wet even though two empty attaches resided in the other detective's bottom desk drawer. "Couldn't sleep."

"Because of Size-Two Fitted Bodice?" Ben shrugged out of his slicker and tossed it on an unused desk. "What's the story?"

Daniel scratched his jaw and felt the stubble of hair where he'd missed a swipe with the razor. He grimaced. Now he would be aware all day long that that thin line of whiskers was there and it would drive him crazy. "No story."

Ben snorted. He unpacked the notebooks from the trash bag—probably containing lists of his interminable lists—then threw the bag next to the slicker. "Everybody in the department knows there's a story. And the sheriff's office. And the fire department. A man doesn't leave first responders' night two-thirds through a perfect game without a story."

Daniel looked over his shoulder. There was a nighttime desk officer on, but they had so few walk-ins that he spent most of his night in the dispatcher shack chatting. All he'd done this morning was stick his head out the door when he heard Daniel come in, wave and settle back in.

"We're both early," Ben said. "Let's get breakfast at Mom's." He left the rest unsaid—*we can talk there*—but it was implied.

"Yeah, sure." Not that Daniel particularly wanted to eat breakfast or talk, but since the time difference kept him from doing what he did want, he might as well do something besides brood.

Mom's, known as Creek Café outside the Little Bear family, was eight blocks east of the police station. They could have run it easily, could have walked it even

more easily, but they took Ben's car. Even though neither of them was on duty yet, if they did get a call,
the chief would be annoyed if they got caught without
transportation.

The café was located just west of the bridge that
spanned the creek, the building high enough above
the stream that it couldn't really take advantage of the
view. Instead, when a customer looked out, he saw
the rocks that lined the creek bed twenty feet above
the water's surface. When Ben told him it was because of occasional floods, Daniel hadn't quite gotten
it. Sitting now at a table against the side windows, he
glanced over the water, swirling and splashing fifteen
feet higher than usual, and he got it.

Mrs. Little Bear came from the kitchen when she
heard Ben was there. She hugged him, combed her fingers through his hair then turned her attention to Daniel. "You look pale," she said, catching his chin in her
fingers and studying his face. "You didn't get enough
sleep last night. You young people think you can get by
on coffee and your good looks, but take my word for
it—you need a good night's sleep every single night."

"It wasn't for lack of trying, Mrs. Little Bear," he
said drily.

She gave him another appraising look. "I'll fix you
something special. You'll feel better in no time."

She left without taking their orders. The first couple of times that had happened, Daniel had been openmouthed, trying to say, *Wait, you don't know what I
want.* He'd learned that it didn't matter much what he
wanted, because everything Mrs. Little Bear and her
kitchen staff made was excellent, and she always chose
well for him.

"Am I getting chicken soup for breakfast?" he asked as a waitress filled Ben's coffee cup. She didn't offer him any. Her boss had probably told her not to.

"Could be. Or maybe her special grits. They have healing powers. So do her breakfast casseroles. And her sticky buns. With Mom, you never can tell." Ben sipped his coffee, no cream, no sugar, then fixed his attention on Daniel. It was rather an unsettling experience. "The fire department won last night. It would have been different if you hadn't run out on us."

Daniel shrugged. The first responders' competition was just for bragging rights. No one took it too seriously, but it did keep the three departments in touch with each other.

"So, what's the story?"

The waitress provided a brief respite by bringing Daniel a glass of pulpy orange juice poured over ice. He didn't have to ask to know it was freshly squeezed. Archer wouldn't drink it any other way, and so, beyond a one-time try in middle school, Daniel never had, either.

After a long, sweet drink, he set the glass down and shrugged. "Nothing much. Old girlfriend. Wanted to talk."

"So, your old girlfriend from Los Angeles just happened to show up in Cedar Creek, Oklahoma, and tracked you down not once, not twice, but three times, and it was nothing much?" Ben gave a sorrowful shake of his head. "You're a cop, Daniel. People lie to you every single day. Surely you can do better than that."

He wished he was more comfortable with lying, because he really would rather not talk about Natasha. Or think about her. Or remember. Or wonder…

Nope, he wasn't going there. He'd spent half the

night wondering. How good things had been. How bad they'd become. How they could have turned out differently. How much happier he'd been with her. How she'd shattered his hard-won contentment simply by walking through the police station door.

Whether he was in danger.

Whether *she* was in danger.

The man in him wanted her to go away, to leave his memories as well as his life this time. The detective in him was curious about the events she'd described, and the cop in him felt an undeniable need to do what he'd always done: protect people. Not her specifically, just *people*. That was why he wore a badge and carried a gun, why he'd become a cop, why he'd committed so much of himself to the job.

That was what he'd been telling himself the past ten hours.

Ben was waiting, and Daniel knew it wasn't just the detective in *him* that was asking. They were friends. Not bare-your-soul-share-all-your-secrets friends—Daniel had only ever had that sort of relationship with his fathers and, he grudgingly admitted, Natasha. But still friends. And if there was any real threat from her stalker...

"Long story short," he began, scratching that bit of hair on his jaw again, "we were engaged. She changed her mind a week before the wedding. Ended it at a pre-wedding party with all of our friends and families there." A pause as Ben grimaced. "By proxy. She sent her sister to give me back the ring."

"Damn." One word, a lot of sympathy. "I'm guessing that happened about five years ago."

Daniel nodded.

"Why is she here now? Did she change her mind?"

A snort escaped him. "Oh, she's good at that. I'm the third of four jilted fiancés."

This time it was Ben who snorted. "Did you know she'd dumped two other guys before you?"

Daniel grudgingly nodded. "I did, but…it's complicated."

"Women always are."

The waitress appeared, delivering eggs, bacon, biscuits and gravy to Ben and the biggest omelet Daniel had ever seen. She grinned at his wide-eyed look. "Cheese, bacon, sausage, ham, chorizo—oh, and veggies and avocado for our California boy. Miz LB says that'll give you the energy to get through the day. Eat up."

"Or die trying," Ben added.

"That's a distinct possibility." Daniel took his first bite. The omelet was hot and steamy and meaty; the seasoning perfectly balanced; the cheese melted and smooth; the tender-crisp vegetables just the way he liked them. "Man, your mom can cook."

"Good thing, too. This restaurant supports our whole family, except Great-Aunt Weezer."

Weezer might be the only member of the extended Little Bear family that Daniel hadn't met. She hadn't been particularly sociable before she won half a million dollars in the lottery, and she was even less so afterward, afraid people wanted her money.

Daniel didn't have to worry about that. He would never make the kind of money his fathers did, but he got by. The cost of living in Cedar Creek was nothing compared to LA, and generous people like Ben's mother gave discounts or free meals to officers. It helped a so-so salary go further.

They were finished eating and Daniel had half of his omelet in a box when the sound of a Federal siren winding up caught his attention. He and Ben both looked toward the fire station across the street, where one engine was pulling out of the station and a second, lights flashing, its own siren engaging, waited to follow.

"As wet as it's been, you've got to be determined to burn something," Ben remarked as they walked out to his car.

"Determination might be the number one character trait of criminals."

"Or stupidity. It's funny how often you hear the phrase 'criminal mastermind,' but in all my years on the job, I've never met one. I think Mila's stalker came closest."

Daniel agreed with him there. Though Sam had passed on information to various police departments, the number of murders that one had committed was still unknown. There had been three in Cedar Creek alone, plus two attempts on Mila and one on Sam.

Mila's stalker had been deadly. Was Natasha's?

A black plume of smoke rose to the west above downtown. Ben's expression went grim as he turned onto First. They would have headed in that direction anyway, but to the police station, not a fire. Daniel hoped it was just a small fire and nothing that required their presence.

The smoke grew thicker, dimming the emergency lights on the engines parked half a block from the courthouse. Ben set the siren to yelp, easing past cars stopped in the street, parking sideways to block the nearest intersection.

"Looks like a car fire," he said, shutting off the engine. "Damn, and the rain's starting again."

Daniel pulled his slicker closer as he got out. A sedan parked across from the courthouse was engulfed in flames, patches of its bright red paint blistering and peeling off, a Dodgers sticker on the rear bumper melting from the intense heat.

He stared at the ruins of the sticker. He knew that sticker—had seen it just last night. Firefighters wielding a powerful line blocked his view of the license tag, but he didn't need to see it to know it was white with blue numbers and the state's name in red script across the top.

Natasha's stalker had set her car on fire.

Now where the hell was she?

When the first raindrop splashed on the tip of Natasha's nose, she wasn't surprised. She didn't even stifle a groan. The dreariness seemed fitting. Her life was figuratively pretty dark. Why shouldn't it be literally dark, as well?

Grumbling, the people around her started moving away, going on about their day or seeking shelter. Most of the buildings farther down the street had awnings that would keep them dry, but the closest ones were beyond the firefighters' barrier. Here by the courthouse, there was nothing but sidewalk and grass, and her feet had rooted themselves there. She didn't like being in the open, but at least no one could approach her stealthily. No one could sneak up and scare her. No one could observe her fear closely.

Not *no one*. RememberMe. *He* couldn't sneak up. But he'd already scared her.

She wore her slicker, zipped to her chin, and hugged the purse tucked underneath with both arms, her gaze locked on the flames with macabre fascination. Fire-fighters called to each other and to the police officers who had arrived to assist, and the engines' sirens droned in a low hum, matched by a toneless numbing hum inside her.

He was here. Maybe in one of the groups of gawkers, maybe down the block or in one of the nearby buildings. Maybe he'd driven away after starting the fire, but he wouldn't have gone far. He could be parked on a side street, watching his handiwork. Watching her.

She didn't glance around. It was too damn hard to look at strangers' faces and wonder, *Is it him? Is it that man wearing the suit that looks like a lawyer? Is it the mechanic-looking guy with the grease rag hanging out from his back pocket? Could it be that firefighter in all that gear? Is one of them capable of doing this? Are all of them capable?*

Was it even a man? She had assumed, and Stacia and Felicia Martin, but none of the communications made that certain.

Hey, RememberMe? How about a new name? I'm thinking ScrewYou.

Yeah, she liked the sound of that. It made her sound brave and bold, even though she was quaking inside.

She saw two figures approaching in her peripheral vision, but she couldn't make herself look their way. Strange that, even after five years, she needed to see no more than that dark blur to know the shorter of the two was Daniel. She needed no more than to remember the way he'd left last night to know his expression was going to be as dark as the smoke, that he was going to be wound as tight as she was and more ready to explode.

He stopped directly in front of her, too close, invading her space. She wanted to step back, but her feet wouldn't move, so she slowed her breathing and dragged her gaze slowly to his face.

Dark. Angry. Hostile. Very tightly controlled.

"Are you all right?"

The question startled her, making her blink slowly. The unexpectedness of it struck her at the same time the ridiculousness of it did. She was standing there unharmed, wasn't she? The firefighters weren't offering her medical care, were they? Of course she was all right. Though how the hell could she possibly be all right when her stalker had just set her damn car on fire?

She wanted to laugh and to cry, but instead clenched her jaw tightly and nodded.

"Do you know what happened?"

Before she could remind herself to maintain her control, an answer slipped out. "Well, it didn't spontaneously combust. I'm guessing *he* did it."

"Who?" That came from the second man, a few feet behind and to the side of Daniel. He'd been at the desk beyond Daniel's yesterday afternoon when she returned to the police station, and seeing him now confirmed her first impressions: he was big, dark and gave off a calm, solid sense that nothing ever got past him.

How much did he know? Had Daniel told him anything? Everything?

Squeezing her eyes shut, Natasha wished herself someplace else. It didn't work, of course. When she opened them again, the big man was waiting for an answer. Daniel was looking hard at the people who watched the firefighters working.

"Someone's been harassing me," she said stiffly.

He politely reworded it for her. "Someone's stalking you."

She nodded.

"And you think he followed you here from California?"

Yes, Daniel had told him something. She couldn't tell by the man's impassive expression how much he'd confided, how much of his hostility he'd passed on.

Wishing for a deep breath that would erase the tension contracting every muscle in her body, she nodded. "He sent me an email saying that he would find me. After all, Cedar Creek isn't very big."

The other detective's expression didn't change. "When did you get here?"

"Yesterday, around noon."

"Who knew you were coming?"

"My sister." She hesitated, glancing at Daniel, still intensely observing the bystanders as if she and his friend didn't exist, then added, "Daniel's parents."

"Who would they tell?"

"Nobody." Stacia was scared to death for her and viewed anyone who even casually mentioned Natasha with suspicion and wariness. Archer and Jeffrey didn't know about the stalker, but she'd asked them not to tell anyone about her visit. They hadn't even told Daniel, so they certainly wouldn't have confided in anyone else.

Abruptly, Daniel turned back to her. "You should get inside."

"The fire department evacuated the hotel. Besides,

the chief said the fire marshal would want to speak to me. He told me to wait here."

"I'll go find Jamey and tell him she'll be at the station." The other detective walked away before either Natasha or Daniel could protest.

Though the flames were apparently out, the firefighters continued to spray the wreckage. As if the clouds had decided to help, the scattered raindrops multiplied into a deluge. Water running over her scalp and pouring down her neck, Natasha gave her car one last woeful look then turned toward the police station. She didn't want to go there, but where else could she go?

Daniel walked beside her, turning several times to study the people scurrying behind them, before he spoke. "So you weren't wrong."

The last thing in the world she expected was a smile, but a wry one pulled at her mouth. "Some people might say I was actually right." God help her, she wished she hadn't been.

His only response was a grunt.

They passed the gazebo, pretty and invitingly dry underneath its roof, then approached the steps to the police station. Still hugging her purse, she was thinking of her ruined plans for the day—heading out of town—and wondering if RememberMe was Karma's way of repaying her for her fickleness in love and dreading having to replace the car, which she'd just paid off six months ago, when a short, sharp curse from Daniel drew her out of her gloom.

She'd gone a few strides past him and turned back to see him lifting one foot from a puddle at the base of the steps. His pants leg was drenched to the calf, and water streamed from his boot.

"That's a word Archer would say," she commented mildly. How had he not seen the puddle? This was only her third visit here, and she'd noticed it.

"Where do you think I learned it?" Grimacing, he shook his foot to dislodge the excess wet then looked back toward the courthouse. "You don't need to mention that to Ben. Forgetting it's there three times in two days isn't a very detective-ly thing to do."

Her smile came back, this time without the wryness. "So that's why you were barefoot yesterday."

He shrugged before climbing the rest of the steps, holding open one of the tall doors, then following her inside. This time, instead of stopping at the counter, she walked behind him around the end, down a hall and into a conference room. Silently he extended one hand, and she slipped out of her jacket and gave it to him, then he left again.

After going to the far end of the table, she sat in the single chair there to survey her surroundings. The room was about as dull as any she'd ever seen. It looked like the place office furniture went to die: a table that had clearly seen better years, file cabinets with broken drawers, mismatched desk chairs—not wooden ones that got better with age but the cheap kind with five wheels and ugly vinyl or fabric seats—and lamps of varying sizes and styles.

Ironically, the bones of the room were beautiful. The walls needed something more imaginative than drab white paint that looked as if it had come out of the can already dirty, and the ceiling could definitely benefit from a new coat of paint as well, but the vintage black-and-white floor tile and the elaborate trims around the doors and windows were lovely, and the eighteen-inch-wide crown molding was incredible. She should take a picture to send her brother, Nick, a finish carpenter, who complained he'd been born in the wrong century to do really beautiful work.

It was nice to let her mind wander from her current problems, but voices at the door snatched her back to the seriousness of the moment. Daniel came in first, carrying a couple of fat white bath towels and a space heater. The other detective, Ben, was behind him, improvising a clipboard as a serving tray.

No one said anything. Daniel handed the towels to her then plugged the heater in nearby, turned it toward her and flipped the switch on. Ben set a cup of coffee in front of her, along with packets of sugar and tubs of cream, then took a seat on her right. He turned toward her and began writing on the clipboard's legal pad, adding to the stuff that already filled half of the page.

Daniel sat down on her left, sipped his coffee then leaned back in his chair. He didn't speak. Ben didn't. Natasha felt oddly as if she shouldn't, at least not until the coffee, the towel wrapped around her shoulders and the warm air of the heater chased away her chills.

Rain lashed the windows behind her. She turned to glance out. Second Street wasn't nearly as busy as First, but there was an occasional vehicle passing and cars were parked across the street. Someone was waiting in one of those cars, visible only as a vague shape through the side-to-side swipe of the windshield wipers. Goose bumps appeared on Natasha's arms. The car's engine was running, sending little puffs of exhaust into the chilly air, and the headlights were on. Could that be him? Could he have seen her and Daniel come to the police station? Could he have known they would wind up in the conference room and which windows looked into it?

Suddenly a small blur of energy raced out of the building where the car was parked. Between the rain hat, slicker and boots, it was impossible to see anything about the child, though the pink of the clothing suggested a girl. She ran through puddles instead of over them, pulled the car door open and flung herself into the front seat.

You're paranoid. Are you going to start cringing from old people and their canes next?

She hated paranoia.

The door opened once more to admit a woman in uniform, a smile wreathing her face and blond hair showing gray roots, and a man dressed in the same uniform as Daniel and Ben. He couldn't be much older than them, but Natasha assumed he was their boss. His quiet, confident demeanor just said so.

He sat next to Daniel, the woman next to Ben. Natasha regretted picking the seat at the head of the table. It put her at the center of their focus and gave her an instinctive me-against-them response. She should have chosen a chair along the side, where someone would have been forced to sit next to her.

"Close those blinds, will you, Daniel?"

Natasha hadn't thought to do it herself or to ask, but the instant the gloom deepened in the room, she felt better. Safer. "Thank you."

"I'm Chief Douglas. This is Officer Gideon, you've met Detective Little Bear, and of course you know Detective Harper."

Daniel's jaw tightened in her peripheral vision, so she shifted her gaze the other way, to Detective Little Bear. The *bear* part suited him well; being fierce would be no stretch for him. But at six foot four and all broad shoulders and muscles, he'd surpassed the *little* part a long time ago.

"Let's start with the car," the chief said, "since that's our immediate issue. We were waiting for the fire marshal to join us, but he's tied up elsewhere. Tell us what you know, Ms. Spencer."

She took a long drink of coffee then wrapped her fingers around the edges of the towel around her shoulders and held it tightly as she began to talk.

Chapter 3

Daniel fixed his gaze on the coffee cup in front of him. It was made of sturdy cardboard, not as good a choice as reusable mugs, not as bad as the foam cups they'd used when he first came here—and safer to look at than his ex-fiancée.

Natasha's voice was soft, level. She didn't sound hurt or angry, but the stress came through. So did bewilderment and fear. She was entitled to all of it, and he hadn't done anything to ease any of it. Leaving her alone at the restaurant last night… He should have followed her back to the hotel, should have looked at more of the emails, should have checked security on the building and the car. Instead, he'd been a jerk.

But the car had been parked street side, downtown, right in front of the hotel. How much safer could it have been?

"I was getting dressed," she was saying when he tuned back in, "when Claire Baylor screamed up the stairs that there was a fire. I put on my shoes, grabbed my purse and jacket and left with the other guests. It was too hot to go out the front doors, so we used the rear entrance, went down the alley and crossed to the courthouse lawn. The firefighters moved us farther away when they arrived."

"Your room…is it at the front or back of the hotel?"

"Front. Second floor. But I didn't look out. I didn't hear anything."

"How many guests did you notice?" Ben asked.

"Um, there's an older husband and wife down the hall from me. Four women on a road trip who had adjoining rooms in the back. There's a businessman on the third floor, and a military family visiting relatives on their way to his new assignment."

"That's John Weaver's oldest," Lois said. The databases in her head rivaled any law enforcement database. No matter how many times she snatched some detail out of thin air, Daniel was still impressed. "The road trippers—they come through here every fall. Their husbands think they're nature nuts, following the autumn color, but what they're really doing is taking the scenic route to hit every winery in this part of the country. The businessman—he's really cute. He checked in Tuesday and is from California. Somewhere around San Francisco. He's been here the second week of every month for the past three months. Computers."

"Okay, come on," Ben said. "Did you already know this stuff, or have you been talking to Claire this morning?"

Lois gave him a chastising look. "I know all…except

about the older couple. I will, of course, find out the scoop on them when we're done here."

"Did you see all of them outside this morning?" Sam asked.

Natasha thought before nodding. "Yes, I think so. The winery women went off for breakfast, the older couple were in their pajamas and taken in by some store owner down the street, the family was going to his parents' house and he was arguing that they should have stayed there in the first place, and the business guy left for an appointment."

"Can we just get to the point?" It was the first time Daniel had spoken since returning with the towels. His voice sounded thick, and his teeth hurt from clenching his jaw. There was a reason for routine questions, but that didn't make them any less intolerable. He wanted to discuss the real ones, the who and why and how did they stop this guy.

"What is the point, Daniel?" Lois asked in her motherly, understanding tone.

"She's got a stalker. He's sent her thousands of emails, texts, cards and gifts. He knows she's in Cedar Creek. He's here, and he's sending a pretty clear message."

"He's here because you're here, not me." Natasha let go of her towel long enough to lift her coffee and take a long drink. She liked her coffee lukewarm; all she wanted to do when it was hot was breathe in the steam. Daniel kept an electric warmer on his desk because he couldn't stomach it if it dropped much below scalding.

He spent a moment wishing he didn't remember that about her—that he didn't remember anything. Like how she put pepper on watermelon and preferred long drives without the chatter of the radio and how she wore summer clothes no matter how chilly the weather might get and how her snores were more of a quiet hum that lulled him to sleep. But he remembered all that and way too much more.

Including that damnable moment when Stacia had approached him at the party, pale and stunned and shaking as she offered him the ring. *I'm so sorry*, she'd whispered, but his heart had been pounding so hard that he'd barely heard her. The moment, the shock, the disbelief, the hurt, were branded into his mind with an intensity as fierce as the ice that had spread through him that night.

He heard words, just a rush in his ears, saw a flush creep into Natasha's face, giving her some color for the first time this morning, then felt a small foot thud against his shin. His gaze jerked to Lois, who was giving him a none-too-subtle pay-attention-to-the-boss look. Sam's expression wasn't stern, but there was a new interest in it.

"I'm sorry. What?"

"I asked how you figure into this."

He couldn't believe Lois hadn't absorbed the information from the molecules in the air or that Ben hadn't passed it on. But Sam wouldn't be asking if he already knew. "Uh…we were…"

When he didn't continue, Natasha picked up. "We were engaged. I think my stalker is holding a grudge against my former fiancés. All…" She grimaced. "All four of them."

A laugh burst from Lois, followed by a grin. "Honey, are you that impulsive or that slow to learn?"

Daniel thought the glance the chief sent her way

might have translated to *Don't insult the victim, please.*
He didn't know whether Natasha was embarrassed by
her runaway-bride status, but he was embarrassed by
his left-behind-groom status. For a long time, he'd been
so humiliated that he couldn't look anyone in the eye—
tough when everyone in your life witnessed your jilting. Moving to a place where no one knew anything
but what he chose to tell them had saved his sanity.
And now they got to hear about it anyway.

Daniel folded his arms over his chest while Natasha
told them about Kyle's accident, RememberMe's email
and her interpretation of that as a threat. Last night, he
hadn't given it much weight—bad on him—because
he'd been ticked off about seeing her, having to deal
with her, finding out there'd been another engagement
after him. Even he would have taken a third failed engagement as a warning and kept his distance from her.
Two he could overlook, but three was a pattern. Only
a fool would try to disrupt a pattern.

"Do you have that email?" Ben asked.

Natasha pulled her tablet from her oversize purse
and called up the mail program. She selected the specific message then handed the tablet to Ben, who read
aloud:

> "'How was your Saturday, Nat? Lunch and a
> movie with your sister. So predictable…you need
> to get out more. I had a great visit with Kyle…
> gorgeous view. Did you choose those great colors
> when you were together? I'm looking forward to
> meeting Eric, Daniel and Zach, too, and hoping
> those visits will be just as satisfying. Don't let
> the Monday blues get you down. RM.'"

Something nagging settled in Daniel's gut. Being told about the email hadn't had much impact. Hearing it in the guy's own words raised several issues suggestive of his danger. Calling her Nat, a nickname she hated and refused to answer to, letting her know that he didn't care what she wanted. The comment on her and Stacia's day, showing he'd been keeping tabs on her. The remarks about Kyle's house, implying that he'd been inside and knew whereof he spoke. The satisfaction he'd spoken of and naming the fiancés by name.

"The RM is short for RememberMe, his email address," Ben added before turning to Natasha. "And Kyle's accident happened that day at his house?"

"Yes."

"Does it have a gorgeous view? Are the colors great?"

"Yes." The word was little more than a whisper.

"Are you feeling a little threatened, Daniel?" Sam asked.

He didn't want to admit it. Didn't want to believe that Natasha could actually be right. Especially didn't want to believe that she truly was in danger. But no stalker went around trying to kill the people in his target's life, then suddenly decided to leave her in peace. He would try to win her in his own warped way, and when he failed, he would kill himself because he couldn't have her, or would kill her because if he couldn't have her, no one else would, either.

"Maybe I am, Chief." Not by the fact that RememberMe had put Daniel on his must-die list, but by the fact that the arson this morning put this whole mess squarely in their laps. There would be no quick exit from Oklahoma by Natasha. There would be no

timely start to purging himself of all the emotions she'd
brought back to life. *I listened to you, now go,* wasn't
going to fly anymore, because she was the victim of a
crime in their jurisdiction. Neither the chief nor Ben
nor Daniel himself could overlook that, even if Natasha asked nicely. Overlooking criminal activity wasn't
a cop-ly thing to do.

She would stay. They would work the case. They
would keep her safe, and they would find and lock up
her stalker.

And once again, she would blast his life all to hell.

He hoped surviving the second time was easier than
the first.

By the time Natasha was free to leave the police station, the fire chief had allowed staff and guests back
into the hotel. The assistant fire marshal, Jamey Moran,
who'd surprised her with his youth, his New York accent and the pistol on his belt, offered to walk her to
the hotel, and she gladly accepted. He was a quiet man,
comfortable with silences, she suspected because his
brain was working on a dozen subjects at once.

The meeting with Daniel and the others had seemed
endless. She'd been dreaming of begging a bottle of
wine from the women down the hall, getting out of
her damp clothes and into a warm bath and sipping
her cares away. But cares weren't so easy to banish
these days.

"We took your car for examination," Jamey said
when they stopped at the curb to cross First Street.
The rain was doing its best to wash away the signs and
smells of the ugly scene, but there were scorched marks
on the pavement and soot on the hotel windows, and

singed odors still hung in the heavy air. He gestured toward the buildings across the street. "It would have been a shame if those windows broke. They're original to the building, you know."

"I would have hated that." She shoved her hands into her pockets and sighed. "It would have been easier for everyone if I hadn't come to town."

"It's not your fault some crazy guy set your car on fire."

"It is when the crazy guy followed me here."

"Nope, not even then." They trotted across the street once there was a break in the traffic. "You okay with staying here?"

Jamey had been part of the conversation about that in the conference room. She had suggested a move one town over. There were bigger, more anonymous hotels in Tulsa. Anything Jamey or the detectives needed from her, they could get by phone. She could hide there until their investigation went nowhere, and then she could leave. Go. Hide someplace else for a while.

She'd thought Daniel, at least, would have supported her. After all, if she moved temporarily to Tulsa, she would be out of his way. No accidental meetings, not even distant glimpses. But he'd remained tight-jawed, silently agreeing with the others. They wanted her to stay in their jurisdiction, Chief Douglas had said, and that had been that. She'd looked at Daniel's face for disappointment or satisfaction or some hint of anything, but his features had been as blank as a wax doll's.

She and Jamey stepped around a cleaning crew that was scrubbing the hotel's large windows, and he opened the door for her. Behind the desk, Claire's color was slowly returning. She sighed heavily as she stood.

"Natasha, I'm so sorry! I feel so bad that I told you to park out front last night. Your car would have been so much safer in the back lot. None of the cars back there had any vandalism at all."

Jamey tilted his head to one side. "You think it was random? Her car was the only one on the block and that's why the guy chose it?"

Claire's eyes widened. "What else could it be? You know how kids are. Used to be, they'd drive down the road at night and bash mailboxes. Now they bash car windows or store windows. Sometimes they start fires. You've investigated enough of them, Jamey. And she hasn't even been in town twenty-four hours. No one could have made an enemy that quick."

The fire marshal looked as if he was giving her remarks some thought, and a tiny bit of hope sparked inside Natasha. Could this have been totally random? It wasn't RememberMe targeting her but kids with enough booze to impair their reasoning abilities, a firebomb that needed testing and the lone vehicle on the block? They might not even have realized that Prairie Sun was a hotel. They would have thought all the businesses were closed for the night; there would be danger only to property, not people.

"We have to look at all the possibilities," Jamey said. "It just might be as simple as that."

Claire didn't seem to hear the unsaid part that rang in Natasha's mind: *But I doubt it.*

"Don't worry about it, Claire," she said with the best smile she could summon. "You suggested parking out front, but it was my choice to actually do it. Insurance will take care of it." At least, part of it. She turned to thank Jamey for the escort, but he moved to the foot of the stairs, gesturing for her to go first. It had been a long time since a man had walked her to her door. Daniel had been the last, in fact. Zach hadn't really registered on the gentlemanly or protective scale.

Weariness washed over her as she climbed the stairs. She felt as if she'd been running all day, but it wasn't even noon yet. But she hadn't slept well, hadn't had breakfast, had been chilled and scared and damp all morning. She was tired, hungry and blue.

Don't let the Monday blues get you down, RememberMe had written. The bastard had turned every day into blues day.

"I notice you carry a gun," she remarked as she dug her key from her bag.

"I've been through both the fire academy and the police academy. Fire marshals have powers of arrest."

"So you could be a cop if you wanted." She swung the door open just in time to be startled by a heavy blast of water against her windows. She didn't realize she'd gasped until Jamey touched her arm.

"It's the cleaning crew." He pointed across the room, where sudsy high-pressure streams sprayed across first one window, then the other. He didn't remark on her jumpiness, but he did step past her into the room, look around, open the bathroom door and look inside. "I could be a cop," he said laconically, "but a lot of people don't like cops. Everyone likes firefighters."

"And women go weak for them." Her smile was faint but genuine. Jamey was no taller than her, compact and muscular, with his head shaved and his eyes blue, and she imagined a lot of women went weak for him. Stacia would drool over him, given the chance.

His grin was compelling. "Good thing, too, because

I certainly go weak for them." That sharp gaze connected with hers. "You gonna be okay? Do you need anything?"

Her mouth compressed into a line she hoped passed for a smile, and she shook her head. "Thanks a lot, Jamey."

When he closed the door behind him, the room suddenly grew small and quiet. The only sounds were the rain and the water spray still sweeping across the front of the building. Tiredly she stripped off her slicker, shoes and jeans, pulled on a pair of cotton shorts then sank onto the bed. There were things she needed to do—call Stacia, unpack the suitcases she'd packed late last night, get some food before her stomach turned rebellious, forget everything that had happened in the past twenty-four hours—but first she needed rest. Just a quick nap, if sleep would come.

It seemed as though she'd just lain down, but when she rolled over to face the clock, nearly an hour had passed. She didn't feel any better—something vaguely uneasy had settled over her, as if her dreams had been bad—but the immediate rumble of her stomach suggested that nap time was over. Eyes closed, she lay there a moment, listening, wondering what had awoken her. The rain continued, but the sounds of water directed at the building were gone. Everything was still and should have been peaceful, but she felt…

The knock at the door startled her into a sitting position. Tasha chastised her with too much snark, *You think ScrewYou's gonna come here in the middle of the day and knock politely at the door?*

"Natasha?"

It was Daniel. The knowledge calmed her and, at the

same time, disturbed her even more. On the one hand, she'd always felt safe with him—and liked spending time with him—and found such pleasure in him. But on the other, he wasn't dealing with this whole stalker thing the way she'd expected. His anger bothered her, stirred up her guilt, made her remember such better times, and there were those occasional moments that made her wish…

"Natasha." His voice was louder now, his tone more urgent.

"Yeah, just a minute." She scrambled from the bed, glanced in the dresser mirror to make sure she didn't look too much the worse for wear then padded to the door. Without bothering to check the peephole, she unlocked the door, stepping back as she opened it wide.

He didn't look much drier than he had when he'd left the courthouse while she talked to Jamey. His pants legs were wet to the knees, his hair was slicked back from his face and the plastic bag he carried was splattered with raindrops. He made no move to enter the room until she gestured.

"I'd feel more comfortable with the door closed." And not just because she wore only a T-shirt and snug-fitting shorts.

He stepped in, waited until she closed and locked the door, then glanced around before going through the open bathroom door. The bag crinkled as he set it on the counter. He then deftly untied the knots that secured it. No point in tearing up a perfectly good bag, she thought, suppressing a grin that unexpectedly raised her spirits a mile or two.

He came back out holding a paper-wrapped deli sandwich in each hand. After laying them on the desk, he added two bottles—one water, one her favorite pop—then pulled napkins from a pocket. "I brought lunch," he said unnecessarily when he finally looked at her.

Her stomach roared happily. "I was wondering if a run to Judge Judie's would be okay."

He scratched subconsciously at a place on his cheek. "Probably, but it would be wiser not to go out alone. Taryn would probably be happy to deliver something."

Taryn, whose face had lit up and whose voice had gone husky when she'd seen him yesterday? Natasha wasn't sure she was hungry enough to trust her.

She pulled a chair to one end of the desk and chose the smaller of the sandwiches. Though there really wasn't a huge difference between her and Daniel as far as size, her appetite was normal while his had always been... Healthy, Archer said. Enormous, Jeffrey disagreed. Daniel claimed he burned a lot of calories just thinking.

He used to claim he burned a whole lot more thinking about her.

He probably still did. It was just that the passion these days was negative.

After hanging his jacket in the bathroom, he took the chair opposite her, unwrapped a foot-long cheesesteak with all the trimmings and took a bite. "They said Jamey brought you back."

She nodded, but he wasn't looking at her. "Yeah. He carries a gun."

"I know," he said drily. "But he's more Stacia's type than yours."

She wasn't surprised he remembered Stacia's type. Wasn't surprised he remembered her own favorite sandwich, right down to the dressing. She was kind of surprised that he admitted to it. Wouldn't it have been easier for him to claim amnesia? She would even have gone along with it, though deep in her heart, she knew he never forgot anything that had been important to him.

But then, neither did she. Every major fact about him was seared into her memory.

That he'd loved her more than he should have.

That she'd loved him as much as she could but just not enough.

That she'd broken his heart.

That she'd damaged her own heart.

And that he would never, ever forgive her.

They'd eaten a few bites in silence when Daniel took a good look around the room. His first glances were always fairly comprehensive. In an emergency, he didn't have time to scrutinize every detail, but he'd learned to see enough. This time he noticed the fussy bed that Jeffrey would describe as whimsical, the old armoire that Archer would admire the workmanship on, the marble top on the dresser and the two suitcases standing next to it.

Suitcases in a hotel room were hardly out of place, but their presence gave him a jolt. He'd traveled with Natasha enough to know that the first thing—well, sometimes the second—she did in a hotel room was unpack, even if they were staying for just one night. She hung clothes in the closet and folded them in the drawers and put the suitcases out of sight, wanting no reminder that the stay was temporary.

He shifted his gaze to her. She'd noticed what caught

his attention and was plucking off little pieces of bread from her sandwich, her cheeks tinged pink.

"You were planning to leave this morning."

Her shoulders jerked in a shrug.

Without calling. Without letting him know. After telling him someone was stalking her, she'd intended to load her car and take off and leave him to figure out where she was going on his own. He wanted to think, *Of course. That's what she does. She runs away.* But how could he hold it against her when his last words to her had been, *Don't feel like you need to stick around any longer*? When his last action had been driving off and leaving her to make her way back to her hotel alone after she'd just told him she was being stalked?

She'd intended to do what he'd told her to do. What he'd wanted. Sort of. Mostly.

He chewed another bite while getting a firmer grip on his control, then asked, pretty calmly he thought, "Where were you going?"

"I hadn't decided."

"What about staying with Stacia?"

"I won't put her in danger."

"Your parents?"

A snort escaped her. "Mom's on husband number five, Dad's with girlfriend number eight and husband number three has taken up with girlfriend number three and they're staying at the house between their travels. Between all the extended families, grown kids, grand-kids, kids' friends and such, when Stacia and I went there for the Labor Day cookout, we didn't know most of the people living in our house."

Daniel winced for her inside. People always thought his upbringing had been unconventional because his fathers were gay and he had no mother figure, but his life had been predictable and boring compared to Natasha's. Her parents had never shared a responsible day in their lives. The only constancy in their house had been inconstancy. He couldn't remember a time when fewer than five adults had lived in the house—not counting any of the Spencer kids—and their romantic entanglements had been more complicated to sort out than the cleverest criminal enterprise ever. The best thing he could say for her mom and dad was that they did love their kids.

But, apparently, they loved anyone. Everyone.

After another bite, she changed the subject, at least to another aspect. "Claire thinks this was just vandalism. That my car was picked because it was parked on the street instead of the lot out back. Wrong place, wrong time. Do you think…?"

The hope in her voice was faint, and he didn't like being the one to shoot it down. "No, I don't. I think he figured out that you were planning to leave and wanted you to stay. He lured you here, Natasha. Maybe he knew that you would have to locate the other two. Maybe he knew you were friends with my fathers and they'd give me up in a heartbeat. Maybe he was prepared to play out the game wherever you ended up. But now that you're here, I'm guessing he doesn't want you to leave until he deals with me."

It felt funny saying those last words. He wasn't superhero material, but he'd always taken care of himself. When kids had bullied him about his parents in elementary and middle school, he'd been unflappable. No one had ever been able to get under his skin. No one had ever *dealt* with him, and some idiot who called himself RememberMe—the guy had probably been going for romantic, but gagging was Daniel's first impulse—wasn't going to be the first.

"How could he have known I was coming here? I was on the road for two and a half days. Do you think the same car could have been behind me all that time and I didn't notice?"

He shrugged. "Maybe he had a tracker on your car. Maybe he's bugged your phone. Maybe he's hacked your tablet. Maybe he knew you contacted Archer and Jeffrey and assumed this would be your destination. Jamey'll look over your car for anything that survived the fire. Our IT guy will check your cell and tablet. We'll need copies of those emails and texts anyway. Did you by chance bring the cards and gifts?"

She left her chair, hefted a suitcase onto the bed and unzipped the outer pocket. "The gifts were in the trunk of the car. I thought I should keep them, but I didn't want them in my house." Pulling out an armful of thick envelopes, she laid them on the table between them. The top one was labeled "Emails #1." The envelopes were full but not so stuffed that the edges were wearing. He counted seven of them.

After adding her phone and the tablet, she sat down again. Ignoring what was left of her sandwich, she folded her arms over her chest. "Could someone give me a ride to a store to get a prepaid cell? I'm really not comfortable with the idea of sticking my head out the window and yelling, 'Nine-one-one!' if something happens."

The room had a phone, Daniel had noticed, but landlines could easily be cut. "We'll take care of it." He could pick up a cell phone when he left here, activate it and send one of the uniformed officers over with it. About a half dozen of them who'd seen her yesterday or this morning had already asked if she was single and if there was anything going on between them.

Ben thought the first few had seriously wanted to know. He thought the last few had done it just to see steam rise from Daniel's ears.

Steam had *not* risen from his ears. His blood pressure hadn't risen, either, and he hadn't practically ground the top layers off his teeth.

"I tried to call Flea." He wasn't used to having to redirect his thoughts all the time—or, actually, not at all. The chief had told him on more than one occasion that he sometimes had a bad case of tunnel vision, looking straight ahead and not opening to all the possibilities. This morning, the only time his focus had been good was at the hospital when he'd interviewed their domestic violence victim.

"She couldn't talk," he went on. "Said she would call me back later. Jamey says there was definitely some sort of solvent used. Of course, they could smell that. He and Ben are checking the surveillance cameras that had a view of the car overnight. The nearest camera is at the courthouse door, so it's not great footage. They're not done yet, but the only thing that's caught their attention so far is that no one went near the car in the hour preceding the fire."

"Maybe it really was spontaneous combustion."

He remembered her flip comment when he'd first approached her outside that morning. "About the only thing that spontaneously combusts around here is hay."

"Really."

"Yeah. If hay has more than 22 percent moisture

when it's stacked or baled, it begins to release flammable gases that will auto-ignite when the temperature inside the hay gets hot enough."

"I actually meant 'really' in a dry, surprised way that you know anything whatsoever about hay. In LA, you only knew what it looked like from what you'd seen on TV."

She was right. "Cedar Creek's not LA. We deal with different types of situations here."

"What other types of situations besides self-burning hay?"

"Well, you do not honk at cows that have gotten out of their pasture onto the road. They surround your vehicle and stare at you while chewing—" he mimicked their big eyes and exaggerated mouth action "—waiting for the treats they expect you to give them. And some people here do their gift-shopping at the feed store. Oh, and the best frog legs in town are at the gas station on South Hickory but only on Fridays."

She laughed. She didn't intend to—he could see it in her surprise—but it burst out anyway. It eased the lines of her face and the pallor of her skin and reminded him like a punch to the gut why he'd fallen in love with her. She was funny and optimistic and lighthearted and beautiful and smart and sexy, and she'd loved her family and their friends and his parents and their dog and him... She'd loved him most of all.

For a while.

Good times. Bad times. Times that made him just the slightest bit wistful.

"How is Stacia?" he asked before starting on the last chunk of his sandwich.

"She's great. She got a recurring role on one of those

crime-drama shows. She plays twins, one who died in the first episode and the other who wants justice for her death. It was creepy, seeing her made up to look dead, even though she was sitting right beside me when I watched it." Natasha suppressed a shudder.

"If it pays the bills…"

"You still don't watch television. Just the documentary stuff, right?"

"And the occasional old movie. Last weekend I saw *The Thin Man* series, and this weekend it'll be Cary Grant. *Arsenic and Old Lace. His Girl Friday. The Philadelphia Story.*"

Emotion flitted across her face, amusement there and gone almost too quickly to identify. *Sometimes I forget you have a sense of humor,* she'd said last night.

"I know. You still think it's weird I like comedies."

"Old comedies," she stressed. "When the writing was intelligent, the actors were talented and the setups were more sophisticated. I think it suits you." She sat back, legs crossed, fingers loosely clasped in her lap. Her T-shirt was thin and long-sleeved, clinging to her breasts and waist and hips, and her black shorts did the same. They could have done double duty as a bikini bottom—they were that skimpy—and he wondered if RememberMe had ever seen her in them.

Under normal circumstances, it would be none of his business. They had been together, and now they weren't. If another guy saw her in the tiny shorts or the fancy lingerie she'd always preferred, if he'd seen her in nothing but her skin and they'd done wild, wicked things together, that was fine. But the key word there was *together*. If RememberMe was spying on her, if he was watching her dress or undress, shower, do any of the million intimate, basic, everyday things she did and she didn't know it, the pervert level went high enough to launch it into Daniel's business.

That aside, she presented an intriguing picture. Her legs were long and the muscles were lean. She claimed her only interest in physical activity was watching the Dodgers play, but they'd walked thousands of miles when they were together. Running errands back home, she would say, *Why drive from the restaurant to the store? It's only a mile and a half.* Go to a restaurant, then decide she'd prefer the one ten blocks away: *Hey, let's leave the car here. We've already got a parking space.*

She was curvier than she would prefer and exactly the way *he* preferred—nice hips, narrow waist, luscious breasts—and the way she held her head had always seemed regal. Even with the short, sleek hair, mostly shorter than his own, she looked very elegant. Beautiful. A vision that should be frozen in time.

Daniel would bet RememberMe had more than a few images of her. Probably an entire wall of them, candid shots taken at a distance, hiding in a crowd, capturing private moments he had no right intruding on.

He didn't realize he was rubbing his stubble again until she gestured. "Did you miss a spot shaving, or are you developing a nervous habit?"

Temptation tried to pull his face into a rueful smile. "I didn't notice it when I was at home and could do something about it, of course."

Rising gracefully, she pulled a plastic zippered bag from her second suitcase, removed the razor inside and laid it on the table. When she sat, she pulled her feet onto the chair and wrapped her arms around her knees.

For an instant, she looked so vulnerable. He had to look away, and when that wasn't enough, he took the razor into the bathroom, wet it, shaved that narrow strip then dried both his face and the razor.

For a moment, he looked at his reflection in the mirror. His own color wasn't so good, his hair was drying in an unruly manner and the muscles in his jaw and cheeks and forehead were taut, forming lines where a man his age shouldn't have them.

He exhaled heavily, rotated his neck and lifted his shoulders, but none of it made him feel any more relaxed. He grabbed the plastic bag he'd brought lunch in and returned to the room.

"Feel better?"

"I wish all my irritants were that easily taken care of." Another emotion flashed across her face, guilt this time or maybe hurt, and everything inside him got tighter. He fixed his gaze on the items she'd stacked on the table, and then he placed them inside the bag. "Someone will stop by in the next hour or two with a cell phone, and we'll be in touch about dinner, any shopping you need, whatever. We'll also need whatever information you have on Kyle and Eric and Zach—full names, birth dates, where they last lived, what kind of work they did—so if you could write that out and have it ready…"

He had edged halfway to the door when she stood. "Daniel, I'm so sorry—"

Because she looked so sincere and familiar and dangerous, and because he was remembering too much and feeling too much, he went past the control he'd always exercised right back to verging on hostility. "You're always sorry, Natasha. You make everyone else sorry, too. You don't need to apologize for the guy stalking you and setting your car on fire, and I don't need an apology for you dumping me. Sometimes…" He picked up his jacket then unlocked and opened the door before looking back. "Words just aren't up to the job."

Nothing brought out the need to be active like the inability. Natasha spent fifteen rushed minutes on the phone with Stacia, blurting out everything on one of her sister's breaks. She unpacked her suitcases. Stood near—not at—one window or another and watched the rain. Paced the length and the breadth of the room. Put on the makeup she'd never gotten around to that morning.

She would have played *Candy Crush*, but it was on the electronic devices Daniel had taken. She could have lost herself in a book, but all her books were on the same devices. She could have surfed the internet—she'd been known to pass countless hours on Wikipedia, clicking from one link to another—but that access was on the devices. She had nothing to do but read a glossy twenty-four page magazine put out by the Cedar Creek Chamber of Commerce, and she'd done it. Twice.

After two hours, she was ready to climb the wall.

Daniel had said it wouldn't be wise to go out alone, but he hadn't said she had to stay locked in her room. After trading her sleep shorts for a much more *there* pair, she shoved her feet into running shoes, grabbed her purse and went downstairs to the lobby.

Claire was behind the check-in counter, typing on the computer. "Hey. How are you?"

"I'm good. A little bored."

Claire's gaze shifted outside. "Yeah, I'm wondering if we should start building an ark. I heard Polecat Creek is within a few inches of spilling out onto the street and Cedar Creek has already covered the beach and some of the picnic tables."

Natasha had no idea where either of those streams were but figured they must be significant if Claire found them worth mentioning. "I have to say, floods aren't the first thing that comes to mind when I think of Oklahoma."

Claire snickered. "I bet not. Not with a guy like Daniel here."

Natasha rested her elbows on the mahogany counter. "You know him?"

"Just to say hello to. After all, he's swoony, and I'm...me."

Wincing inwardly at the woman's self-deprecating shrug, Natasha wanted to tell her that Daniel was too genuine to care if she carried a few extra pounds. He never took anyone at surface value. A pretty face might turn his head, but it wouldn't earn his interest if there wasn't a lot of substance underneath.

"Ooh, by the way..." Claire opened a desk drawer and pulled out a small shopping bag and handed it over. "Officer Simpson brought this by a little bit ago. He got a call as he came through the door and asked me to give it to you. Don't worry. I wouldn't have forgotten it for long. That drawer's where I keep my candy."

Hmm, chocolate sounded good. Natasha hadn't had anything sweet since arriving here, and that was a long time for the sugar fiend inside her. "Two questions, Claire—do you have anything I could read? And do you have a vending machine?"

Claire's answering smile was amazingly cheery, re-

minding her of Stacia's normal happy-happy mode—
though her sister had had little to be happy about lately
where Natasha was concerned. "I have bookcases over
there—" she waved toward the lounge around the corner, past the stairs "—and the vending machine is in
the first room down that hall, on the right. It's dis-
guised as a refrigerator. There's candy and chips and
cookies, too."

"Thank you." Natasha turned down the passageway
that led to the back parking lot and went into the first
room. It wasn't much bigger than a closet and held a
small fridge with bottled water and pop, a coffee maker
with a selection of brew pods and a nice mix of sweet
and salty snacks. An honor sheet hung on the refrigerator door: no need for money, just add her name and
choices to the list.

Armed with pop, M&M's and a bag of barbecue
potato chips, she returned to the lobby. After taking a
couple of books from the case, she sat in a cozy chair
in the corner that was almost big enough for two. A
knitted throw was draped over one arm, and a hassock
stood a few feet away. She felt almost giddy at being
out of her room, though not overly exposed. The windows gave her a great view of the entire block outside,
the chair dwarfed her, and if worse came to worst, she
could hide underneath the throw and possibly go unnoticed.

Too easily, she could see Daniel rolling his eyes
at that.

First things first: with three M&M's melting in her
mouth, she took the phone and an accompanying note
from the bag. She would recognize Daniel's handwrit-
ing anywhere; back home she had dozens of notes he'd

written her, everything from asking her to buy bread
to suggesting dinner out that evening to professing
his love for her.

This note was much more impersonal.

The phone is activated. The number is 918-555-
0949. The chief's, Ben's and my numbers are
already programmed. So are Stacia's and your
insurance agent's.

Insurance. Ugh, she hadn't even thought about that.
Would a photo of the twisted metal frame that was all
the fire had left be enough to convince them the car
was totaled, or would they still need to send an ad-
justor?

She stuck the note and the bag in her purse, the
phone in her pocket and examined the two books she'd
grabbed: both hardcovers, one a psychological thriller
and the other *The Unlucky Ones*. Oh, great: terror and
gore. Crazy-making and dead-making.

Instead of getting up, though, she kicked off her
shoes, propped her feet on the hassock, covered up
with the throw and opened the second book. *I've heard
that book will give you nightmares*, she'd told Claire
last night. Well, it wasn't as if that would be anything
new, would it? And it might be a nice change of pace, to
dream someone else's nightmares rather than her own.

The story was true, according to the blurb on the
cover: "The experiences of a young girl whose parents
were serial killers." It could also be nice, Natasha reminded herself, to remember that a lot of people had
problems far deadlier than her own.

Please, God, let it stay that way.

Music played softly in the distance, probably from the private office behind the check-in counter, and traffic splashed by on the street. The sidewalk was empty of pedestrians—really, who wanted to do anything that wasn't absolutely necessary this afternoon?—and Natasha lost herself in the book. It was scary, yes, and poignant and sad, and every few pages, she kept reminding herself of what Claire had said about the author: *she survived horrible things and went on to live a good life.*

Gradually, she became aware of the fact that she was no longer alone. The hairs on her neck and arms prickled, and fear spasmed in her gut as she slowly drew her gaze from the book page. A man stood at the edge of the carpet—his raincoat and shoes damp—depositing a dripping umbrella into a nearby stand. Obviously he'd just come in, but she hadn't heard the door open, hadn't caught a whiff of rainy freshness or a cooler breath of air. She thought her senses were more attuned to her surroundings than that and was faintly disturbed that they weren't.

He shrugged out of his coat, revealing dark trousers, a gray button-down and a black tie. Her heart rate slowed as she recognized him as the third-floor guest. In the business of computers, Officer Gideon had said, which made Natasha's skin crawl just a little, and from California, which made it crawl more. But the officer had also said he was a regular, same week every month, and he'd arrived in Cedar Creek this time before she'd even crossed the New Mexico state line. He wasn't in the running to be her stalker.

He could be, Tasha nagged. *Anyone could be. Even Claire. Even Daniel.*

After an instant, the irritable voice reconsidered. *Well, not Daniel. He's too…*

Sane? Normal? Uninterested?

The computer guy seemed to notice her for the first time and cast a cautious glance her way. Great, was she so consumed by her stalker that she was starting to act like one herself?

She smiled at him, hoping for polite, not wanting conversation or company. When he took a few steps her way, her hopes sank, but his destination was the bookcase, not her. He ran long fingers across the spines of the hardcovers that stretched across the top rows, apparently looking for a specific title.

Natasha picked up the book she was reading. "Is this the one you want?"

When he turned, his glance went to the book she offered, then to the thriller sitting on the table "Nah. *That* one is. Claire said it's very good."

She offered it, too. "You can go ahead and take it. I haven't started it."

"Well…are you sure?"

"One's enough for me. My eyes aren't used to these things called paper books. They're accustomed to the tablet, where I can change the size of the font and look up things in the dictionary right on the page and change pages with a tap."

He laughed as he came forward to take the book. "I'm old-school. I still prefer the feel and the smell and the weight of a real book."

"Isn't that heresy for an IT guy?"

His brow crooked up, and she shrugged. "Claire mentioned it." Not to her, granted, but she didn't want to acknowledge being the person who, however inadvertently, had disrupted the guests' trips and brought a criminal investigation into their lives.

"Rob," he said then stuck out his hand. Unfortunately, it still held the book. He switched hands and offered his again. "I'm Rob Miller."

"Natasha." She half rose and shook hands. His palm was damp, his grip unimpressive. She wasn't crazy about bruising handshakes, of course—Archer had one of those unless he remembered to tone it down in time—but she liked to know she was shaking hands with a live person. Rob's fingers had barely closed around hers before he let go and pulled back. It was forgettable.

They stayed there, out of words, it appeared, and a little awkward, when a colorful movement outside caught their attention. An instant later, the door opened and in breezed the four wine-trip women. They wore bright clothes and carried brighter umbrellas, and all four of them carefully clutched large, heavy shopping bags to their chests. One of them flashed Natasha and Rob a far-too-cheery smile. "We thought we might have to swim Cedar Creek—"

"Or go down with the wine," a second one interjected.

"—but we made it, and we're celebrating with a wine-tasting in our room tonight. Wear your jammies."

The third one subjected Rob to a sly up-and-down look. "You, too, if you have 'em. But join us even if you don't."

"I'm not much of a drinker," Natasha said with a smile.

"Neither were we when we started these trips. Come see how good we've gotten." The woman winked, then her gaze narrowed. "Hey, you're the owner of the formerly-red-car-now-scorched-heap-of-twisted-metal, aren't you? Honey, we've got a bottle of blackberry wine with your name written all over it. Room five, any time after seven."

They thundered up the stairs, still clutching their purchases, then Natasha shifted her attention back to Rob. "Glad I don't have the room above them." At his slight frown, she hastily went on, "They can't get too bad. Claire keeps letting them back every year."

Instead of relaxing, his frown sharpened a few degrees, his gaze directed toward the stairs, where the women had disappeared. Abruptly, he gave his head a shake, then smiled at her. "I'll be in my room tonight with pizza and a good book, thanks to you. Perfect ending for the week I've had."

With a nod, he left, too, so quiet on the stairs that compared to the wine women, he was damn near stealthy.

Settling back in the chair with the thriller she'd rejected earlier, she sighed softly. When she thought someone was stealthy because he didn't walk like a herd of elephants, maybe it was time for her to take that blackberry wine and drink down every drop.

Chapter 4

"I have better ways to spend a Friday evening," Daniel announced sourly as he waited for traffic to pass before opening the door of the SUV and sliding out.

"What? Watching cop TV?" Morwenna took her time circling the vehicle, and why not? She wore a lime-green raincoat that reached below her knees with purple-and-black checked rain boots that ended in the same vicinity. The coat's hood was pulled over her head, casting her face in deep shadow and giving a glimpse of its red-and-yellow striped lining. It would take a flood of biblical proportions to get her wet.

"I don't watch cop TV," he said with a scowl. "Unless it's to laugh at the mistakes."

As she strolled across the street, he took her arm, trying to nudge her to go a little faster. "Don't worry, Dan'l. Nobody's going to miss seeing me in this outfit."

"No, but it might make them run you down on purpose."

Under the hotel awning, he let go, and she shook impressively before pointing one chastising finger at him. "You have no concept of fashion as a statement. As art."

He wiggled his fingers in the air. "Remember? Dad? Supermodel? I grew up in designer diapers and jammies. I had the best coordinated wardrobe of any nursery school student in Malibu. I know fashion. I also know color-blind I-don't-give-a-darn, too."

"Jeffrey's style is as classic as classic can get. My style is funky."

"Your style is close your eyes, grab some garments and throw them on." As he reached for the door, movement in the lobby shifted his gaze past her, poking the ember of annoyance in his gut. Natasha sat in the corner, shoes kicked off, snuggled in as if she were safe in her own living room instead of a hotel lobby with plate glass windows from side to side, there for anyone to see from the sidewalk, the street or the other neighboring buildings. Why wasn't she in her room with the door double-locked and the blinds drawn?

Because it was an awfully small space to be confined to for hours on end, and he hadn't actually told her to stay there, which she would be quick to point out if he made a fuss. And there'd been no direct threat against her yet—just her fiancés and her car. The only person even remotely threatened was him, and he'd been two dozen places today without looking over his shoulder even once.

Well, maybe once.

Not noticing his hesitation, Morwenna pushed past

his outstretched arm, opened the door and went inside. "Evening, Claire," she called, hanging her coat on the rack and taking a few steps toward the desk, stopping at the edge of the rug. "I won't come any closer because I don't want my wellies to drip all over your floor, but how are your cat babies? And how's your mum?"

Daniel dried his boots on the rug, intensely aware of Natasha's speculative gaze on them. She had more color than when he'd last seen her, and less hurt, and an air of boredom that practically vibrated. Placing a finger in the book she was reading, she closed the cover and waited.

His boots squeaked a few times as he moved from the heavy-duty rug at the door to the braided one where the furniture sat. He thought of a dozen things he could say—shouldn't say—and settled on the least offensive. "Did you get the phone?"

"Yes, but I didn't get to give the officer this." She pulled a sheet of hotel paper from the back of the book and laid it on the coffee table between them.

He had to take a few steps more to pick it up. Identifying information for her other fiancés: Kyle, Eric, Zach. When they were together, everything was always *Natasha and Daniel. Natasha and I. We.* He'd been able to ignore *Natasha and Kyle* and *Natasha and Eric* because he'd known this time was different. *They* were different.

And then there'd been *Natasha and Zach*, and before long, there would be *Natasha and someone else*, because while he might have been different, she wasn't. She was the same unable-to-commit woman who'd broken hearts both before and after his.

"Thank you for putting Stacia's and my insurance agent's numbers in the phone."

He shrugged. Serve and protect—that was what cops did. His gaze fell on the book she was reading, a cover he knew well. *The Unlucky Ones.* "You're reading—" At the last instant, he bit off the words. No more than a handful of people in town knew that author Jane Gama was Mila Douglas, the chief's wife, and that that nightmare had been her life. Any time Mila wanted to spill the secret, great, but he wasn't going to spill it for her.

"Kind of creepy reading given the circumstances," he said instead.

"It's easier to worry about Jane than myself."

"She survives," he said drily.

"I know. I don't think I could have started it if Claire hadn't told me that."

She looked past him, and he realized that Morwenna and Claire's conversation had ended. Morwenna was still standing on the rug instead of stepping onto the wood floor, but her curiosity was sharp enough to minimize the distance between them. She looked from him to Natasha, then back again, rolling her eyes. "Where are the manners Jeffrey taught you, eh? I'm Morwenna Armstrong. I work at the police department. And you're the size-two beach goddess with OMG shoes."

Natasha's expression was part amused, part wry. Daniel knew she wouldn't waste time wondering if that description had come from him. His fashion sense extended only to his own clothes, he wasn't sure he'd ever used the word *goddess* in his life, and he was very sure he'd never said *OMG* in his life.

Natasha set the book aside, threw back the afghan and stood, coming around the furniture to shake hands

with Morwenna. When he saw that she'd changed out
of the tiny shorts she'd worn earlier, something crazy
like disappointment surged through him, but he ruth-
lessly pushed it away.

"I'm Natasha Spencer." She gave Morwenna a look
then said, "I like your outfit."

As Daniel joined them, Morwenna punched him on
the arm. "Ha! She's clearly got better taste than you."

Or lies better, he thought, because he was pretty
sure Natasha wouldn't be caught dead in leggings, a
miniskirt and layered T-shirts, snug-fitting in eye-
spasm-inducingly bright and clashing colors. Granted,
Natasha could catch every man's attention wearing
olive drab camouflage.

"You look incredibly comfy," Natasha said, and
Morwenna nudged him again.

"I know! No one seems to understand the concept
of comfort today. Mum spends half her life in leggings
but still gives me the evil eye when I leave the house
wearing them."

"The difference is your mum is running marathons
in her exercise clothes while you're going to work and
on dates in yours," Daniel helpfully pointed out. "To
say nothing of the fact that hers tend to match."

"It'd be a sad world if we all had to match, wouldn't
it?" Morwenna shifted closer to Natasha. "We're here
to take you to dinner. You might want to put on something that covers more. The rain's got a chill to it tonight. I'll escort you upstairs to change while Daniel
turns the vehicle around to park in front of the door
the way I told him to when we got here."

He watched the thoughts cross Natasha's face:
amusement, fading boredom, curiosity, surprise. Was

she wondering what his and Morwenna's relation-ship was? Did she assume Morwenna was a cop, too, maybe even a detective working plainclothes, not that the phrase even existed in Morwenna's vocabulary?

Or was he projecting his own thoughts on her? He'd seen the man talking to her the first time he'd driven by. He'd noticed how reluctant the guy seemed to walk away from her. He'd texted Ben and asked him about the information they'd dug up on the only single guy on the guest registry.

Daniel didn't like her hanging with the man, he'd decided after scanning his photo, his identifiers, his job information. He was sure of that. But it was okay, because he was equally sure that his only objection was Natasha's stalker situation. Having possibly put Daniel's, Kyle's, Eric's and Zach's lives in danger, the least she could do was delay looking for number five until that was resolved.

Jealousy had nothing to do with it. He was just try-ing to do his job.

He tuned back in to find both women watching him. Morwenna wore her exasperated face, and Natasha still looked faintly amused. For what was probably the second—or fourth—time, Morwenna said, with impossibly unhelpful hand gestures, "We go upstairs. You get car. Turn around. Park at door."

Daniel scowled at her. He wasn't about to admit that he'd been too deep in thought about Natasha and that guy and jealousy to hear what either woman had said, so he just turned toward the lobby exit. Natasha never dawdled getting ready. Changing shorts for jeans, sneakers for boots…a couple minutes, tops. They would be back in the lobby by the time he drove far enough down the block to make a U-turn and came back.

Morwenna had been right: with the setting of the unseen sun, the rain had picked up a chill. Misty auras circled streetlights and headlights, and denser pockets of fog floated free-form a few inches above the concrete. For just a moment, as he turned the truck's heater on and waited to pull out of the parking space, he felt a tug of homesickness. He wanted to see sunlight, to smell the ocean brine on the breezes, to feel the heat of the sun and the air and the ground combining to warm him all the way through. He wanted to be dry. Comfortable. Peaceful. Was it so much to ask? Of course not. Was it going to happen?

He glanced into the hotel lobby, where Natasha and Morwenna would appear any moment, and found the answer there.

No. Not any time soon.

"So, this stalker of yours... Is he shy and quirky or just totally creepy?"

Natasha pulled a pair of jeans from the armoire and went into the bathroom to change, closing the door only partway so they could talk. "Well, he's been around two weeks short of a year, and I've never seen him. I think he pushed my ex-fiancé down the stairs, he followed me to Oklahoma and he set my car on fire. What do you think?"

In the mirror, she watched as Morwenna considered her words. "Well, pushing the guy down the stairs was horrible. Not having the backbone to out himself and meet you... I have some friends who could overlook that. Probably the fire, too. You know the type—my friends, not him. They grew up thinking that the absolute only thing they could be as an adult was married, and now they're twenty-four or twenty-seven and still single, and it's upset the balance of the universe so much that it's about to explode." She made an explosive sound, miming a nuclear mushroom cap.

Grinning, Natasha came out of the bathroom, retrieved socks from a drawer and boots from the armoire then sat down. "What about you? Is marriage in your plans?"

"God, no. Not for at least another twenty years. My mum and dad are married. She lives here. He lives in London. My brother's married, too, to a total prat whose whole family are prats. When they came here to visit, they had to stay here at the Prairie Sun because Mum doesn't tolerate prats, and Fee got little bird-wing and beak bruises all over her backside." She gestured to the string of birds decorating both headboard and footboard of the bed. "She offered to show proof to Claire when she complained—and trust me, Fiona *always* complains—and I was like, 'Ew, no! Are you trying to scar her for life?'"

This time Natasha laughed out loud, easing the tension in her neck by a few degrees. There were times when she felt like Morwenna's friends whose universe was on the verge of exploding, though for clearly opposite reasons: theirs for lack of a man, hers for the presence of one. If she couldn't laugh now and again, she would cry.

"Going back to the subject of marriage..."

Ah, Tasha said in her smug tone. *See what happens when you ask people personal questions? They get to ask them right back.*

"You've been engaged four times, so it's safe to assume that you want to get married. But you've called off four weddings, so it's safe to assume that you don't want it as much as you thought. What's the deal?"

Natasha shoved her feet into the boots then zipped each one. "That's the million-dollar question," she said drily, one she'd discussed multiple times with everybody who'd thought they'd had any kind of stake in the event. That had included her father's girlfriend's grown daughter, her mother's third mother-in-law and pretty much anybody who'd bought a wedding gift.

Except the fiancés. She hadn't seen Eric or Zach, and apologizing to Kyle and Daniel didn't constitute a discussion.

"I really did love Kyle…and Eric…and Daniel…and Zach. At the time, we seemed such perfect pairs. But as the weddings approached, the perfection looked more and more an illusion. It seemed ridiculous to think that I could make a marriage work when so many smarter, braver, more normal people than me couldn't. Suddenly I couldn't see us five years down the line, still happy and in love. I couldn't see us five *months* down the line. I couldn't invest one more minute in a marriage that wasn't going to last."

"But every marriage, no matter how improbable, has a chance," Morwenna said quietly.

"Your mom and dad, married and living half a world apart. My mom and dad still live together but have been divorced for fifteen years. Mom's added four more husbands, and Dad's had eight girlfriends. Most of them moved in with him and Mom and the husband of the moment."

"Ew. No offense, but that's just…" Morwenna shuddered for emphasis. "Is that all they do together? Live together? I mean, it's not like some kinky sex thing?"

It was Natasha's turn to shudder. "I try not to think about my parents having sex, with each other or anyone else." *Or everyone else.* "No, as far as I know, it's just weird." After a quick look in the mirror, she picked up her slicker and purse. "This isn't the same room where your sister-in-law got cozy with the birds, is it?"

Morwenna laughed easily as she crossed to the door. "Oh, no. And trust me, Claire sanitized every little feather and beak on that bed. I still don't want to imagine how Fiona's bum came into contact with them."

They left the room and headed down the stairs. At the bottom, Daniel's dark SUV came into sight, parked only a few steps from the main entrance. "I told him to park here before," Morwenna commented, "but he was talking to Ben about the man you were talking to. He can be so stubborn."

So he'd seen her with Rob, which meant that Rob checked out okay. If there had been anything questionable in his background, anything to indicate he could even possibly be her stalker, Daniel would have warned her.

Even if it was just out of an abundance of caution and lacking even a whiff of jealousy.

Breathing deeply, Natasha climbed into the back seat while Morwenna settled in front. As Daniel pulled back into traffic, he told them to let him know if they got too warm from the blasting heat. Morwenna *hmm*ed in response. Other than that, the only sound was the swiping of the wiper blades as they tried to keep up with the rain.

Natasha didn't have a chance to get uncomfortable in

the silence, or to even get warm. A couple of minutes, and they'd reached their destination. They approached from the rear, the headlights flashing across a faded sign for Creek Café. The area was too dimly lit, too wet, too shiver-inducing to be appealing, with ruts in the driveway practically deep enough to swallow the SUV.

"Poor Mrs. LB," Morwenna said, twisting to see Natasha as the vehicle rocked from side to side. "This street is city property, which means it's their responsibility to maintain, but the only place it goes is to the back of the diner. Mrs. Holcomb, who owns two of the competing restaurants in town, is a city councilwoman and she keeps them from ever doing work on the road. Luckily, only stubborn people ever come this way because if we'd gone 'round the block and used the main entrance, we would already be seated by now."

Even in the dim light of the dashboard, Natasha saw the look Daniel gave her. To someone who didn't know him, he might appear annoyed, but she knew the annoyance was feigned and the affection was genuine. He really liked Morwenna, and it was clear as air that she really liked him, too. Natasha wasn't sure how far it went, or in which direction, but she was glad for both of them. Daniel deserved every friend, girlfriend and so much more. He really did. And she really was happy.

Really, damn it.

There was a large ill-defined lot behind the restaurant, four rows of vehicles parked in crooked rows on puddle-saturated gravel, with a tall chain-link fence providing a barrier on the east side. Daniel nosed the vehicle into the space between it and an oversize black pickup truck.

"I guess we're going in the back door," Morwenna said brightly.

"Remember? Keeping a low profile?"

She paused, her open door lighting the vehicle. "Then why'd you invite me? I've never kept a low profile in my life."

"You invited me. Remember? Better things to do?" Abruptly, his gaze met Natasha's, as if his mouth had spoken without permission and he'd heard the words the same moment she did. Discomfort played around his mouth, then after Morwenna slammed the door shut, he stiffly muttered, "Sorry."

Not sorry he'd thought it. Just sorry he'd said it. Aloud. To her.

Natasha forced a smile and opened the door. The powerful rushing of water immediately filled her ears, drawing her gaze past the fence and below. Even with illumination from the restaurant and along the street in front of it, it was impossible to make out anything but shadows: big solid ones hunched in piles down the hillside, and rushing swirling ones that cascaded past with enough force to carry a good-sized vehicle along like a leaf. Mother Nature's fury was impressive.

"Cedar Creek." Daniel's voice came from nearby. He'd circled to the back of the vehicle and stood a short distance away. "Normally, you can't hear the water over the birds singing."

"It's scary." Could anyone who fell into such tumult make it out alive?

"Yeah," he agreed. Awkwardly he gestured toward the restaurant. "We should get inside."

Before she'd taken more than a few steps, the flood-light nearest them flickered then went out, leaving only a small bright glow in the center that was slow to fade. Natasha wasn't sure whether the sharp intake of breath was hers, or if it had come from Daniel, since the tiny hairs on her nape had risen and his right hand automatically pushed back the edge of his slicker to reach his gun. She had a crazy urge to grab onto him with both hands, or to shove him out of the way and make a wild zigzagging run to the rear door of the restaurant, but by the time she'd managed to suck in a breath, that same door opened, spilling light into the night.

Ben Little Bear stood there beneath the protective overhang, his dark gaze directed to the light post. "Damn light always goes out at the worst time possible. Come on in."

"Wouldn't the worst time possible be any time it's dark?" Morwenna asked as she slipped past him.

In spite of the recent spike of her blood pressure and the new high she'd reached on her thrill meter, Natasha couldn't resist smiling at the other woman's response. Behind her, Daniel snorted.

Ahead of them, Ben did nothing but give Morwenna a stark, flat look that should have cowed her but made her smile sunnily instead.

"I like her," Natasha whispered, expecting no one to hear. Of course Daniel did. Of course he snorted at her, too. It felt familiar. Comfortable.

The small room they entered appeared to serve as both a coatroom for employees and an overflow storeroom. They left their raincoats there before following Ben through the kitchen, where a lot of people called hellos to him, nudged or swatted him on the way past or ignored him pointedly. Mrs. LB owned the restaurant, Morwenna had said—no doubt, Mrs. Little Bear.

A family business, and maybe a few relatives on the line tonight who were jealous of the one who had his Friday off to do what he wanted.

Even if he was apparently babysitting her. And even if Morwenna and Daniel had confessed to the babysitting gig from the beginning, she still would have come along. There was only so much sitting alone in a room she could bear.

How much sitting in a room with Daniel could she bear?

Ben got sidelined by his mother, so Daniel stepped around him and proceeded through the kitchen. At the front, a door led into a hallway that bisected the building from side to side. The main dining rooms were to the left; the bathrooms and Mrs. Little Bear's office were the other way. Past the office, an unmarked door was their destination: the family dining room.

The hallway was the only place they risked being seen by other diners, and he said a crisp, "Hurry up," when they reached it. He stepped out, scanned the dining room, then motioned for the two women to turn right. Seeing only familiar faces in the dining room eased his nerves somewhat. He wasn't a strong proponent of letting people in danger go out and about as they pleased, but Morwenna had insisted dinner would be safe, and when Ben had taken her side, Daniel been outvoted.

The only other option, she'd said, was for him to take Natasha home and cook for her.

Not in this lifetime.

"It's a shame he's not warm and fuzzy like his dad,"

Morwenna said, "but no, he's gruff and grumpy like his father."

"Oh, you know Jeffrey and Archer?" Natasha responded. Their voices were soft, vastly familiar and different and…important.

"Yes! Aren't they great?" Morwenna paused, and her comes-and-goes British accent came. "Though Archer gets pretty warm and fuzzy with Jeffrey."

"I know," Natasha agreed. "They're really sweet together."

Daniel stepped past them to open the dining room door. What would tough-guy Archer think of being described as fuzzy and sweet? He would probably consider the sources, then take it as a compliment. He liked Morwenna and, together with Jeffrey, he had loved Natasha more than anyone else could have.

Except Daniel. With the emphasis on *had loved*. As in *no longer did*. He was one of those people who learned from the past, so he wasn't doomed to repeat it. When RememberMe was out of Natasha's life and she'd disappeared again, he would be okay again. Satisfied again. Good without her again.

He would.

Absently rubbing his chest, he walked the perimeter of the room, adjusting the blinds on one window, lowering them the last inch on the next. The room wasn't overly large; getting between some of the tables required turning sideways and squeezing past the chairs. Like the main dining room, it had a tile floor, but this one was mostly covered by area rugs. There was a fireplace at one end, with a couch, a cradle and a changing table grouped around it. Family pictures hung on the walls, and decks of cards and board games were stacked on the fireplace mantel.

"This looks more like someone's house than a restaurant."

He glanced over his shoulder as Natasha came to stand beside him. Somewhere between the last two feet of the hallway and the room, they'd lost Morwenna, probably gone to say hello to someone. It seemed she knew everyone.

Daniel leaned against the back of the sofa, his hands resting on the frame at his sides. "When Mrs. Little Bear started the diner, she never was home for dinner. They didn't have enough customers to use the whole place, so she had this room blocked off and made it into a family room. The kids came here after school, did homework, watched TV and ate dinner with her before going home."

While tables for four were pushed against the walls, the main tables were two old trestles, rough and primitive, bearing the scars of decades of work, enough chopping to dull a thousand blades and carved hearts and tic-tac-toe games. Mismatched wood chairs butted up to the sides with armchairs at the ends: one for Mrs. Little Bear, the other for Great-Aunt Weezer.

Now *there* was someone who was gruff and grumpy. She made Daniel appear the soul of friendliness and light.

Natasha walked in a slow circle around the trestle tables. "I used to think that the smaller the family dinner, the better. In our case, it meant the people eating with us were actually family and not girlfriends, boyfriends, exes, prospective exes, friends, neighbors or casual acquaintances. Usually at our table, everyone there was someone's family. Just not ours."

Which had left her and her siblings feeling marginalized. It had been hard to believe she was important when the elder Spencers had treated everyone equally. The mailman's daughter or a regular customer's son got the same praise and ego strokes as their own children did. Mom and Dad were proud of everyone; they were happy for everyone; they loved everyone.

In theory, such harmony and balance sounded good. In reality, it had hurt six-year-old and eight-year-old and ten-year-old Natasha to never be singled out as special. There had been a time when Daniel had thought he could make that up to her. It had lasted right up until that last party.

That spot on his chest ached again. Probably the chocolate bar he'd had for a late-afternoon snack. He'd better not let Mrs. Little Bear know, or she would surely have some dietary solution that would prevent him from ordering her excellent fry-bread tacos.

"Your parents meant well," he said as he went to one of the smaller tables and pulled out a chair facing the door. True to stereotype, he didn't like having windows at his back, but with the blinds closed, no one could see in and, with the iron grates outside, certainly no one could come in. Any threat they faced tonight would have to use the door, like everyone else, or hunker in the parking lot shadows.

"They did." She took a seat, too, directly across from him. "I swear, I was switched at birth. Somewhere out there, an incredibly free spirit is having dinner with her hidebound, traditional nuclear family and wondering, '*How* did I get here?'"

Daniel didn't expect the smile that tugged at his mouth. "That would be easier to believe if you didn't look just like your mom."

A smile tugged at her mouth, too. She fingered the faded flowers embroidered on the place mat for a moment, a sign she was about to change the subject. "I like Morwenna."

"So do I."

"Do you two date?" She was trying to sound perfectly casual, as if she had zero interest in his personal life—as if she hadn't once *been* his personal life—but he heard the emotion in her voice, saw the intense curiosity in her eyes. Like it somehow mattered.

How could it? She'd dumped him. Broken his heart. Discarded him like all her other fiancés. He hadn't mattered enough to her then; he didn't matter now.

"No."

He didn't need to say more—that they'd considered it, that they were aware enough of their mutual attraction that it had been worth a discussion. It was none of Natasha's business. Just as it was none of his business that there was a hint of relief in her blue eyes.

"So…" She rested her hands in her lap. "What were your better things to do tonight?"

Now it was his turn for nervous behavior, lining up the silverware, straightening the edges of the faded linens that, a long time ago, someone had taken the time to embroider with a fancy, curlicue *LB* on one point per napkin.

"Did you have a date?" she pressed.

"No."

"Aw, come on. I remember how girls approached

you everywhere you went, even when I was standing right there."

"Yeah, I remember when you were one of those girls," he muttered.

"I wasn't—" Her protest broke off. "I guess I was."

It had been at a food festival. He'd been standing in line for Korean barbecue and kimchi fries, and she'd walked right up to him. As it happened, one of her friends had known one of his, and they'd spent the rest of the afternoon together. And the evening. But not the night. She might approach strangers, she had told him, but she wasn't casual about sex. That was an entirely different matter.

For...eh, maybe ten days, and there had been absolutely nothing casual about it. It had been... It sounded sappy, but he couldn't think of a better way to describe it. Life-changing.

But that was a long time ago. A time best left in the past.

Luckily for him, because his brain insisted on recalling the way she'd looked that day—long hair in a ponytail, shorts that revealed a mile of leg and a tank top that clung so sweetly it was almost better than seeing her naked—the door opened, admitting loud conversations and laughter, along with Morwenna and Ben. Her British accent was noticeable again as she ragged Ben about something his mother had said.

The two joined Daniel and Natasha at the table, sitting opposite each other. "We have to separate them so they don't poke and kick each other during the meal," Daniel said.

Morwenna reached across to pinch his arm, but he anticipated it and leaned away far enough that she mostly caught his sleeve. "It's not our fault you're an only child and have no concept how siblings behave."

"I was happy being an only child." It was true, as far as it went. Though sometimes he'd envied Natasha's intimacy with Stacia or Ben's affection for his sisters. But not all siblings had that kind of closeness. Morwenna rarely saw her brother and didn't know what to do with him when she did, and Ben's own younger brother had abandoned the entire family years ago.

But Daniel had had it good: all his fathers' love, all their affection, all their attention.

Ben handed Natasha a menu, and she opened it before glancing around the table. "No menus for you? What are you getting?"

"Fry-bread tacos," they answered in unison. Ben added, "It's the Friday-night special."

"Then that's what I'll have, too."

She would be surprised when she saw it. Mrs. Little Bear didn't skimp on quality or quantity. But given the way the last day had gone for Natasha—the last year— a good surprise was in order. Daniel could use one, too.

He just didn't see one coming his way any time soon.

Natasha didn't want to move. Between the taco the size of a dinner plate, necessitating a fork and a knife to eat, and the comfortable presence of her dinner companions, she'd been lulled into a sense of security that wrapped around her like a warm blanket. Her senses were dulled, her brain too relaxed to think about something as ugly as danger. She wanted to stay there. Didn't want the night to end. Didn't want to go back to her hotel room or the fear and the dread.

But Ben had already hidden a few yawns, and Morwenna hadn't bothered to hide hers. Natasha had also caught Daniel sneaking glances at his watch. Unlike her, he wasn't one bit relaxed. He was counting down the minutes until he could go home, close her out of his mind and get on with whatever he'd planned before dinner had interrupted.

"Sorry, guys, but I'm pooped." Morwenna stood and stretched, an eye-popping flow of colors, then stepped away from the table. "Mum never learned the concept of being quiet while others are sleeping. She'll be waking me at five when she goes out to run."

"If you got a place of your own, she wouldn't wake you," Daniel pointed out as he, too, stood.

"A place of my own? On what the city pays me? We dispatchers don't make nearly as much as you detectives do."

"I got my first place on way less than you make," Ben said.

"Yes, but you were living with your mother, three sisters and two brothers. You had incentive. And I'm sorry, but I will not live in a mobile home in Oklahoma. I need a solid foundation when the tornados come blasting through."

"It wasn't a mobile home," he retorted. "It was a travel trailer in Weezer's backyard. My great-granddad moved it in twenty-five years ago, and it hasn't blown away yet."

Natasha smiled as she pushed her chair back. She missed friends and dinners out and good-natured squabbles. In the past year, her world had gotten progressively smaller, until the only person she spent much time with now was her sister. Stacia couldn't be Natasha's whole life, even though she was willing.

And Natasha had better not get too attached to this warm, pleasant feeling. These people weren't going to be around for long. The police would catch RememberMe, or *he* would catch her, or when the investigation stalled, she would eventually be forced to move on. However it went, she would probably never see Morwenna or Ben again.

Probably never see Daniel again.

She'd had five years to get used to that idea, but she never had. Even the night she'd pressed his ring into Stacia's hand and begged her sister to return it to him, she'd known she would miss him like crazy. She was ripping apart the very essence of who she was, and she'd hated it, but she had done it anyway. Despite its incredible wrongness, it had seemed her only option.

How sad that loving him so totally hadn't been enough to make her stay. She had joked about her family earlier in the evening, but seriously, what would it take to make her settle down? It was what she wanted— a husband, kids, a dog and a cat—and she'd had four chances to get it. What was wrong with her that she'd kept running?

"Natasha?"

Daniel's voice startled her. He hadn't spoken much through dinner—no need with Morwenna and Ben there to entertain and probably no interest on his part— and he sounded tired but patient. He was almost always patient.

While she'd been lost in her thoughts, he'd crossed the room and now waited at the door. The other two were already down the hall.

With a mental slap from Tasha, she pushed her chair in then slung her purse strap over her shoulder. Daniel stepped back, letting her leave first, then closed the door, caught up and walked beside her down the hall and through the kitchen.

Ben was staying at the restaurant to help out, so Natasha, Daniel and Morwenna put on their slickers in the storeroom then headed into the night. The light that had gone out earlier was burning again, flickering, buzzing loudly enough to be heard over the rain and the rushing creek water. They walked quickly to the truck, climbed in and fastened their seat belts, then Morwenna heaved a sigh. "I wish Mum cooked like Mrs. LB. Can you believe, all the years we've lived here, Mum's never had fried catfish or chicken or chicken-fried steak?"

When Daniel didn't respond, Natasha did. "You said she runs?"

"Like a crazy woman. Seriously, seventy-five to a hundred miles a week."

"That makes my joints hurt just thinking about it." Natasha liked to walk. She liked hiking, too, but in her opinion, time outside should be peaceful and relaxing, not jarring your bones pounding the pavement for mile after mile. Though, given the circumstances, it probably wouldn't hurt if Natasha could run a little faster and a whole lot longer. Just in case it was necessary to save her life.

The time to start training would have been a year ago. Not now, when he's followed you halfway across the country and set your car on fire.

A year ago, Natasha hadn't known she was getting a stalker. She'd thought the next ten years of her life would go on like the last ten: normal, average, unique only to her.

She gazed into the dreary night as Daniel drove back the way they'd come, slogging over potholes and puddles, and she let her weary body sway in time with the truck. Only a few feet after reaching pavement, they rattled and bumped over railroad tracks, then it was a smooth drive back to the hotel.

Until Morwenna yawned loudly. "I'm knackered. Drop me off first, would you, Daniel?"

Natasha fancied she could actually see the tension shimmering around him. He turned his head slightly, giving Morwenna a long and most likely meaningful look. "You live two blocks from me."

"It's not that far out of your way, taking me home, taking Natasha back to the hotel, then going home yourself. Don't be a prat."

It couldn't be too far, Natasha agreed, but tonight it was the company that mattered, not the distance. Was he thinking he'd already been bullied into having dinner with the fiancée who'd jilted him? That he'd done his duty and shouldn't now have to endure extended time alone with her? If she thought even remotely that he might let her, she would ask him to stop at the corner and leave her to walk the last few blocks by herself.

After another moment of that heavy look, he turned on the blinker, turned left and, a block later, crossed First Street, heading south.

Poor Daniel. Despite her occasional wishes, Natasha hadn't been switched at birth. She was proving to be a true Spencer, creating chaos everywhere she went.

Now that he'd acceded to Morwenna's request, the other woman's exhaustion morphed into energy. "My best friend from high school used to live in that white house on the corner, and our family doctor lived in the brick house next door. That empty lot over there has been turned into a community garden, and that's the church our neighbor took me to as a kid. Sunday is the only day Mum's guaranteed off, so she tries to run twenty to twenty-five miles then. I had to put on dresses, listen to sermons and be on my best behavior while she worshiped at the church of endorphins.

"Oh, and this house on the corner—" She twisted around to point in the dark. "That's Daniel's house. The south half of it, at least. The entrance is on the other street."

Streetlamps were evenly spaced along the block, but with mature trees mostly still in full leaf, much of their light got lost in the crowns. Natasha had an impression of a house old and solid and traditional, vastly different from the sleek glass-and-steel contemporary he'd grown up in. In Malibu, he'd had a deck overlooking the ocean, but he'd wanted a porch overlooking a yard with big trees and lush grass and room to run. It looked as if he'd gotten it.

At least a few things had worked out for him since she'd ripped the rug out from under him. He had good friends and a great place to live. He probably, at least sometimes, had someone to share it with.

Odd how it could hurt her heart that it wasn't her.

Morwenna's commentary continued until the moment Daniel pulled into the circular driveway of another traditional two-story house. She leaned around the seat to smile. "I'm so glad you came to dinner. You can't imagine the headaches those two give me sometimes. We'll do this again, as long as the guys say it's safe, okay? See you."

Before Natasha could form a *thank you*, Morwenna had slid to the ground and slammed the truck door behind her. In that one moment, damp air rushed into the vehicle, bringing a chill but also a fresh, clean scent that reminded her of mountain hikes on drizzly days. Snuggling with Daniel under the waterproof blanket she always kept in her pack. Talking or kissing or just being still together, listening to the rain dripping from branches overhead. They'd had some lovely conversations at those times. They'd had some lovely quiet, too.

She glanced at him. His attention was on Morwenna, illuminated by the porch light and shielded from the rain, wiggling a key into the lock. When the door opened, she turned back, grinned and gave them a thumbs-up, and he slowly began pulling out of the driveway. Morwenna was locked inside the house before they drove out of sight.

Chills shivered through Natasha. In a few minutes, Daniel would park in front of the hotel, get out and walk her inside to her room. He would check to make sure it was empty and safe, and then he would leave her to spend the night there alone. That reality made her warm pleasure in the evening trickle away. How could she sleep knowing that RememberMe had found her yet again? Sleep was her most vulnerable time, when he could come right up to her so easily, could have his hands around her throat before she knew what was happening. Sleep made her an easy target.

One that RememberMe might be watching even now.

Chapter 5

Despite Daniel's friends' early end to the evening, it wasn't late. Barely eight, according to his watch. Ben and Morwenna really were the early-to-bed, early-to-rise type. Keeping them out past ten was almost impossible. Tonight he shared their longing for their beds and a night of restful sleep, but he was almost too tired. He felt like a spring that had been wound too tightly and was just waiting for the worst possible time to come undone. His head hurt, and so did his jaw, and he was pretty sure the muscles in his hands were strained from clenching everything too tightly—his keys, his glass, his fork, the steering wheel. He needed a few hours of oblivion. Eight sounded good, twelve even better.

He would pencil them in on his schedule after this case was done.

There were no cars parked in front of the hotel.

After this morning, the other guests most likely thought the tiny little lot out back was perfectly fine. At least *their* cars hadn't self-combusted.

He lined up the vehicle's back door with the hotel door to minimize the time Natasha would be outside, visible to anyone who might be watching. There were no guests in the lobby, no sign of Claire Baylor and no one on the outside who appeared to be watching. That didn't mean the stalker wasn't nearby. He could have broken into one of the other businesses on the street or be staying in one of the apartments above them. He could be hiding in the empty building two doors down or even renting a room in the hotel.

Except every guest in the hotel had checked in at least two days before Natasha had arrived, and a cursory background on each of them had checked out.

"Are you waiting for me to get out?" Natasha sounded unsure, because he'd never failed to walk her to the door, and timid, because she didn't want to go inside by herself. He'd never seen her scared, and he didn't like it.

"No. Just..." Grimacing, he shut off the engine, pocketed the keys then withdrew his pistol from the holster and slid it inside his jacket pocket. "Wait until I come around."

"All right."

He'd never seen her so compliant, either.

After a quick look up and down the street, he got out, circled the truck with long steps and opened the back door. She slid out, close enough for a moment for him to recognize the exotic floral scent that clung to her, the fragrance that had clung to his bed and his clothing and every single item in his house for months, it had seemed, after she'd left him. Quickly, he forced himself back a step, filled his lungs with fresh air, closed the door and gestured toward the hotel.

Claire locked the exterior doors at 8:00 p.m., so Natasha had her key ready. The door was original to the building, but the lock was well oiled and smoothly tumbled to the open position. They ducked inside, and Daniel twisted the lever to secure it again before they headed to the stairs.

How many flights of stairs had he followed Natasha up, admiring the way she moved and smelled and sounded, wanting all things she promised with the slightest look or smile, wondering how he'd been lucky enough to meet her? Not enough. Not a lifetime's worth. That was all he'd wanted.

All he'd wanted. Just the entire world.

The stairs were grand, still in their original stain, broad and heavy with carved balusters and elaborate moldings on the risers and treads. So many feet had trodden them in the past hundred years that there was a noticeable dip in the center of each step. Natasha kept to the right side, her hand sliding along the polished railing. When she reached the landing, she turned toward her room, and he followed her.

At the door, he drew his pistol from his slicker pocket, took her key and went inside. She'd left a light burning on the desk, the blinds open, the book she'd been reading on the bed. The bathroom door was open, a night-light giving the room faint illumination, and nothing appeared out of place. More importantly, nothing felt out of place.

"You can come in." Putting the gun in its holster, he went to the window and closed the blinds. The window locks were secured, but that was just a precaution. Fifteen feet above the ground and twenty from the roof, with no ledges, balconies or trelliswork nearby, they weren't a likely point of entry.

Natasha's steps were hesitant as she entered. She dropped her slicker on the bathroom counter, set her purse on the dresser then stood beside the bed, looking like the proverbial deer in the headlights—more than a few of which he'd seen since moving to Cedar Creek. "I appreciate…" A gesture finished the sentence for her: dinner, the room check.

It seemed ungracious not to respond with *You're welcome*, but he hadn't wanted the dinner, and the room check was part of his job. So he let the comment slide and shoved his hands into his pockets. "Nice room. Archer would love that bed."

"And Jeffrey would cringe in horror."

"Yeah." His dad claimed he'd spent forty years trying to teach his father some class, and Archer gleefully insisted the lessons hadn't taken yet. Maybe after another forty.

"Well…" It was time to go home. Get out of these perpetually damp clothes and into bed. Make a start on his Cary Grant comedy marathon. But despite his brain's command, his feet didn't carry him to the door. They just stood there. *He* just stood there.

Natasha just stood there, too, looking cold and edgy and awkward. "I—I like your friends."

"They're good people." Geez, how inane was that? Would they discuss the rain—again—next?

She looked about to speak when a shriek sounded down the hall, sharp and piercing. The color drained from her face, and his heart thundered as he fumbled beneath his slicker for his weapon. Before it cleared the leather, there came a round of feminine laughter, and Natasha sagged with relief.

"It's the wine women," she explained shakily. "They came back with armloads of wine today and said they were having a party in their room this evening. Pajamas. Wear 'em if you've got 'em and come anyway if you don't."

Her knees gave way, and she sank onto the bed. He could count the number of times he'd seen her looking so vulnerable—generally only when they'd visited her family and gotten proof once again that she was just one of the multitude her parents loved. But that was a whole different level of vulnerability. That was purely emotional—tough, sure, but no one at Casa Spencer was actually dangerous.

RememberMe was. To Natasha. To Kyle. Maybe to Daniel himself. Unlike Kyle, Daniel had been warned. He was naturally cautious and made cynical by the job. He was suspicious of others, always alert, an excellent shot and difficult to catch off guard.

Even if Natasha's appearance at the courthouse yesterday had done just that.

He wasn't scared. He'd held his own in plenty of dangerous situations. Had always Tased or handcuffed or pepper sprayed the bad guy in those situations. A few times he'd even talked his way out of trouble, but RememberMe wasn't the type to respond to reason and logic. If he was, he wouldn't be stalking Natasha, she wouldn't be here in Cedar Creek and Daniel would still be blissfully ignorant, thinking that he was totally over her and ready to move on.

Damn. He didn't want to even consider that last thought.

"I should go," he said, moving toward the door. "You've got my number. If anything happens..."

Still wearing that look of helpless fear, she nodded.

At the door, he hesitated. He couldn't spend the night here. Wouldn't. He was one of RememberMe's targets; his presence in the hotel might drive the guy to take action, and Natasha or someone else might get hurt. Besides, one night of protection wasn't going to fix things. The stalker had been hanging around for nearly a year, and he hadn't gotten caught yet.

Still, it felt wrong, walking away, leaving her there alone. He did it—gave her a somber nod, closed the door and waited for her to lock it, and then he headed toward the stairs—but it gave him a vague feeling of dissatisfaction deep inside.

A door at the opposite end of the hallway opened, spilling light out onto the faded hardwood floor, and Claire Baylor appeared. Her face was flushed, either from the party behind her or the half-empty wineglass in her hand, and her smile was pretty. "Detective Harper," she said, carefully enunciating the syllables, and he decided to place his bet on the wineglass. "Are you leaving?"

"I am. Do you mind coming down to lock up behind me?"

"I'd be happy to." She swayed a bit on her feet. "But I'd be safer giving you a key to the doors. You're a cop. I can trust you, can't I?" Fumbling in her pocket, she pulled out a key, studied it front and back and then offered it to him. As he came close to take it, she leaned forward and lowered her voice. "Can you believe this is only my second glass? Compared to them, I am such a lightweight. The amount of wine those girls can hold would put me in a coma."

He lowered his voice, too. "Then you'd probably better stop after this one so you don't put yourself in a coma going down the stairs."

"I will." She nodded seriously, drained the rest of the wine, handed the empty glass to him and returned to the party.

Daniel set the glass on a table against the wall then headed down the stairs. He was glad someone was having a carefree evening. Too bad it wasn't him.

Daniel had showered, crawled between warm sheets and made it through the opening credits of *Arsenic and Old Lace* when his cell phone rang. He wished he was an ignore-the-phone sort of person, mindful that people had survived for centuries without being available to talk at any time of day or night. But it wasn't in his genes to not even glance at caller ID, and the name displayed there made him answer before another ring sounded.

"Flea?"

"Don't make me come there and shoot you, Harper. My name is Detective Martin."

"And to your friends?"

"That is my friends. Sorry I couldn't return your call earlier. You know what it's like out here. LAPD is saving money by working us to death."

He settled more comfortably in the bed. "They still training everybody else's police officers?" It had happened with their own academy class. Only a third of those who'd started had graduated, and most of them had left within two years for better-paying jobs with other police departments in the area.

"They are, which means I'm doing the job of three detectives. So you mentioned Natasha Spencer in your message. Please don't tell me I was wrong and Mr. Aw-He's-Harmless killed her."

His gut clenched at the thought. No matter how angry or bitter he'd gotten with her, he couldn't imagine the world without her in it. Not necessarily within his sphere of it, but out there somewhere. "No, he hasn't hurt her. But he set her car on fire yesterday."

"Damn. He didn't happen to leave his driver's license behind, did he? Or look at the camera pointed right at him? Maybe live stream it on social media?"

"Could we be that lucky?"

"Sometimes the gods smile on us, Detective." Flea paused, rustling in the background, then cautiously asked, "How are you dealing with this?"

This was such an innocuous word to describe the upheaval in his life. But he ignored that thought. He was becoming very good at ignoring things. "I'm dealing. Is there anything you can tell me about your conversations with Natasha that she wouldn't have passed on?"

"That I was skeptical from the start? Damn, Harper, I thought I was more professional than that. I never thought my personal feelings would get in the way. But here I was, dealing with real tangible threats against real innocent people, and in walks Miss Princess with her complaint about her latest admirer. I told her to change her phone number and her email address. I told her to be careful, to let me know if things escalated."

"Did she tell you she'd already changed her phone and email?"

"No, she didn't."

Flea sounded abashed. Daniel knew the feeling was useless. A cop needed the whole story to do the job, but too many people left out pertinent information. *I didn't think it mattered. I forgot about it until now. It just seemed so trivial.*

A sigh sounded before she went on. "I contacted the internet service provider, but that was a dead end. The guy was good at covering his tracks. The texts traced back to a burner phone. We checked the security cameras at the apartment complex where she lived, and we ID'd a guy leaving flowers at her door. He was paid in cash by some other guy, not too big, not too small, wearing shades and a baseball cap, and the delivery guy had the impression that the baseball cap guy had been hired by some *other* guy. The security footage only went back a couple weeks, so that was the only thing we saw. After that, like I said, I had a heavy caseload."

So she'd put Natasha's case out of her mind.

"Do you have anything at your end?"

Daniel pinched the bridge of his nose. "Nope. She came to town, told me I was in danger, planned to leave again the next morning, and her car, parked all by itself on the main drag, caught fire. The guy knows she's here—he sent her an email last night—but he hasn't tried to contact her since the fire. We've got her electronic devices. Our IT people are trying to find something."

"Do you think he's responsible for the first fiancé's accident?"

"My gut says yes. He told her things about Kyle's house, so he had to have been inside. Emailing her on the day Kyle fell couldn't have been coincidence. He mentioned the rest of us by name. Yeah, I think maybe he wants to punish her or to punish us, because we had her—temporarily—and whenever he met her, he didn't even register on her radar."

"Has he tried to contact you?"

"No. I wish he would. I'd rather face him head-on than go through this stalker crap."

"If he were capable of facing you head-on, he wouldn't be stalking. Daniel, I'm really sorry. I wish I could have done more—gotten surveillance footage from the areas where we knew he'd been, pinged the towers for his cell phone, interviewed more people. But I honestly thought..." She was silent a long time, and when she continued, despite her words, there was doubt in her voice. "I honestly thought he was harmless. And I honestly believe I wouldn't have done anything different even if she'd been a total stranger. I do."

Daniel considered it a moment. "I do, too, Flea."

They talked a few moments longer—her husband and kids were fine, his fathers were fine, life was good—before ending the call. He leaned back against the pillows, staring at the image of Cary Grant frozen on the TV screen, wondering if he really wanted to watch a funny movie or if, maybe, he *needed* to, when a distant sound made him stiffen.

It had come from downstairs and outside. Not the elderly man who lived in the other half of the house; he was spending the week with his granddaughter in Texas. Besides, when he was home, he was in bed by eight. Early to bed and early to rise might not have made him wealthy and wise, he said, but it had gotten him through eighty-seven years of living.

The sound came again, a scrape of wood against brick, below Daniel's bedroom window. Someone bumbling about in the dark on the patio, bumping into the chairs there?

He grabbed his cell and pistol, shoved his feet into running shoes and dashed down the stairs. He didn't pause to yank his slicker from the hook but quietly opened the front door a few inches, eased out and headed toward the west end of the house. He knew where every planter was placed, where every shrub grew, knew not to trip over the downspout at the corner that was flooding the yellowed grass with rain.

Cold, soaked, wishing for something more than boxers and a T-shirt, he paused at the corner, drew a deep breath and darted a look at the back of the house. The only light was faint, what little seeped around the blinds in his bedroom windows, and it dissipated long before reaching the ground. He waited a moment, let his eyes adjust to the darkness then looked again. Nothing appeared out of place. No shadow seemed more substantial than any other. Nothing moved or stood unnaturally still. Nothing *felt* wrong about the scene.

Except the chair on the patio, moved only inches from its usual spot. It wouldn't have been noticeable to most people, but at home Daniel, like his dad, was a little fixated with balance and symmetry. The chair nearer the house, normally aligned with its mate, was tilted now at an awkward angle.

Trying to ignore the goose bumps rising on his exposed skin, he stealthily crossed the patio, his gaze searching for any other sign of an intruder. He went around the far corner of the building, checking the other half of the house, and wound up a few moments later back at his front door.

It could have been a dog. The neighbor three doors down had a fat cat who was more than capable of re-arranging furniture with her heft, and he'd seen plenty of possums and raccoons who could do the same. He could have bumped the chair himself when he'd last used the grill.

Could have been. But it hadn't been a dog, a cat, a possum, a raccoon or his own carelessness. Deep inside, he knew.

While he stood there, willing his heart rate to settle, a form detached from the shadows of a tree across the street and trotted his way. "You're getting awfully wet, Detective Harper."

For an instant, Daniel's grip on the gun tightened, but recognition set in quickly enough to relax it again almost immediately. "Have you seen anyone around here, Ozzie?"

"Just you and me, Detective. Everyone else is smart enough to be inside." Ozzie pushed back the hood of his slicker to reveal his ever-present grin. He was a fixture in Cedar Creek: in his fifties, always cheerful, rambling his way around town for hours every day. Everyone knew him—nice guy, sweet guy, not *quite right*—and looked out for him when he let them. That wasn't very often, which was why *ornery* was another description they applied to him.

"You're getting soaked. You want my raincoat, Detective?"

"No, thanks, Oz."

"I don't mind. I've got another one at home. Maybe two or three."

"No, really. I'm going in in a minute." Daniel pushed his hair back from his face. "What have you seen, Ozzie?"

It was the man's favorite question to answer. He'd once described a patch of ragweed in precise detail to Daniel, as if it were the most beautiful of all God's creations. He was fascinated by trains and sirens and cracks in the sidewalk. There was nothing too small, too insignificant, to deserve his attention.

"I saw that car burn up this morning. But you saw that, too, 'cause I saw you there. You was talking to the girl that owned it. She's from California, where the ocean is. Have you ever seen the ocean, Detective?"

"I lived on the beach when I was a kid."

"You didn't have a house? Gee, that's too bad."

Daniel dismissed the thought of explaining himself as soon as he had it. He'd tried it before, but it was anyone's guess what Ozzie understood and what he merely glossed over because it seemed the right thing to do. "Have you seen anything else interesting?"

"More rain than I thought the skies could hold. Everybody hurrying to get where they're going. Nobody takes the time to enjoy a walk in the rain anymore." Ozzie tilted his head back and smiled toward the sky, blinking when water splashed in his eyes. "There are strangers in town. The girl who owned the car that burnt up. The wine women. Look what they give me today." He reached into an inside pocket and removed a small canning jar, bearing the name of an Oklahoma winery and filled with wine-grape jelly. "It's my favorite. They remembered from last time."

People were kind to Ozzie—all the locals and apparently the visitors, too. "That was nice of them. Don't eat it all on one piece of bread."

Ozzie's grin widened. "You're teasing me, Detective. I didn't know you knew how." After carefully returning the jar to his pocket, he said, "Even with it dark out here, I can see you're turning blue. Are you sure you don't want my raincoat?"

"No, thanks, man. Do you want a ride home?" It was a question asked without much risk. Ozzie never wanted a ride, no matter the weather.

"Naw. That's what God give me good feet and strong legs for." He pulled his hood back in place, walked a few feet along the sidewalk then turned back. "And there's the man who watches her."

Daniel had reached for the doorknob. His fingers clenched it so tightly that it required conscious thought to let go of it so he could face Ozzie fully. "Who does he watch?"

"That girl. The one with the car."

Sleep was overrated. Natasha could get by on two or three hours of restless tossing and turning. She'd done it in high school and college. So what if she was ten years older? And twenty years more tired. And thirty years more worried. A cup of coffee, and she would be fine.

She told herself that before meeting her haggard reflection's gaze in the mirror and scowling. All the coffee in the world wouldn't make her feel any better than she looked, and that was pretty damn scary. The shadows beneath her eyes had turned from bags to a full set of luggage, and the lines across her forehead and around her mouth looked as if they'd been etched with a chisel. Even her hair was limp, lacking the energy to develop a case of bedhead.

She showered, dressed and did her best with makeup to conceal some of the damage. She had no appetite, but her stomach was rumbling anyway, and though she was jittery enough on her own, that aforementioned cup of coffee sounded good. Not that she knew how to get a real breakfast. Should she ask Morwenna to play delivery person? Get Daniel's okay to go to Judge Judie's? Call the lovely Taryn who had an obvious thing for Daniel and ask her to send a meal over?

She would start downstairs. She could get coffee in the lounge, and maybe her stomach would be happy with a chocolate rush instead of the bacon and eggs it was starting to crave. After peeking out the door, she let herself into the hallway, locked up and headed down the hall. Halfway there, the sound of solid footsteps descending the stairs stopped her short.

A pair of feet came into view first, shod in clunky running shoes, showing only a thin line of socks above. Tanned and muscular legs followed, then a pair of faded black shorts and a T-shirt with the faintest remains of a logo. Dodgers. They had fans everywhere.

Rob Miller reached the landing, glanced her way and stopped. "Good morning."

Her stomach was knotted, her chest tight. Everything inside her wanted her to run back to her room like a frightened little mouse, but she squared her shoulders and breathed deeply for courage. "Morning."

Though he kept a polite distance, his gaze moved across her face, as if his blue eyes were cataloging her features on a checklist. It was a familiar interest, one she'd been aware of since she'd become aware of boys, and was usually pleasant, mildly satisfying, occasionally annoying and rarely thrilling. Like when Kyle had looked at her that way, or when Eric had. Or Daniel.

Oh, especially when Daniel had.

This morning, the interest made her feel vulnerable and afraid, wary and suspicious and all those ugly things she didn't want to feel. Even if it was naive, she wanted to believe in the general goodness of people, the way she always had.

"Are you going down?" Rob gestured toward the stairs.

Instead of believing, she was doubting everyone. Instead of living her life, she was on the run, and instead of standing up to RememberMe, she was quaking in fear. But how could she stand up to a phantom?

"Yes." It took determination to walk to the landing, to pass him and start down the steps with her back to him. "Are you going running?"

"I'm hoping I can get a few miles in. When I looked out the window, the rain had stopped, but if there's one thing I've learned on my trips here, it's that the weather can turn on a dime. Do you know one time I was here, and at 3:00 p.m., it was sunny and seventy-five, and by seven o'clock there was two inches of snow on the ground?"

"Really," she murmured, conscious of the relief sweeping through her. His visit to Cedar Creek was business; he'd been coming here on a regular schedule long before she'd ever heard of the town. He wasn't RememberMe.

There were a lot of people out there. She needed to be afraid of only one. She would make a point of reminding herself of that every so often.

Still, she couldn't deny the lightening of her tension when she reached the bottom of the stairs and Rob stepped past her. "Have a good morning," he said on his way to the door.

"Fingers crossed you stay dry," she responded, and he waved one hand in the air to show he heard her before stepping outside.

To Natasha's left, the married guests shared a sofa and drank coffee while discussing where to have breakfast. They both smiled and nodded when they noticed her. Back to the right and behind her, Claire's voice came, soft and sweet, in answer to a deeper, masculine rumble.

When Natasha was little, she'd often lain in bed in the room she always shared with Stacia, sometimes with their brother, Nick, and often with the children of strangers her parents had brought into the house. Her bed was next to the window, and she'd gazed at the night sky while listening to her parents talk. The words were indistinguishable, but the sounds were always a comfort: her father's voice, deep and gruff, her mother's like delicate high-tuned chimes. Years later, she'd done the same—different window, different night sky—while listening to the pure comfort of Daniel's voice.

She'd found a home in his voice.

And she'd given it up when she'd broken his heart.

When she turned to head toward the coffee maker, she saw Ben Little Bear, towering over Claire at the counter. Of course, Ben appeared to tower over everyone. His back was to Natasha, but his attention seemed laser-focused on the innkeeper. He was easy on the eyes, once they'd made the long journey up to his face, and he didn't wear a wedding ring. It was hard to say whether Claire was turning on extra charm, since she was always pleasant, but her smile was certainly satisfied as they'd talked. Whatever reason he was there, it didn't seem to upset her, so maybe it wasn't business. Maybe—hopefully—it was as personal as things could get between a man and a woman.

She returned Claire's little wave and turned into the back hall. The smell of fresh coffee tantalized her, reminding her of cartoon animals from her childhood, so entranced with aromas that they floated on air to reach the source. If she'd delayed five more minutes, the captivating, enchanting scent of life-giving caffeine might have made her float, too.

At least, until she reached the break room door.

Where Daniel was grumpily stirring powdered creamer into a mug of coffee.

For one moment, the language part of her brain stopped functioning while the drooling part took over. The man who made a rumpled T-shirt and boxers look *GQ* appeared to have slept in his khaki tactical pants and polo shirt, so much that she suspected he'd done something he'd probably never done before: dragged them out of the bottom of the laundry hamper. His hair, as short as it was, was rumpled, too, as if he'd repeatedly dragged his fingers through it. His jaw was unshaven—a sexy look on him—and tension began radiating from him the instant he became aware of her presence.

She hadn't made a sound. He hadn't glanced around. He hadn't seen her reflection, because there was nothing in the room shiny enough to reflect. But he knew someone was there, and he knew it was her.

Once she had asked him how he always knew, and he'd shrugged. *I don't know. Maybe it's pheromones. Or the missing piece of my soul coming back.* He had considered it a moment while she got all swoony, and then he added, *Maybe you emit some kind of spores.*

She had refused to cuddle with him until he'd insisted he loved her spores with every spore of his own.

Heart aching with the memory—all of them, sweet and sad and steamy and innocent and tragic—she stood where she was, doing nothing, and he stayed where he was, acting as if she didn't exist.

Finally her beleaguered brain found some words. "Really? You move to cow country and switch to powdered creamer?"

His expression was sour with distaste when he finally looked at her. For her? she wondered. Or the sacrilege he was committing with the coffee?

"When I have the time and the inclination, I go to the dairy over in Claremore and buy raw cream for my coffee. This is for Little Bear, who, despite growing up with fresh milk from the family's cows, thinks powdered creamer is the best add-in ever."

She shuddered playfully, and the tension around Daniel eased a little. "Some people." It was a phrase Jeffrey used a lot—often in reference to Archer, though always said with love.

The machine signaled the finish of another brewed cup with a gurgle, and Daniel set it aside, leaving space for her to start her own. Though her olfactory neurons were actually dancing in anticipated delight and her mouth was beginning to water, she hesitated to enter the room. It was so small, and she would have to be so careful not to bump into him because if she did… If she did…

Oh, the things she could do with him. Had done. Had wanted and loved and needed and given up because they weren't enough. *She* wasn't enough.

He added three packets of sugar to Ben's coffee and grabbed a plate holding a cinnamon roll as big as his head then waited for her to move aside. She did so, stepping back into the hall, first blocking the way he needed to go, abashedly switching to the opposite side. After a moment lost in the past, she stepped into the break room.

Just inside the door, she stopped, closed her eyes and took a deep breath. Coffee, sugar, butter, cinnamon—all tempting enough for a hungry woman. Shampoo, cologne, man—more than tempting enough for any woman. When scents evoked as many tender memories as these did, they were a threat to her composure and her emotional balance.

With her knees more than a bit wobbly, they were apparently a threat to her physical balance, as well.

She chose a pod of coffee and started a cup while focusing on the food choices available. A box of pastries sat on the counter next to the microwave with a note that read *Guests, please eat so I won't*. It was signed with Claire's name. There was a bowl of oranges and apples, some packets of instant oatmeal and grits—*seriously?*—and the candy, chips and cookies she'd seen yesterday.

No eggs, no bacon, no biscuits and gravy.

She was mourning that last bit when Daniel returned. Warm pleasure rushed through her that he'd come back for another round, but then he reached for his coffee. Of course. His hands had been full with Ben's stuff.

He added sugar and a tiny cup of half-and-half before moving back to lean against the doorjamb and fix his gaze on her. "Aren't you going to ask why we're here this early on a Saturday?"

She studiously avoided looking back at him and shrugged. "Because you couldn't wait until Monday to see me again?"

He'd told her that the first time he'd stayed overnight at her apartment. He'd left the next morning, but he came back five minutes later. *I couldn't wait until tomorrow to see you again.*

And another time, she'd awakened in the middle of the night to find him leaning on one arm, gazing down at her, the gentlest look in his eyes, and he'd whispered, *I couldn't wait until morning to see you again.*

She'd realized in that very instant that she loved him—bigger, deeper, better than she'd ever loved before.

For whatever it had been worth.

The coffee machine gurgled and hissed, and she had just lifted the cup out when he went on. "There was a prowler at my house last night. Also, we have a witness who says he's seen a guy watching you."

Her muscles froze, leaving her unable to breathe or process his words. She didn't feel the trembling that started in her hands until she saw rings spreading across the surface of her coffee. A tiny wave was forming, rising heavy on one side of the tilting mug before it crashed back to the other, about to splash steaming brew over—

Daniel's hands appeared in her narrow field of vision, taking careful hold of the cup, pulling it from her grip, setting it on the counter. For a moment, his right hand retained its hold on her left, and she reflexively grasped it, squeezing tightly, focusing all her energy on maintaining contact with the one person who'd always, always made her feel safe.

"What— Are you— Did you—"

His thumb rubbed across the heel of her palm with a slow, easy gesture that eased tension with each press. "I didn't see anything. I'd just gotten off the phone with Flea, and before I started the movie again, something ran into one of my deck chairs. By the time I got out there, he—it—was gone."

He had it right the first time: not *it*. *He*. RememberMe.

"You went out there by yourself? Knowing that he wants to—" She finished with a gesture of her free hand, unable to put it into words. The mere thought of the danger she'd brought into Daniel's life could break her heart and her spirit.

"I wasn't alone. I had my weapon." He laid his free hand on the pistol snugged on his belt. "You know I never leave home without it."

The small smile that touched his mouth was reassuring, but Natasha couldn't stop the ominous words going around in her head. RememberMe was here in Cedar Creek, and he knew where Daniel lived, and he wanted him dead.

And it was all her fault.

Daniel wasn't a touchy-feely sort of person. Between his coworkers' general friendliness, dates and the people he handcuffed, searched or restrained, he had plenty of physical contact in his life. He never found himself longing for the feel of someone else's skin against his.

Except Natasha's.

The import puzzled him. He was holding her hand. Nothing momentous, nothing special. People held hands, shook hands, offered hands to other people on a daily basis. One bit of work-worn skin pressing against another bit of work-worn skin. No big deal.

But this was a very big deal. It was chemistry, according to his dad. His father shrugged. *Beats the hell out of me.* But, he went on, he didn't have to understand the mechanics of something to appreciate it.

Daniel was appreciating this far more than was wise.

He cleared his throat, relaxed his fingers and tugged his hand back. She didn't let go easily, and he didn't blame her. He was mostly annoyed today—who wouldn't be when his calm, peaceful life was turned upside down by some whack-job he'd never met?—but Natasha was scared. Danger was new to her and, like any normal person, it frightened her.

After clearing his throat a second time—the last thing he wanted to let her know with a quavery voice was that his fingers were still tingling from hers—he said, "Sam is going to meet us at Judge Judie's for breakfast. Bring your coffee and grab a coat."

Her face pale except for twin red spots on her cheeks, she nodded, picked up the cup and started out. It was a sign of how shaken she was that she gulped a huge drink of hot black coffee without noticing it wasn't lukewarm, sweetened and creamed.

He walked as far as the desk with her. Ben was polishing off the last of the cinnamon roll while Claire continued their conversation about the hotel's guests.

Daniel hadn't done more than take a few sips of his own coffee when Natasha returned, a dark blue sweater pulled on over her plaid shirt, her purse strap slung over one shoulder.

Even with the time it took Ben to finish talking, they were walking into the diner less than three minutes later. It was early for the breakfast rush—even farmers and cowboys liked a later start on Saturdays, it seemed—so they had their choice of seats. Ben headed for a table for four at the back and took a seat facing the door.

At least he hadn't chosen a booth, Daniel groused as he settled into the chair next to Natasha. Her movements brittle, she scooted her seat closer to the table, emptied a packet of sugar into her coffee and stirred it. When droplets splattered from the shaking of the spoon, she stopped and clasped her hands in her lap. "What about this witness who saw him?"

"Hold that question." Ben nodded toward the door. "Here comes Sam."

They all watched the chief approach. When Daniel first came to Cedar Creek, Sam had been up every morning, at about five o'clock, for a run, but that routine had slacked off some since he married Mila. Who wouldn't prefer a warm bed with a wife who adored him over pounding the pavement? Heck, Daniel preferred a cold bed alone. He only ran so he could chase, and usually catch, suspects.

Sam hung his cowboy hat on a hook on the wall then sat down next to Ben. A nod served as a greeting for all of them, and his gesture to the waitress showed he wasn't starting this morning in any better shape than Natasha and Daniel were.

Natasha waited long enough for the waitress to deliver coffee to Sam, her gaze sharp on him, though it appeared it was taking all her effort to not snatch away the cup and do the doctoring herself. The instant Sam's spoon clinked on the saucer after he'd finished stirring, she pounced.

"Who is this witness and what does he know?"

Sam gave her his customary smile, the one that made young girls giggle and elderly women blush, that left all the women in between feeling noticed, appreciated, acknowledged and protected. "Good morning."

"Good morning. What does he know?"

Sam scratched his jaw. "First, you've got to understand that Ozzie is..." He looked at Daniel and Ben, and they finished the statement with him. "Not quite right."

"I don't know what his official diagnosis is," Sam went on, "but he's...delayed. He lives in a group home, but he doesn't require care. He goes everywhere, and he never met a person or animal or inanimate object that didn't interest him greatly."

"So he's not a credible witness." Disappointment rang in Natasha's voice and rounded her shoulders. Had she thought Ozzie could lead them to RememberMe today and she could be on her way back home tomorrow?

"Oh, no, he's very credible," Sam said, and Ben added, "With us. Maybe not so much in court. It would depend on how many of the jurors knew him."

"The thing is, Ozzie notices stuff. Big stuff, little stuff," Daniel said then grudgingly admitted, "and occasionally nonexistent stuff. You got here at noon Thursday. By that night, he'd seen you at the hotel and the diner and the police station. He knew you drove a red car, that you're from California, that you knew me. He's curious, he asks questions, and because he's Ozzie, people tend to answer them.

"During the fire Friday, he saw you again. He also saw a man watching you. He saw the same man outside the hotel later that day, and he saw him again outside Mrs. LB's restaurant last night."

The waitress brought menus, and they took a break to place their orders. When they got back to the subject, Natasha looked not so much disappointed as reluctantly accepting. "I'm guessing he doesn't know the man."

"No. It was raining. He can tell us it's a white guy, taller than him—"

Ben interrupted. "But Ozzie's only five foot five, so most men are taller than him."

"—and he wears a blue slicker with the hood pulled up."

"I've seen at least twenty blue slickers since I got here," she pointed out glumly. "I thought I was pretty alert during the fire. I looked at people, every single person on the street, on the sidewalk, sitting in a car. I probably stared right at RememberMe, and he looked so normal that I didn't notice him. Hell, I didn't notice Ozzie watching me, either. I thought I was so alert when really I must be clueless."

When she hid her face in her hands, both Sam and Ben gave Daniel meaningful looks. *Do something. Say something. She's your ex-fiancée.* What could he say? She *was* on the clueless side. Everybody was. Normal people didn't go around in a state of high-level paranoia, constantly searching for the tiniest hint that something wasn't as it should be.

Awkwardly he said, "Look, I didn't notice Ozzie

then, either, and I'm supposed to be more aware of my surroundings than you are."

Sam's response was dry. "Really? You're a cop. She's got a stalker who's tracked her every move for a year, tried to kill her ex-fiancé and followed her more than a thousand miles, where he set her car on fire. People don't always like you, but none of them have tried to kill you."

The chief pulled a creased email from his pocket. "I got a report from Jamey. The fire was caused by white phosphorus. Apparently, it's reasonably safe as long as it's submerged in water, but when it's exposed to air, it eventually dries out and spontaneously ignites at a certain temperature. RememberMe—" He grimaced with disgust. "Jeez, I hate calling a suspect that. Anyway, he rigged it so that the water drained very slowly and then the fire started. And wherever he gained access to the car, it wasn't on the street. According to the surveillance videos, between the time she parked and went into the hotel and the fire started, no one went near the car."

So he'd broken into Natasha's car before the last time she'd driven it. While she and Daniel were at McDonald's, not drinking coffee? Could he have sneaked up then without either of them noticing?

Daniel didn't think so. She'd spent too much time staring out the window, watching the rain and avoiding him. The car had been less than thirty feet away. Surely one of them would have seen someone tampering with it.

At the bowling alley? The parking lot was well lit, but everyone had been hustling in or out. They probably wouldn't have paid attention to anyone messing with a car, thinking some poor schmuck had locked himself out. But *probably* still left room for risk.

"My money's on the hotel parking lot," Ben said at the same time Daniel's thoughts turned that way. "There's only the one light. There're no cameras. It's hidden from view, and there's very little traffic. Chances of being seen are minimal."

If Natasha wasn't already pale, the color would have drained from her face. "So I was driving around town with a dangerous chemical that spontaneously ignites in my car? Aw, jeez, I'm going to start walking everywhere I go."

"You practically do that anyway," Daniel absently reminded her. It was a nothing comment, but for a moment, everyone went still. Ben wore his usual unflappable expression. Sam was looking curiously from Daniel to Natasha and back again.

Daniel didn't look to see what was on her face. He didn't want to think about all the hundreds of miles they'd walked together—in the city, the country, the mountains, on the beach. They'd talked and laughed and sometimes argued and sometimes been silent, but they'd always been close in a way that his rational brain could never completely figure out.

Like his father, he hadn't needed to understand it to appreciate it.

Gradually, the conversation resumed, small talk about car insurance, reports, paperwork. When the food came, the grimmer topic obviously hadn't affected anyone's appetite. Even Natasha ate as if she didn't have a care in the world.

Everyone needed a break from reality now and then, or they would all go insane.

After they'd made a dint in the food, Sam turned the focus of the discussion Daniel's way. "What are we going to do with you?"

His fingers tightening on his fork, Daniel forced a grin. "Chief, you've been asking that since the day you hired me."

"You've got the potential to be a good detective. Little Bear and I have put enough work in on you that I'd hate to lose you now."

Daniel took the dry comment the way it was intended. He *was* a good detective. Sam wouldn't have kept him on if he wasn't. Every chief, if he held the title long enough, had to lose an officer someday, but Sam hadn't yet, and he really would hate it. Though only a few years separated them in age, Sam was mentor to everyone in the department, and he took that responsibility seriously.

"He knows where you live," Ben said.

Daniel didn't insult them by suggesting that his prowler could have been anyone, two-legged or four. They knew, just as he did. "He didn't try to get inside."

"Maybe because he didn't have a chance."

That came from Natasha in a soft, unsteady voice. Her eyes seemed unusually blue in the porcelain of her face, rousing every protective urge he'd ever possessed. He wanted to promise her he would survive this. Wanted to squeeze her hand the way she'd squeezed his back at the hotel. To take away her worry and fear and give back the security she was so desperately in need of. To—

Whoa. This was Natasha, he reminded himself. Who got engaged on a whim then fled like a frightened deer. Who had humiliated him in front of God and everyone. Who had broken his heart and driven him nearly fifteen hundred miles away from her, his fathers and his job. Who'd been the best and worst and most disastrous thing to ever happen in his life.

"I have an alarm system," he said in measured tones. "I sleep with a gun and a Taser and pepper spray. I'm not going to let some stranger in my house. I'm not going to be taken by surprise."

That much was said to the table in general, but he paused, locked gazes with her and added just for her, "I'm not Kyle."

Chapter 6

He certainly wasn't Kyle, Natasha reflected once Daniel finally broke eye contact with her. Kyle was kind, good-natured and expected the best of everyone. He was friendly and helpful, and while he knew there was an uglier side to people, he didn't experience it often enough to be wary.

Kyle had been an easy target for RememberMe. Daniel wasn't. But RememberMe knew that, knew Daniel was a cop and therefore was well armed and suspicious, and he wasn't put off by it. He wasn't heading out of town in search of Eric or Zach instead, both of whom were certainly easier victims.

Which meant he was prepared.

So was Daniel, she had to admit.

But there wasn't enough preparation in the world to make the idea of someone wanting him dead bearable.

The chief pulled another piece of paper from another pocket and handed it to her between bites of ham with thin, dark gravy. "Redeye," the waitress had called it. "Your guy doesn't yet know we've got your devices. Your texts and emails from yesterday."

Hands trembling, she unfolded the paper. Probably unaware of it, Daniel leaned close to read it with her, so close she smelled his scent and felt his warmth, his solidness, real, tangible, assuring. For a long time, she couldn't focus on the words printed on the paper, not because she was afraid to see what her nightmare had written. She was concentrating on breathing deeply of Daniel, on absorbing as much of him as she could, on reveling in the fact that he was there beside her, exactly where she needed him.

After a moment, he pulled the printout from her and settled back in his chair. He scanned the messages in silence, his mouth thinning, his jaw tightening, then he snorted and dropped the page in the middle of the table.

"You want to read it next?" Ben asked her. "They're your messages."

She tried to reach out, but her hand wouldn't cooperate. After a tiny shake of her head, he picked it up and, more courteous than Daniel, read the words aloud. "'Did you like my surprise this morning, Nat? I thought it was pretty spectacular, all those beautiful flames on such a gray day. Don't worry about the car. I'll get you a new one. A better one. You should know, there's nothing small about my romantic gestures.'"

"Any of his gifts been over-the-top before?" Chief Douglas asked.

"He sent a bouquet of roses once that was almost as big as my dining table." It had been relatively early in their—their whatever-it-was, and she had been disturbed that he knew where she lived and concerned that the gift was far too extravagant. But a small naive part of her had been impressed. All the flowers she'd received prior to that time combined still wouldn't have matched the size of that single huge, glorious bouquet.

It was the first time Stacia had said, *This is creepy.* Far from the last time she would say it.

"He thinks he's romantic," Daniel muttered.

"By crazy stalker standards, he is." Ben went on to the next message. "'Should I be worried that my surprise this morning had you spending half the day with Daniel? If I didn't know you so well, maybe I would be. Have you told him everything about us? Are you going to? That I was the reason you broke your engagement with him?'"

Alarm shivered through her. "That's ridiculous. I never knew he existed until last Halloween, and he certainly had nothing to do with—with what I did."

"Crazy stalker," Ben repeated with agreeing nods from both Daniel and the chief. "He believes you're soul mates. He loves you, and you love him, and once he's removed the obstacles, you'll never want to leave him again. Isn't that what he said in Thursday night's email?"

She nodded glumly. "The only way I'd never want to leave him is if I'm dead."

The last three words boomed in her brain, echoing ominously, tumbling her stomach about so violently that she couldn't possibly take another bite of food. It had an effect on the men, too, leaving Ben and Chief Douglas unusually somber.

Anger, fierce but protective, flashed in Daniel's eyes

and made his voice harsh, his words clipped. "That's not going to happen."

Natasha couldn't fill her lungs enough to steady her voice. "But…it does happen. Sometimes. Too many times." When stalkers finally had to face the truth of their delusions, when the knowledge somehow penetrated their fantasies that they would never possess the object of their desire, no matter how hard they tried, no matter how many obstacles they removed, their mindset too often turned from *You'll always be mine* to *If I can't have you, no one can.*

RememberMe would want her dead because that was the only way she would ever, ever be his.

Daniel shifted in his chair, brushing her leg, drawing her stricken gaze to him. "I'm not going to let that happen." A pause, a small frown wrinkling his forehead, and he amended the promise. "We're not going to let it happen."

She believed him. Believed he and Ben and Chief Douglas would do everything in their power to keep her safe. But the sorry truth was that they couldn't stop RememberMe without finding him, they couldn't find him without identifying him and the sole identifying bit of data they had came from Ozzie, who was *not quite right* and sometimes saw things that weren't there.

She felt sick and helpless. She wanted to throw a full-blown tantrum, shrieking out her rage and frustration. Wanted to know why this bastard had decided to destroy her life. Wanted to run outside into the middle of the street and scream at the top of her lungs, *Here I am, you sick, sleazy coward! You have something to say to me, say it to my face. Step up. For the first time in your life, be a man. Then burn in hell.*

At least she would have the satisfaction of knowing he would hear her. He'd gone every other place she'd gone. He was surely skulking around out there now.

"There's only a couple more." Ben's quiet, calm voice helped tamp down the hysteria rising inside her. "From last night—'Why did you take him to your room? I saw how quickly you walked inside, trying to get away from him, but then you invited him upstairs. I'm trying to give you the benefit of the doubt, Nat, but sometimes you make it hard. Like leaving home without telling me. Like taking your former fiancé to your hotel room. Sometimes I think you don't understand what you and I have. We're destined to be together. You and me. Forever. Everything's already in motion. You can't stop it. You can't save Daniel, Nat. You can't save him. You can't save him.'"

Stillness surrounded them as Ben's voice faded. They were just words, simple ones, harmless in themselves, but together they made a chilling reminder that words had power.

The bell over the front door rang, and a group of grumbling old men, by the sounds of their voices, came inside. Natasha wanted to take a casual glance over her shoulder, just to confirm that, but couldn't dredge up anything the least bit casual inside her. If she looked, she would search their faces, then she would look outside. She would be drawn to the large windows, and she would frantically study every person, every car, every doorway or window or bush that might offer a man concealment. She wouldn't be able to stop looking, staring this way and that, panic building until she lost all semblance of control.

She could even imagine how mad she would appear

to everyone. She only had to look to Stacia, whose first network acting job had been playing a hysterical woman running for her life down the street before the unknown villain caught and killed her.

"There's one more, a text that came this morning while you were getting coffee at the hotel." Apparently having memorized the text, Ben folded the paper and stuffed it into his own pocket. "'You can't even save yourself, Nat.'"

Into the stillness came a great wheezing sound, interspersed with choking sounds. Her face burning, she realized the awful noises were coming from her. She couldn't take a breath, and her lungs were burning and tight. Daniel pushed his chair back and stood, pulled her to her feet and the short distance down the hall marked Restrooms. There was a door for the men's room, another for the ladies' and a third that led outside to a tiny lot. Outside, in the cool morning air, he pushed her against the wall, nudged her feet apart with his boot then maneuvered her until she was supported by the building, thighs angled, and she was bent at the waist, head close to her knees, staring at mangled asphalt.

Parts of him came into her field of vision when he crouched in front of her. "Shallow, easy breaths, Tash. Just a little one in and blow it out. Then another little one in."

Hearing him call her by the nickname that had only ever been his was almost enough to undo what effort she'd made to calm herself. She pushed it to the back of her mind, to marvel over later, and forced short breaths in, short breaths out.

It worked, tiny bubbles of sweet air squeezing into her lungs, relaxing the strained muscles in her chest and her throat. Each breath grew a little bigger, and the roiling in her stomach shrank in response. Her eyes were watery but clearing, and her panic was receding like the tides she'd watched so many times: retreating, returning, retreating a little more, each time leaving behind a wider strip of sand.

After a minute—or ten—Daniel peered up into her face. "Okay?"

She wiped her face with one hand then heaved a sigh. "I see wet sand but no water."

He didn't frown in bewilderment. He just shook his head and remarked, "And your family thought I was the odd one."

Slowly, not wanting to jar any part of her that hadn't regained its steadiness yet, she straightened but continued to lean against the wall. Daniel shifted to lean beside her. "My family didn't think you were odd. Just black-and-white."

"In their fifty-six-million-color world, that was odd."

"The entire world thought—thinks they're odd. They're proud of it. Stacia, Nick and me not so much, since we desperately wanted to be seen as normal." Her laugh, meant to be normal as her family never was, wobbled instead. "I'd take their kind of odd happily right now. RememberMe wouldn't be interested in me at all if I were Mom-and-Dad weird."

"I don't know. Men will overlook an awful lot for a beautiful woman." There was a pause, broken by a series of honks from the sky. A flock of Canada geese flew overhead in loose formation.

"Aren't they headed west?" she asked, part of her

mind still focused on returning her systems to pre-panic state.

"Male navigator. I imagine one of the females will take over and turn them south soon." He watched until the higher buildings blocked the geese from view, and then he stared at something on the ground. "I think you should leave Cedar Creek."

Of course he did. He'd said so Thursday night, and he'd probably said it again Friday. Still, pain, tiny but vicious, pricked at her insides. She managed to keep her voice steady, though. "What if he finds me again?"

"I think he found you here because he knew you would try to warn the rest of us and I was the only one you could find. By the way, Ben told me this morning that Eric is in Seattle, and Zach is in Hawaii."

She had no clue what had drawn Eric to the Pacific Northwest, but it was a no-brainer what had drawn surfer-boy Zach to the Big Island. "I never told him I knew how to find you. Hell, I never told him anything after the first few months."

"He had you under surveillance, Natasha. He knew where you were going, what you were doing, who you were talking to. He was smart enough to realize if you were in touch with the Harper fathers, they would tell you where to find the Harper son. I'm betting he already knew where I was, just like he knew where to find Kyle."

Finally he gave her a sidelong glance. "If we can get you out of town without him knowing, he'll stick around to take care of me. If he's here, trying to kill me, he can't be wherever you are."

She swallowed hard. "If he's following me some-place else, he can't be here trying to kill you."

Irritation flashed across his face. "You want to take

this guy on face-to-face? Natasha, he's nuts. He thinks you belong to him. You were right in there. If he ever gets control of you, you're not going to live up to his expectations. His illusions will be shattered, and he'll blame you, and he will almost certainly try to kill you. What kind of chance do you think you'll have alone with him?"

Staving off a resurgence of queasiness, she smiled thinly. "You're awfully sure I'll disappoint him."

"You gonna fall madly in love with him?"

"Hell, no."

"Then you're gonna disappoint him."

She sighed, her first deep breath in a while. "At least he'll have company. The list of people I've disappointed is long."

The quiet between them was sharp-edged. She waited for Daniel's response, dry or bitter and accusing. He opened his mouth, but then closed it again and continued to gaze off toward his boots.

They stood there a long time. The sun went behind the clouds, came back out then disappeared again, and the air seemed to cool a few degrees with the next breeze. More rain? Bring it on. If she couldn't drown her troubles, maybe the rain would drown her.

"You good to go back in?"

She pushed away from the wall, testing her legs. They were steady. She didn't need the building to hold her up anymore. "I'm good." She walked to the door before stopping to face him. "Daniel..." She needed to apologize, but as he'd told her at lunch yesterday, sometimes words just aren't up to the job. So instead, she said something else she needed to say. "Thank you."

Without waiting for his response, she stepped inside and walked quickly down the hall.

* * *

Daniel had learned as a young Harper that arguing with people who held authority over him was rarely a good idea, but that didn't stop him from disagreeing—loudly—with Sam. "If you force us both into hiding, it's just going to cost the department time and money, and I'm going to turn into a crazy-maker."

"You already make me crazy, Harper."

He jabbed one finger in the air toward his boss. "You haven't seen anything yet."

In his peripheral vision, he saw Natasha press her lips together, a sure sign she was trying to resist a smile. "He's right, Chief. He can drive a sane person straight into the heart of Loony Land in no time flat. And I grew up there, so I know loony."

Sam's smile was for her only. When he turned back to Daniel, he was scowling. "Can't you get it through your thick skull? This guy wants you dead."

Daniel snorted to go along with his gesture. "People want all the time. They don't always get." He was living, breathing—and, for a long time, broken and bleeding—proof of that. All he'd wanted was Natasha. All he'd gotten was betrayal.

And a new job. A new place where he belonged. New friends.

And maybe another chance with Natasha.

Aw, jeez, which would be worse? Getting outmaneuvered by a guy who called himself by such a goofy name or falling for and losing Natasha a second time? He'd barely survived the first. He might not survive the second.

Grinding his teeth until his jaw hurt, he fixed his attention on Sam. "I've got a job to do. I've got cases. I'm supposed to appear in court next week on the Hilliard case. What do you think? This guy's going to stroll into the police department and shoot me?"

"It's happened before," Sam said stonily.

"Yeah, well, people who open fire in police stations tend to get shot themselves. He can't get himself killed, because to get Natasha, he's got to get rid of us all and there are two more besides me. In public might be the safest place for me."

Sam stared at him a long time. Daniel had no idea if his statement had swayed him, or if Sam was considering the consequences of forcing him into hiding: a lot of resistance, a lot of annoyance, a lot of whining. Hey, Daniel tried to be dignified most of the time, but he wasn't above juvenile pettiness to get his way.

After a moment, Ben elbowed Sam. "We don't let him go out by himself very often. We can watch out for him."

Sam sighed heavily. "If you get yourself killed—"

"Yeah, I know, you'll kill me." With one victory down, thanks to Ben, Daniel pursued the next. "Natasha needs to leave town."

He didn't expect her to sit there quietly, and she didn't disappoint him. "You can't make me go."

"It would be safer."

"Only if he leaves with me."

"Damn it, Natasha!" An instant after his outburst faded, he realized all three of them were staring at him. She knew he swore on occasion; she'd heard it. Sam and Ben had probably heard it a time or two, but there had been too much teasing from everyone in the department about the times he didn't swear for them to remember. Okay, so what? Now they knew this was beyond important to him. Figuring out stuff like that was what they did.

He pinched the bridge of his nose then glanced around the room. The restaurant was three-quarters full, and two more customers were coming in the door. "We should move this conversation someplace else."

"Like the holding cell back at the office?" Sam asked drily. He picked up the checks and paid all four at the cash register, then they followed him outside. When he started to cross the street, like sheep, Daniel and Ben fell into step.

Natasha stopped short. "You're not putting me in a holding cell."

Sam backtracked and took hold of her arm. "The sooner we get you inside, the better I'll feel. Just come along, Nat."

She bared her teeth at him, reminding Daniel of the day they met. Does anyone call you Nat? he'd asked, and she'd growled. *Only once.*

She grudgingly let Sam pull her along. Once they reached the opposite sidewalk, he released her, and the four of them quickly covered the short distance to the courthouse. The entire time, Daniel's head was swiveling left to right, ahead and behind, searching for anyone who fit Ozzie's description and anyone who didn't. Even though relief spread through him as they climbed the steps into the department—without him stepping in the puddle—there was frustration, too. There had been no one paying attention to them.

At least, no one he could see. But there were all those buildings, all those windows. Who knew what was hiding inside and looking out?

Natasha looked relieved, too, when Sam turned into

the conference room they'd occupied the day before. Had she really thought he might lock her in a cell?

If the decision were Daniel's, he would go for it. A bed, three meals a day, someone always in the building to keep an eye on her... They had bathrooms, showers, televisions, even computers with games and Wikipedia to pass the time. And she would be safe. What could be better?

His house offered that and more. Comfort. Privacy. They had always been compatible as roommates. They kept the same hours. They both liked it cold at night. They both woke slowly and easily and usually in a good mood.

She fit just right against him in bed.

Before he walked once more into a room with Natasha in it, he needed to go down the hall to the holding cell and beat his head against the iron bars. This situation was making him crazy. She was making him crazy. The thought of her being in danger. The memories that kept dragging themselves from the darkest parts of his mind right back center stage. The awareness. The disquiet.

The possibilities.

No possibilities, his self-preservationist side insisted.

Always possibilities, his argumentative side disagreed. For some reason, it always sounded calm and rational like Jeffrey while the other side sounded like Archer in a snit because he knew he was going to lose.

As long as there's breath in your body, Jeffrey would say.

At least one person didn't intend for Daniel to die of old age.

Pushed against the wall in the conference room but seldom used was a couch that had once sat in the lobby. The story was that the chief before Sam had moved it back here because it invited people to sit down and stay a while, and he didn't want people sitting down and staying a while in his lobby. Sam and his people sat and stayed a long while in this room, but not on the couch. No one ever got too comfortable in this room.

Except Natasha. She'd kicked her shoes off, tucked her feet onto the cushions beside her and folded her arms across her chest. Without being asked, Sam got the space heater from against the far wall, stretched out its cord and turned it on where it would warm her corner of the world.

"So, no one ever calls you Nat?" Sam asked. The bared-teeth outside hadn't gone unnoticed.

"No one who knows me. Not ever. Back in the beginning, I told RememberMe I didn't like the name, and he ignored me."

Didn't like it because it was too similar to the pesky little insect that sucked a person's blood. When they'd been out once with Flea Martin and her husband, someone from work had jokingly called them Gnat and Flea, the bug girls. Neither woman had been amused.

Sam sat in one of the desk chairs, turning it to face her. "You're not setting yourself up as bait to draw this guy out."

Natasha's gaze flickered around the room, from Sam to Ben, settling in another chair, and finally to Daniel, who was taking the opposite end of the couch. "There's not one woman in my life who tries to tell me what to do, but you guys…"

"I'm getting closer to forty every day, I'm the chief

of police and my mother still tells me what to do," Sam remarked.

"So does mine." Ben grinned.

"I don't have a mother," Daniel said, "but both of their mothers boss me around. So does Mila's grandmother." Another thing on the plus side of his life since his bride-to-be abandoned him.

Sam leaned forward, elbows on his knees. "Look, I know this isn't fun, and we don't have any legal authority to make you stay in town or to stick to your hotel room or to only go out when you've got an armed escort. But this guy's got damned impressive computer skills. About the only thing he doesn't know is that we took your computers and phone. I think you're pretty safe at the Prairie Sun, because the guests are familiar with each other and Claire knows everyone. But if you leave town and he follows you…it's not carved in stone that he has to kill the exes before he can kidnap you. He just needs them dead for everything to be perfect between you. If you leave, you've got no one to call for help, no one who will even know you're in trouble. And it won't make Daniel and the others safer. It'll just throw Wacko's timetable off a bit."

It was hard asking a person to be rational when every emotion in her body was screaming the opposite. Daniel understood that. Truth was, Natasha had never been the most rational woman, even in the best of times. She was accustomed to being happy and spontaneous and carefree, a grab-your-chances-with-both-hands-and-let-the-chips-fall-where-they-may sort. Live for the moment and think about tomorrow tomorrow.

But she was also a sensible woman. She didn't want to face her stalker alone. She didn't want to just disappear from life, never to be seen again, and she understood that could be exactly what he had planned for her. She didn't want to break Stacia's heart, or Daniel's, or anyone else's because she'd tried to do the right thing and it hadn't been right at all.

And it would break Stacia's heart, and Daniel's and everyone else's, if this bastard killed her.

Especially Daniel's.

"Okay." The word sounded flat, but there was relief and even a touch of hopefulness in it. She didn't have to deal with RememberMe alone. They would be with her. They would keep her safe.

If Daniel had his way, RememberMe would regret he'd ever been born.

It was early afternoon when the chief, accompanied by Daniel and Ben, gave Natasha a ride to the hotel. They'd talked endlessly about dangers and risk and assessments, along with ordering pizza, and she'd listened, swearing to herself she would be the most cooperative person they'd ever seen. They wanted to keep her and Daniel alive. Far be it from her to make it more difficult.

Besides, she wasn't the only one with restrictions. Daniel had been instructed not to answer any calls alone, not to interview any witnesses without a fellow officer, not to leave his house in the morning or go back in the evening without someone to ensure he was safely in or out. His restrictions chafed more on him than hers did on her. She was desperate, not brave, while he was the opposite.

The rain came back in the minutes it took to circle the block to the hotel. Daniel and Ben got out first and ushered her inside, and Ben took her key to go upstairs and check her room. The chief remained parked out front until Ben came back down and returned the key. "I'll be in town if you need anything."

Daniel nodded and gestured toward the stairs.

Natasha twisted around to watch the other detective walk out to the chief's SUV. "Your ride's leaving without you."

"My car's across the street." Daniel indicated the stairs again, and after a moment, she began climbing them.

"Are you the one stuck babysitting me?" she asked, trailing her hand along the banister.

"There was a time when you anticipated afternoons in a hotel room with me." His tone was level, steady, with just the slightest shade of cynicism. "But that was before the time you couldn't bear to be in the same room with me. You remember, when you sent Stacia to give back my engagement ring."

Her foot in midair, she froze. The air that had been comfortable an instant ago now raised gooseflesh even beneath her heavy sweater, and the homey flowers-wood-vanilla scent took on an acrid flavor. The reason was far different from this morning's upset, when she'd realized RememberMe's obsessive love would eventually turn to hate, but the churning in her gut and the tightening in her chest were very similar.

After a moment, she forced her foot onto the next step. Slid her hand. Lifted her other foot. Climbed another step. She'd been preparing for this conversation since she'd left Los Angeles, but on the stairs, halfway between the public area and the privacy of her room, wasn't the place to have it.

Could she ever be prepared to explain decisions she didn't understand herself?

Women's voices came from the second floor—the wine women—filtering out through their open doors. Rob stood in one of the doorways that sat opposite each other, his shoulder against the jamb, his dark hair damp and slicked back as if he'd just come from the shower. He smiled when he saw Natasha and was about to speak when his gaze shifted past her to Daniel. He closed his mouth and turned his attention back to the women inside the room.

Her key turned easily in the lock, and she swung the door open, walking in without apprehension. At least, no stalker apprehension. After all, Ben had cleared the room a few moments ago.

But there was apprehension. It tingled along her spine and made the hairs on the back of her neck stand on end. It made her stomach hurt, and her head, and her heart.

She set her purse down and turned on all the lights. Normally, she loved having the curtains and blinds open, but not today, when she couldn't see anything but rain, and RememberMe was probably out there. Instead, she stopped at the foot of the bed, rested one arm on the rail then immediately pulled it away from the bony birds and their beaks. "Is there something you want to say, Daniel?"

He closed and locked the door and leaned against it. "I had a lot to say five years ago. I just couldn't find you to say it. You skipped our party. You didn't answer your phone. You didn't go back to your apartment. Stacia quit answering the phone after my first two dozen calls. You just…disappeared, Natasha. I deserved better than that."

Clearing her throat didn't help to steady her voice. Taking a breath didn't steady her hands, either, or the thudding of her heart in her chest. "I was a bit crazy those first few weeks."

"I was a bit crazy those first twelve months."

Color warmed her face, and panic fluttered all the way through her. She wanted to talk about it, to explain what she could even if it was pathetically little. If she'd never seen him again, then maybe she could have pushed it to the corner of her mind that kept ravaging guilt and impending breakdowns at bay forever. The more time passed, the easier she could pretend that it didn't matter anymore. The past was past. Words couldn't fix actions.

She used to be better at pretending than she was these days.

But words still couldn't fix actions. And in this case, her words were just a disjointed muddle. Sorry, scared, didn't think, didn't trust, couldn't.

"What do you want to know?"

His scowl deepened. "There's only one question, Tash, isn't there? Everything else is just a variation of it."

Why?

Why did you break up with me? Why did you do it that way? Why didn't you tell me you had doubts? Why didn't you talk to me? Why did you send your sister to break my heart? Why didn't you give me a chance?

She knew the questions. They'd haunted her for a long time. So had the answers. Non-answers, really.

She pulled a chair from the table, sat down, crossed

her legs and folded her arms over her chest. But that position felt too calm, too open, so she undid those things and instead rested her heels on the seat of the chair and hugged her knees. It made her a smaller target, less vulnerable, and would help hold her together if she needed it.

"We never talked about why I broke up with Kyle or Eric."

Daniel took a hesitant step, then another. Keeping a physical distance from emotional involvement was one of his coping mechanisms. He could resist tears or pleading or sorrow from across the room, she knew, but not so much when he was within touching distance. After what seemed forever, he sat down in the second chair.

"Truth was, I didn't much care," he admitted, his gaze on the enamel teapot sitting at the back of the table, filled with mums in glorious shades of copper, auburn and gold. "If you had married either one of them, you wouldn't have been available when we met, so I was glad you hadn't. What went wrong between you and them, I never thought it had anything to do with us. We were different. I was different." He paused, and his intense gaze reluctantly locked with hers. "I was wrong, wasn't I?"

"No. Yes." She rested her forehead on her knees, missing the old days when her hair was long enough to fall around and hide her face. Knowing there was no insight to be found in avoiding his look, his question, she raised her head again. "I can't tell you how many times I've thought about this. It's been a major part of my life from the moment I decided to break up with Kyle."

"So you dealt with it by breaking up with Eric. And me. And Zach."

"I thought... I hoped..." Her deep breath smelled of flowers and herself and that so very special scent of him. It warmed her a little. Scared her a little. Saddened her a lot.

"You know my parents. Relationships have been a revolving door for them my whole life. Even when they were married to each other, they weren't conventional. Nick didn't care so much, but Stacia and me... that's what we always wanted. A conventional marriage, family, home. They were never going to give us that. They just weren't capable of it."

None of this was new to Daniel. He'd told her a long time ago that it was certainly a change with his gay fathers being the traditional, stable, monogamous role models in his and her relationship. She wished her mother and father showed one-tenth the commitment to each other and their children that Jeffrey and Archer did.

"So, your mom's on husband number five, and your dad's on serious girlfriend number eight, with a couple more wives in there along the way. So...what?"

Her resolve crumbled a little. His question wasn't sarcastic; he was sincere in wanting to understand the connection. "I don't know. I wanted to be married. I wanted the whole bit—marriage, kids, house, pets, fifty years with the same man. I thought Kyle was the man I wanted it all with. When he proposed, I was over the moon with delight. Then the doubts set in. Stacia asking me, 'Are you sure he's the one?' Mom saying, 'If it doesn't work out, there are always other chances.' Little voices reminding me, 'You are your parents' child.

You don't know how to commit. You don't know how to be married to one person. You won't be any better at it than they are.'"

Exhaling deeply, she finished simply. "So I left him."

Four words to describe an experience for Kyle that must have been the worst nightmare he'd ever lived through. At least, Daniel's jilting had been his own worst nightmare—and he hadn't been standing at the front of the church when she rejected him. Kyle had had that humiliation to add to the heartache.

No, Daniel had just been surrounded by every person he called family or friend, everyone who was important in his life. And in one of those strange twists, every single one of them had seen Stacia come into the room alone. They'd watched her make a beeline for him, had seen the distress on her face and every single one of them had gone utterly still. They'd known. Maybe even before he had.

Honesty forced him to acknowledge that none of her breakups had been easy for Natasha. She was a good person, kind and generous and compassionate. There was no meanness in her; she never set out to deliberately hurt someone. Marriage was a big deal to her, as it was to him, as he thought it should be to everyone considering it. She wasn't the sort of person who would leap into it with the assumption that if it didn't work, divorce was always an option. It was a commitment to be with one person for the whole rest of her life. Divorce was an option only in the worst-case scenario.

He stared into the distance, his fingers loosely gripped together. In the end, breaking up with Kyle had been the right decision for both of them. It had taken a while, but they'd kept their friendship. He'd fallen in love with someone else, and so had she.

And done the same thing to him. And then to Daniel. To Zach.

And it had obviously been the right decision with Eric and with Zach, but damn it, *he* was different. He had loved her more than anything. He'd wanted exactly the things she'd wanted, and he'd wanted them with her, forever. But she had run from him, too.

She was silent, unhappiness etched in the lines of her face. There was a defeated look about her, enough guilt for a jail full of convicted felons. She deserved the guilt. She'd wrecked enough lives to earn it.

Though the wreckage of Kyle's life had been temporary. Probably, so had Eric's and Zach's. Daniel appeared to be the only one who hadn't gotten over it. Though he'd convinced himself he had, he still hurt so damned much. Still cared so damned much. Still missed her and dreamed about her and wanted her...

Oh, God.

The rain fell harder, a steady drum on the building, the streets, but in the stillness of the room, they were dry, even cozy. Untouched by it. He'd grabbed his slicker when he left the house. It still lay on the passenger seat, one sleeve and hood hanging over the floorboard. A lot of good it would do him there.

He let his head fall back against the wall with a small thud—maybe it would knock some sense into him—and closed his eyes. He wished he could turn back the clock, just a week. Life had been easier then. He'd been living in the present, satisfied with his work, his friends, his dating status. There'd been no constant reminders of Natasha, no threats to his heart or mind or life, no fears for her life. All things considered, he'd been good.

But if he was going to magically turn back time, why not go further? Maybe he could have prevented the breakup. Maybe he could have talked to her, acknowledged her insecurities, convinced her that they were strong enough together to survive anything. A tendency to take relationships lightly wasn't genetic; a lack of positive role models didn't guarantee failure. They could have overcome whatever life chose to throw at them.

"You really are crazy-making, you know?" He opened his eyes as he spoke and saw a great shudder ripple through her.

"You know my mother's motto." Her tone was dry and cautious.

He knew. Libby Spencer had spouted it off often enough. "'If you're not stirring things up, you're not doing it right.'"

"I asked her once how she could stand having things stirred up all the time. She said she was *living*, that the boredom of my life would drive her to violence. She felt sorry for me, and I felt frustrated for her, and we never discussed it again."

Some of the stiffness left her body, relaxing her spine, loosening the muscles in her neck and jaw. The worst of the conversation was over. Her responses hadn't been as black-and-white as he would have liked, but in a world with fifty-six million colors, he'd learned to accept that things rarely were.

He had one more question to ask before he let the subject drop. "What could I have done differently, Natasha?"

Sadness flitted across her face. "Nothing. You were perfect, Daniel. You were everything I wanted. The failing was mine, not yours."

He'd blamed her all along, though not entirely. There was still the fact that he'd proposed to a woman who had jilted two fiancés hours—and minutes—before the weddings. He'd had the arrogance to believe that he was the one who could change her. He was the one who would live happily-ever-after where the others had failed.

But mostly he'd blamed her. Bitterly. Hearing her say, *It was me, not you...* Sure, it was a cliché, but clichés existed for a reason. It tempered his bitterness. It made him feel...

He didn't want to examine what it made him feel. If he could say goodbye, walk out and never see her again, it would be a relief. Closure.

But he couldn't walk out. He couldn't avoid seeing her. He couldn't leave her to cope with RememberMe on her own. He could forgive but not forget. He had a duty here, an official one and a personal one. The official one was easy. He could do his job with his eyes closed and one hand cuffed behind his back.

The personal one was going to get him into trouble. Because there had never been a time, from the very first time Natasha had spoken to him, that being with her hadn't given him a sense of completion. That talking to her hadn't made him want to touch her, that touching her hadn't made him want to kiss her, that kissing her hadn't made him want to do *everything*.

There wasn't a moment in his life that he hadn't wanted her. Needed her. That he hadn't somewhere, deep inside, loved her.

Like it was meant to be. Like they were meant to be.

He took a breath, bringing fresh smells into his lungs, blowing out the old ones of memory. Perfume, shampoo, toothpaste, laundry soap—all had their memories. Flowers, cooking aromas, cooking burns, smoke, salt, ocean, sand—they did, too. Everything about her had been so bright, high-definition, sharp and vibrant and intense, in his memories that in bad times, they'd cut him to shreds. It was a wonder he hadn't gone stalker-crazy himself.

Time had rubbed off some of the vibrancy, and these past few moments—her conversation, his self-admissions—had taken off some of the sharpness. He didn't feel so much like a bitter walking wound but more like a person who'd just discovered he'd survived what he'd thought would kill him. He wasn't whole, but he could foresee the day when he would be. He still didn't understand, but he could appreciate it without understanding it.

Some things, Archer said, were meant to be taken on faith, or not taken on faith. Acceptance or rejection. No dissection, no microscopic probing.

"I honestly can't remember if I said it during this conversation," Natasha began, "but I've said it to so many people so many times that I can't keep count." She blew out her breath. "I'm sorry, Daniel. And you weren't wrong. You *were* different, and you made me different. We were so different and so right that I thought not even I could screw it up. But my dedication to my insecurities turned out to be a lot stronger than I'd expected."

He looked at her a long time, needing to remember every detail about the way she looked right that moment. Her face was fuller, her eyes were bluer and her smile had lost some of its energy. She was five years older, another heartbreak older, full of regrets and apologies and still the most beautiful woman in his world. Still the woman who knew him best, but who somehow hadn't known that he would have done anything to protect her, not just physically but emotionally and mentally, from real dangers to imagined fears.

He would have died for her.

But he hadn't even fought for her. He hadn't demanded that she talk to him. He hadn't insisted on answers and plans and resolutions. She'd wanted to get away from him? Fine. Instead of standing his ground, instead of fighting to protect them, he'd quit his job, packed his stuff and run fifteen hundred miles to nurse his hurt feelings.

But he was five years older, too. Five years wiser. He would still protect her.

Would still die for her.

He would kill for her.

He suspected he would still do anything for her.

Even trust her.

Chapter 7

If the sun were visible, it would be setting when Natasha peeked at the western sky through the narrow space between window frame and blinds. All she saw was dark clouds in the near distance and darker ones farther away. As the afternoon had passed, the temperature had fallen. For the first time since checking into the hotel, she turned the heat on, grateful that the elegant old building boasted not too terribly old central heating. Warm air blew through the vent against the outer wall, fluttering the curtains, perfuming the air with an unused sort of scent for the first few minutes.

Instead of returning to the straight-backed chair at the table, she went to the bed, kicked off her shoes and plumped the pillows against the headboard. "Are Archer and Jeffrey considering it?"

It had been a difficult afternoon that had somehow

turned into a comfortable evening. The conversation had slowly shifted from her fickleness to safer, everyday subjects that didn't trigger either one's more volatile emotions. They'd even laughed about a few things together. One of the few things Natasha and her mom agreed on: laughter was good for the soul. Hers felt lighter. Safer.

Daniel adjusted his chair to better see her before answering her question about him asking his parents to consider Cedar Creek when they retired. "They are. They come to visit at least twice a year, and sometimes Jeffrey stops in when he's traveling on business. They've charmed Mrs. Little Bear and Mila's gramma Jessica, and Archer makes a point of running with Morwenna's mum when he's here."

Natasha smiled at the thought. Both older Harpers—okay, all three of them—were in excellent shape, but none of them were dedicated to working out. She was lazy, and it showed. They were, ah, less active, but when they needed strength or stamina, it was there to draw on. Supermen, she'd called them.

"It's kind of hard to imagine them in small-town middle America," she remarked. "Or retired, for that matter. They have so much going on in their lives. Then again, it was kind of hard to imagine you here, but you've fit right in." Hesitating, she drew her finger over a line of stitches on the embroidered pillow case. "So, you don't miss LA?"

"On occasion. But planes fly that way, too."

"But not enough to go back there."

"No." Like her, he fidgeted a bit, crossing one ankle over his other knee and fiddling with his boot lace. "When I came here, I figured it would be temporary.

I mean, Detective Daniel Harper, LAPD, spending the rest of his life in Cedar Creek, Oklahoma? I wasn't coming *here*. I was just running away from LA, and this is the first place I stopped. I figured a year, maybe two, then I'd head south to Dallas or east to New York. Maybe even just a little bit northeast to Tulsa. But…"

"You liked it." She was genuinely glad for him. God knows, he'd deserved whatever satisfaction he could get after her.

"The work is interesting enough. I haven't died of boredom. Anything I want is within reasonable traveling distance. No rush hour. No traffic jams. No ten million people wanting to be exactly where I am. The people are good, the weather changes and I like it."

He'd found his home.

She was still looking for hers. She'd thought her home was with Kyle, then Eric and the others. She'd been willing to live where they lived, willing to change her life so she could fit in instead of asking for a compromise.

Daniel's home hadn't been a person but a place, maybe even a state of mind. When her life was back to normal, when RememberMe was gone one way or the other, she would think about that.

"What about you?" Daniel asked. "You still a Cali girl through and through?"

She smiled sunnily and would have tossed her hair if it was long enough. "Don't I look it?"

He didn't answer, or ask another question, or do anything but look at her with his waiting-for-an-answer attitude. Her smile became a tad rueful. "Am I going to live and die in sunny California? Not if RememberMe gets his way. Maybe not even if you get your way and stop him. It doesn't have the happiest memories."

"Hey, you fell in love four times there. It can't be all bad."

It warmed her immeasurably that he said the words without a hint of bitterness. She was so very lucky to hear that. "My happiest memories were there, of course. It's just that the last few years have kind of overshadowed them."

He stretched, paced to the door and looked out the peephole, paced back to the window and nudged the blinds apart. He stood motionless there a long time. Looking for the best vantage points? The places where RememberMe could hide and watch them?

"I wonder if his apartment in LA is creepy," she remarked, and Daniel's shoulders stiffened. It didn't stop her from going on. "You know, if he ever has anyone over, if he's got a room padlocked and says, 'Never go in there,' or if he's one of those strange guys whose neighbors would say, 'He lived all alone. He was such a quiet guy.' If he has a hidden room or a basement or a closet that's plastered with pictures of me. I wonder if he's taken anything of mine—maybe a napkin I used in a restaurant or a coffee cup I walked off and left on the table at Starbucks."

"You don't leave empty cups sitting on tables."

He was right. Not leaving messes for other people to tidy was a trait they shared in common. Though she'd certainly brought a big enough mess to his door this time. "I might have been in a hurry."

"You're morbid."

"Stacia says as long as you can joke about it, it isn't a complete and total tragedy. Besides, isn't that what stalkers do? Surround themselves with reminders of the object of their psychoticness?" Another thought occurred to her. "I wonder if I'm the first one."

Finally Daniel let the blind slats fall back into place and faced her. "You're also ghoulish." He scrubbed his hands over his face. "I admit, I don't know a lot about stalkers, other than they're delusional and dangerous. I guess if he can obsess over you, he might have obsessed over someone else in the past."

"If he did, what would have made him abandon her for me?"

"I don't know. The moon entered a new phase. The tides changed. Your smile was prettier or he liked your hair better or—"

"Or he killed her because he couldn't have her." A shiver washed over her. "Great, now I'm channeling Stacia. Did I tell you she's done three slasher films in the past few years? She always plays the too-stupid-to-live girl who goes to investigate creepy serial killer noises by herself. Those movies terrified her as a kid, so she finds it a hoot that she's doing them now."

"She's certainly got the scream for it. When she's excited, her shrieks can burst eardrums. I can't imagine the magnitude of her terror-induced scream."

There was a hint of fondness in his voice. It had been one of Natasha's greatest reliefs that her sister and her boyfriend liked each other. Stacia hadn't been fond of Kyle, thought Natasha could do better than Eric and had been pretty much bewildered by Zach. *His world starts at the surf shop and ends beyond the breaking waves. It's all he talks about, all he does, all he wants to do. He calls you "dude." Offer him serious hot sex when the waves are crankin', and he'll take the waves every time. The guy's taken too many boards to the head, Tash.*

Natasha figured Stacia understood exactly what Zach's appeal was to her, though they'd never discussed it: he was so very different from Daniel. Breaking up with Daniel had been hard, getting over him had been even harder, and she'd sworn the next guy she spoke to would be his complete opposite.

Thus Zach. Their engagement had lasted less than a week. He'd casually asked, she'd casually said yes, and six days later she'd less than casually changed her mind. He'd been cool with it. *No problem, dude. My buds say the only leash a man needs is the one on his board.*

"She hardly spoke to me for two months after she returned your ring." Natasha was rubbing the embroidery pattern again. "Made it kind of tough since we were sharing an apartment at the time. She would crawl in bed with me and let me cry on her shoulder, but she wouldn't say, 'Poor baby,' or 'It'll be all right.'"

He cocked his head to one side. "Did you cry a lot?"

"Enough to solve the state's water shortage for a year."

"Good."

She raised her brows in his direction.

"You break my heart, you don't get to go out and be all happy the next day. If you're going to make me suffer, you need to suffer, too."

She flippantly saluted. "I'll remember that—" She'd been about to say *next time*, but she caught herself. Daniel was the most loyal person she'd met. Because of that, when he trusted someone, it was wholehearted but not easy. She didn't know what kind of treatment he gave someone who betrayed him because she didn't know anyone besides herself who had.

They fell silent for a time, him thinking heaven knew what, her thinking about all her shortcomings and yet how easily it was to rate them from minor to major to worst to absolutely worst. Jilting Daniel definitely took that title, hands down.

But the anger was gone from his eyes, from the set of his mouth, the set of his jaw, his shoulders. He was less stressed, more at ease. He didn't look as if the universe was conspiring against him. He just looked... good. Incredibly handsome. Usually astute, sometimes a bit clueless, serious and committed and reliable and courageous and—

The ring of the bedside telephone, designed to both look and sound old-fashioned, was so unexpected that Natasha gave a pretty good small version of Stacia's shriek. The only phones she'd ever had were cell phones with volume-restricted, programmable tones, so the harsh *ring-ring* of this phone set her heart racing.

His easy manner vanishing, Daniel came to her side of the bed. He picked up the phone mid-ring and sat beside her, holding it between them so she could speak and he could hear.

"H-hello."

"I saw pictures of the room phones on the hotel's website. Bet you almost peed your pants when it rang."

"Stacia." She gulped a deep breath. "You scared me half to death."

"You forget those things aren't just some ugly historical accessory, don't you? Besides, you said they took your cell. How else was I going to get hold of you?"

Daniel handed her the receiver then scooted a short

distance away, the mattress giving under his weight, then resettling. He was far enough away to give her some privacy, close enough that she could feel his strength, the invisible shield that he'd always shared willingly with her.

"How's the job?" Natasha asked.

"Good."

"The boyfriend?"

"Good. Listen, Tash…"

Natasha's fingers tightened. That shift in tone was a warning. Stacia didn't get serious often, and she always prefaced it with *listen*. "Crazy-pants psycho guy knows you don't have your phone, too. He texted me a few minutes ago with a message for you. You ready?"

Natasha was proud that the tremor in her hand was only a small one, not the full-blown panic she'd experienced earlier in the day. She was locked safely in a room with Daniel. Short of a bomb, crazy-pants couldn't do anything to her until she went out, and she just might not ever do that.

She gave Daniel a beckoning nod, and he moved closer again. "Okay, Stacia, go ahead."

Her sister cleared her throat. "'Nastacia, pass to Nat.' No *please* or *thank you*." She *hmphed*. "'Taking your cell and computers won't help them find me. I'm too smart for that. I've forgotten more about IT than they've ever collectively known. Staying in that hotel room won't work, either. When I'm ready, I'll come for you. I've been planning this for a very long time, and I always get what I want. You're my destiny, Nat. Nothing can change that. Not the police. Not Daniel. Not you. You'll always be mine.'"

Okay, the tremor was picking up force, so much that

Daniel had to steady the phone. She inhaled when he laid his hand over hers. In her ears it sounded like a loud, sharp-edged gasp, but neither of the others mentioned it.

"Nastacia?" Daniel said drily. "How did I never know that was your name?"

"Daniel!" Stacia squealed. "Oh, it's so good to hear your voice! It's been so long! How *are* you? Besides the obvious downer of having your ex-fiancée show up to tell you that her new boyfriend wants you dead?" As usual, she didn't wait for an answer.

"Besides, if you were named Nastacia, wouldn't you shorten it? It sounds like some kind of bug you might catch in the garden. So, how are you?"

"Things have livened up here in the last few days."

"In true Spencer fashion. Are you going to catch this guy?"

"Yes."

When he let that short, simple response stand on its own, Stacia said, "You know, you're the only person in our lives who has always, always done what he said he would. That's one of the reasons we loved you. Still love you. I still love you."

Natasha wondered if her sister could somehow feel the heat of the blush seeping through her over the phone, because she awkwardly shifted topics. "Nick's name is Nikolay. Our parents are weird, huh? But you already know that."

"I knew that before I ever met them. Stacia, will you forward that text to me?" He waited for her to give the go-ahead, then he recited his cell number. "I hear your career's going well. Congratulations."

"Thank you. I know you don't watch much TV, but

if you want to catch my smiling face… Well, I don't really smile much on the show because I'm trying to solve my sister's murder…oh, God, that hits too close to home, doesn't it? Anyway… I'm so glad to talk to you! Tasha, I love you. Stay safe."

The call clicked, leaving a faint hum on the phone line. Natasha stretched forward to return the receiver to its cradle then sat back.

"She's like a wave breaking over the rocks at the tide pools. Unstoppable, fierce, a force of nature that leaves a trail of little bubbles popping silently in her wake."

After a moment of surprised quiet, Natasha laughed. It was hardly appropriate, given the situation and the message Stacia had just passed on, but she couldn't help herself. For the first time in weeks, she was overcome with pure, warm, solid pleasure. In that moment, there was no fear, no apprehension, no helplessness. Nothing but her and Daniel and that oh-so-accurate image of Stacia.

And Daniel laughed with her.

Thank God, the sun was shining Sunday morning. The sky was the beautiful clear blue Daniel normally associated with Oklahoma, and there wasn't a cloud visible in any direction. With the air chilly and everything smelling clean and freshly washed, it would be a good day for a long walk. There was a trail that started at the park next to Mrs. Little Bear's café and wound all the way north to Sand Springs, a nice ten-mile stroll, before turning east toward Tulsa.

But he wasn't foolish enough to put himself in some isolated spot like that. Even the thought of it would make the chief's blood pressure rise, and Daniel tried at least marginally not to do that.

Besides, he would worry the whole time he was gone about Natasha.

But if she could go with him...

He had stayed at the hotel last night until they were both fighting to keep their eyes open. After the call from Stacia, the owner of Judge Judie's had delivered dinner to Natasha's room. Daniel had forwarded the text to Ben and Sam, and they'd shared their frustration on a conference call. They were working more or less on the stalker's timetable. His messages were virtually untraceable; so were his packages. The white phosphorus he'd used in the arson was available online and, according to multiple sites, could be made at home.

He was smarter than the cops, he'd bragged in the text. Unlike their usual suspects, this one might be right. At the moment, they had no lead to follow and nothing to do but wait.

And none of them was very good at waiting.

During the call last night, Sam had scheduled another meeting this morning. Ben was due to pick up Daniel in ten minutes, which meant he was probably parked outside, had found the newspaper where the paper guy threw it—never anywhere near the door—and done a few walks around the house. They were using the back entrance of the hotel to pick up Natasha and the prisoner entrance at the jail to get her inside unseen. It wasn't necessary to have the meeting at the station. Sam just figured Natasha could use some sort of break from the four shrinking walls of her room.

Daniel went downstairs and did his own loop around the interior. The windows were locked, the blinds

closed, the drapes pulled. The side door that led from
the mudroom to the yard was secured. At the front
door, he checked out to, indeed, find Ben's dark-tinted
SUV parked at the curb, inactivated the alarm for the
minute it took him to get out, lock up and reset it, then
jogged to the truck.

"Have you pried open your garage door lately?" Ben
asked as soon as Daniel climbed inside.

"No." *Garage* was the name the owner used for the
structure in the back corner of Daniel's yard. It had no
drive leading to it, it was smaller than most of the police department vehicles he drove, a person could see
through the gaps in the old wood slats and the door was
securely sealed shut by years of grass clippings piling
up and breaking down every time the yard was mowed.

"It's been opened six or eight inches. The rain must
have made it easier to scrape the dirt back. There's
no floor inside, just packed dirt, so there weren't any
footprints. I found this, though." Ben held out a small
plastic bag, marked with his precise writing: date, time,
location, his name. "Couldn't have been there very
long. You know what it is?"

There was a lone piece of something in the bag,
thumbnail-size, pinkish in color, sparkly. Daniel recognized it, though the test came in smelling it. Reluctantly, he lifted the bag to his nose and inhaled. Even
with the bag sealed, he caught a whiff of the aroma.
He all but tossed the bag back at Ben.

"It's crystallized ginger."

Ben gave him a dry look. "Someone broke into your
shed to sneak a piece of crystallized ginger?"

"Natasha goes through stages where she eats that
stuff by the pound. I like ginger fine, but she's a fiend

about it. Pretty soon, I'd start smelling it on her skin and in her bed and her car and tasting it on— Well. The food she cooked tasted like ginger even when she didn't add it." He grimaced, still able to smell it though the sample was now in Ben's center console. "If he's been eating that, we should be able to find him easily. He'll be the one everybody's keeping their distance from."

"So to show that they're compatible, he's eating ginger?" Ben shook his head ruefully. "I don't understand crazy people, and I don't want to. Not even the ones in my own family."

Daniel didn't comment on the Little Bear family. He'd been blessed himself with relatively sane relatives, but if he'd married Natasha, he would have married into an asylum full of "free spirits." Too close to crazy for his peace of mind.

"He may have hidden in the shed while he watched the house," Ben went on. "He may have left the ginger just so you'd know it was him. I wonder if it was from last night or the night before."

When he got home last night, Daniel hadn't even glanced at the shed. He and a uniformed officer had walked around inside and out, Daniel had thanked him and gone straight to bed. If RememberMe had been so close then, he regretted that he hadn't gone across the yard with a shotgun and blasted the place to bits.

Or at least caught the bastard off guard, handcuffed him and taken him to jail.

Ben avoided the front of the hotel, turning into the alley from the next side street over. It took careful maneuvering, but he backed the SUV right up to the rear door, underneath the awning that protected from weather while guests dug in bags and pockets for keys.

After a moment, the uniformed officer who'd been inside visiting with Claire since shift change opened the door, and Natasha, unrecognizable in an oversized hoodie that hid her face and her shape equally well, hustled into the back seat.

"You're good to go," the officer said before closing the door. Two seconds later, the hotel door closed, and probably ten seconds later, the officer was back at the desk, as if he'd never moved.

As Ben pulled away, Natasha said cheerily, "I'm so excited. I get to go stare at other walls today." Her voice came from deep inside the black-and-orange hoodie declaring allegiance to the Oklahoma State Cowboys. "Claire suggested the jacket. She tried to teach me a song, too. Let's see…"

She mangled her way through the first line of the fight song, where Daniel and almost anyone else would have stopped her.

He only half-heartedly considered it, and Ben, big surprise, joined in, his ability to carry a tune much better than hers.

Natasha's laughter was light, bordering on giggly, and reminded Daniel so much of the before-Tasha that his breath caught in his chest and spiraled hard, right into his gut.

"Claire said there's a home game next Saturday. She said if I'm still here, she'll dress me up right—even with a cowboy hat—and we can caravan to Stillwater and get lost in a sea of football fans. ScrewYou would never find us."

Ben gave an appreciative chuckle for the new nickname, then grinned at her reflection in the rearview mirror. "You slept well last night, didn't you?"

"I did."

Daniel wasn't going to look at her, he wasn't, but he felt the weight of her gaze on him, and before he could stop himself, his head swiveled around to take stock. Her eyes were clearer, and the shadows beneath them were fading. She looked like she'd gotten good news—though she would have shared that—or found hope in something. Someone.

Stacia had said last night he was the only person in their lives who always kept his word. Maybe Natasha had remembered that about him. Or maybe she'd had doubts with the past between them, but since they'd talked it out, more or less, she was trusting him 100 percent again.

Maybe it had nothing at all to do with him. He didn't care. This Natasha wasn't forlorn or defeated. She wasn't going to collapse under RememberMe's— ScrewYou's—threats. She didn't give off the vulnerable air that frustrated him. He liked that.

They approached the police station from the rear. A narrow lane led through a locked gate, down a slope and through a heavy electronic gate that blocked all view from the outside. An officer and a jailer were waiting inside the second gate.

Daniel got out and offered his hand to Natasha. She didn't need assistance, of course; she looked as if she might jump to the ground and jog a victory lap around the truck. Fresh air, a change of scenery and even the tiniest bit of freedom could go straight to a person's head.

But she politely took his hand and stepped down. Her fingers clasped his a moment longer than was necessary. He didn't mind. He kept his hold loose, allowing her the option of pulling free whenever she wanted.

"Is this a sally port?" she asked. "You've talked about them before, but I've never seen one. It's kind of grim."

He glanced around at bare walls, cameras, automatic gates and bars. "It's a place to safely transfer prisoners from a vehicle to the jail. We can't waste money to pretty it up for them."

"My mom's a pretty good painter. She'd do a mural of sunflowers or buffalo or whatever on these walls and only charge for the cost of the paint." She grinned slyly. "She might try to sneak a few prisoners out with her when she left, just the ones she was sure were wrongly accused, but she'd leave behind a pretty picture."

Daniel called to the jailer, "You want to see some pretty pictures on those walls over there, Tom?"

"Hell, yeah. Maybe Miss July. Miss October. Definitely Miss December."

Natasha made a regretful gesture. "For that you would need my mother's third husband's second ex-wife. Her paintings all depict women with big boobs, thigh-high black leather boots and a whip. But she'd want a commission, as well as expenses."

Tom's gaze narrowed on her, as if he was trying to decide how much she was exaggerating. Knowing what he did of the Spencers, Daniel didn't doubt it at all.

He led the way inside, down a long corridor and up a flight of stairs to the main floor. Lois Gideon was sitting on the edge of a desk, chatting with Cullen Simpson, when they came in. She slid to her feet, took a few steps toward them and then twirled around. "What do you think, guys?"

Daniel wasn't as clueless as people sometimes thought. Yeah, his gaze skimmed over her from top to bottom, noticing that this might be the first time he'd ever seen her in a dress, definitely the first time he'd seen her in a dress with cowboy boots. And yeah, he saw her big dangly earrings first, beads and feathers in a half dozen shades of blue. But he got to the point eventually.

"Your hair is blue." Ben said it in a commonplace, everyday sort of voice.

"It's the exact shade of my favorite old jeans." Natasha moved past Daniel to lightly touch Lois's hair. "It's gorgeous."

"Thank you." Lois beamed. "I turn sixty next week. Figured I might as well officially become a blue-hair."

"You're too young in spirit to ever be an old woman," Simpson disagreed, and she turned the beam on him.

"Suck up," Daniel muttered.

"He knows she can kick his ass," Ben added.

Both Lois and Simpson made faces at them, then she waved toward the back. "Sam's waiting in the conference room. I'll be there in a minute."

When they walked through the doorway, Sam was kicked back in a chair, his head tilted, his boots propped on the edge of the table. The Stetson he'd worn his whole life—except for his years in the Army—was pulled down to cover his face, shutting out the light coming through the open blinds.

Daniel bumped him when he eased past. "The sun's shining. Time to make hay." He felt the quizzical look Natasha gave him as she slid into a chair opposite the chief. Five years ago, he probably hadn't known the meaning of the saying, and he certainly never would have actually said it.

Like he'd told her at lunch Friday, things were different in Cedar Creek.

Sam's laptop was open and booted up on the table. Daniel sat next to him, gestured to it and asked, "Do you mind?"

Slowly, Sam removed his hat and laid it on the table. "Just don't break it."

"Geez, you smash one laptop, and they never let you forget it," Daniel grumbled.

"What did you smash it against?" Natasha asked.

"A suspect's head. Hey, he was pounding Little Bear's head into the floor. I had to do something, and taking him one-on-one wasn't an option. He was six foot six and three hundred pounds."

Now it was Ben grumbling. "Geez, you let one suspect get the better of you…"

Daniel logged into his email and found the usual stuff, plus a long string of emails Flea had sent the day before. Every one of them carried an attachment, but only the first was accompanied by a message. "Assuming you don't have the budget constraints we have (or your personal motivation helps you along), here's traffic camera video from relevant areas on relevant dates. Good luck."

Judging by the size of the files, relevant areas on relevant dates translated to hundreds of hours of footage. Of course Flea hadn't had the time to watch it all herself or the resources to assign others to do so. But none of Daniel's other cases were higher priority than keeping Natasha safe. Except for the court appearance on Wednesday, he could watch videos until he went blind.

As Lois came in with a coffee tray, Ben put the plastic bag of ginger in the middle of the table. Natasha recognized it immediately, having eaten a ton or two of it. She listened to Ben's explanation of where he'd found it, and some of the lightness in her faded. She met Daniel's gaze, the fear back in her eyes, and swallowed hard. Then she took a deep breath and straightened her shoulders. She would be strong, because that was what she did.

Except when it came to saying, *I do.*

"Where do you get that stuff?" Sam asked.

"The grocery store," Natasha and Lois answered in unison. Lois went on. "In the Asian foods section. It's good for an upset stomach, high in sugar and strong in taste."

"And it happens to be a favorite of yours." Sam directed the comment to Natasha, who nodded. "Common knowledge?"

"Common joke. No one else I know will eat it that way."

"I think only one store sells it here. I'll check with them." Lois made a note to herself. Ben made one to *him*self, probably to make sure Lois followed through.

"I asked Morwenna's mum to come by this morning. She wanted to finish her run first, but she's going to give us a brief education in stalker behavior. She's a psychologist," Sam added for Natasha's benefit.

"Do you think Morwenna is the way she is because her mum's a psychologist, or is her mum a psychologist because Morwenna is the way she is?" Ben asked of no one in particular.

"Mum's been a shrink longer than Morwenna's been

alive," Daniel answered. "The fact that Morwenna's gone Bodmin is just a happy coincidence."

With a frankly puzzled look, Natasha repeated, "Bodmin?"

"Gone nuts. The town of Bodwin, the place where Morwenna's from, used to have a mental hospital."

"Hmm. And do you people always say 'mum'? It doesn't sound very Oklahoma-y."

"I call my mom 'Mom,'" Sam said.

"Me, too," Lois agreed, and Ben nodded.

"I don't have a mom." Daniel shrugged. "I guess we only do it with Morwenna's mum."

"Why?"

"Because she's British," they answered together. Daniel accompanied it with a shrug. When she'd spent enough time there, it would make sense to her, too.

If she spent enough time there.

Did he *want* her to spend that much time there?

God help him, he didn't want to think about it, or he would go freakin' Bodmin. It might not be so bad, though. Natasha had made him crazy before. She would probably do it again.

After a few minutes' lighthearted conversation, Ben left with the sealed bag of ginger, but Natasha was pretty sure she could still smell it on the air. When had RememberMe become aware of that particular favorite of hers? Had he watched her at the grocery store? Gone through her trash? Let himself into her apartment and taken a stroll through her things while leaving her none the wiser? Could he possibly have gotten close enough to her when she was eating it to recognize the smell?

All the possibilities creeped her out. In the end,

the "how" didn't really matter. Even thinking about it made her believe that old bit about ignorance being bliss. Now that she was no longer ignorant about some of the things crazy stalker guy did, she had to think about things *she* did. Could she ever enjoy food shopping again without suspiciously checking out every other shopper in the store? Would she walk into her apartment again without sniffing the air for someone else's scent? Would she find herself setting up little tells—a feather that would fall if the door was opened, a string that dislodged when something was moved? Would she have to invest in some sort of device that created a bubble around her when she was outside, so no one could get closer than ten feet?

No. No, no, no. He wasn't going to control her like that. Yes, she was scared and her every move was being shadowed by police officers, but she couldn't live like this forever. She couldn't hide forever. One way or another, she was taking back her life.

And, please, God, she wouldn't die trying. Daniel wouldn't die trying.

When Morwenna's mum texted Sam that she would meet them after a shower, Daniel glanced at her. "You want a tour of the place while we wait?"

"Sure." She liked old buildings. She'd toured dozens of them with Nick, who shared her enthusiasm, and Stacia, who didn't, and more with Daniel, who'd been of two minds. He had a fine appreciation for the workmanship, coming from a father who'd worked his whole life in high-end construction and a dad who understood the value of simple beauty. There had just been limits to how much architectural appreciation and beauty Daniel could deal with at one time.

Besides, having a conversation with him that didn't revolve around danger, heartbreak or pain was too pleasing an opportunity to turn down.

As she followed him out of the conference room, Sam asked, "What's worth seeing upstairs? There's nothing there."

Lois chuckled. "You're still a newlywed, son. Have you already forgotten the lengths you went to to get Mila all by yourself?"

"Mila's his wife," Daniel explained as he turned toward the broad marble staircase.

"I met her at the bowling alley. She seemed very nice."

"She is. She's appropriately named." When she looked questioningly at him, he went on. "Milagro. Spanish for miracle. Mila's pretty much a miracle."

Natasha considered that as she rested her hand on the banister. It was marble, too, and should have been cold and hard, but it was warm to the touch, and the white stone practically glowed.

She couldn't recall Daniel talking like that about another woman. No doubt, Mila Douglas was beautiful. She'd given off an air of serenity, even when talking about her young and bratty cousin-by-marriage, and she'd seemed to have some influence on Daniel. When Natasha had asked Daniel to listen to her, he'd looked to Mila, waiting for her nod before agreeing.

Interesting.

"What's racing through that complicated mind of yours at a thousand miles an hour?"

They reached the landing, old wood planks with an elaborate inlay of a star in contrasting woods. It seemed a shame to walk across it, though it was well varnished and had clearly seen decades of foot traffic. Even so, she skirted its edges. "You always prided yourself on divining the thoughts that afflicted us mere mortals."

"That was before I found out that even when I thought I knew, I didn't always. If I'd known everything you were thinking, I wouldn't have shown up at that party, either." He followed the words with a thin smile. She knew that smile. It was him being adult about something he believed deserved some really juvenile behavior.

"If I were to venture a guess, I'd say you're wondering if I have some sort of crush on my boss's wife." He flipped switches to light up the broad corridor. The fixtures were brass, tarnished and elegant, and they cast as many shadows as they dispelled.

"You're good." This space was cozier than the lobby downstairs, though it, too, had high ceilings and marble and a lot of wood. A beige vine-and-flowers carpet that looked original ran down the center of the hallway, and doors opened off both sides. Dimpled glass bearing names of long-gone officer-holders marked each door, with a matching transom above.

She walked to the nearest door—formal gold lettering reading Mr. J. M. DuBose—twisted the knob and pushed the door inward. Tall windows spilled sunshine into the room, sparkling on the dust motes drifting on the air. She'd half expected to find the office as Mr. J. M. DuBose had left it, but of course that wasn't the case. Except for a few unmarked boxes, it was empty. The wood floor held no desk or chair. The exquisite built-in bookcases on either side of the green marble fireplace were empty, and the elaborate crown mold-

ings, window cases and doorways had long gone un-
admired.

After looking her fill, Natasha closed the door and
faced Daniel. "Do you?"

"No."

"Did you?"

He was leaning against the opposite wall, arms
folded over his chest, one boot propped on the wall.
He looked amazingly handsome in ways that had never
failed to take her breath away. He wasn't tall or muscular or just plain big, like Ben Little Bear. He was a
tad too serious at times, a tad too reserved or, conflict-
ingly, a tad too blunt-spoken. But his dark eyes were
mesmerizing, and he was compassionate and compelling and intelligent, and his touch…

"My last crush was a beautiful woman who came
up to me at a Korean food truck. She was blonde and
was wearing a pair of very short shorts and a tank top
at least two sizes too small, and she ate half of my
kimchi fries."

That was eight years ago. A lifetime. So much joy
and love in those first three years. So much less of everything in the last five. All her fault.

And all she could think to say: "That tank top wasn't
too small. I still have it. I can prove it." Thanks to the
miracle of stretch fibers.

Wearing a faint smile, he pushed away from the
wall. "The first and fourth doors on each side go to
private offices. The middle doors open into common
workspaces for clerical-filing-type stuff."

"Men in the private offices and women doing the
clerical-filing-type stuff." She looked into the next
room. It was much bigger than the first, just as empty,

with the same attention to architectural detail, minus the fireplace.

She didn't open the next set of doors. Her focus was fixed ahead, where a wooden staircase as wide as the corridor climbed a dozen steps to a landing before making a sharp left turn. *Ooh*ing softly, she automatically reached for the pocket where she kept her cell phone but stopped when her fingers brushed across the flip-top burner cell.

"Want a picture for Nick?" Daniel offered his own phone.

Thursday night, when he'd taken her phone to read the texts, he'd made a point of not touching her. She made a point of very definitely touching him, her fingers rubbing across his, as she accepted the phone. She took multiple pictures—overviews; close-ups of the meticulously carved newel post; the balusters, each slightly different from the one before, giving a sense of upward flow as they climbed; the beading on the mahogany rail; the stained glass window on the landing. After sending them off to her brother, she returned the cell and ran up the steps to the landing before facing Daniel. "They never left any question about why it was called a grand staircase, did they?"

"All you need is the right dress, and you'll be 'ready for your close-up, Mr. DeMille.'"

The old-movie reference made her laugh as she began climbing the last steps. Seriously, on a staircase this beautiful, with the marble paneling and the stained glass glowing in jeweled tones, it was hard not to acknowledge exactly what the right dress would be. It was white with a touch of cream, or cream with a touch of white, silk and simple, with a plunging back and beading on the straps and on the back, at the base of all that exposed skin.

Her first wedding dress had gotten the boot the next day. Same with the second, and her engagement to Zach hadn't lasted long enough to even think about a dress. He probably would have wanted a beach wedding with bare feet, board shorts and aloha shirts, and with his board at the ready in case the wave he'd been waiting his whole lifetime for—or even just most of the day—came along during the vows.

But the dress she'd bought to marry Daniel in still hung in her closet. It had been too perfect to get rid of. Too tied to *him.* Even though it had broken her heart to look at it, she'd hidden it inside a heavy garment bag and dragged it along from apartment to apartment, thinking…

She didn't know what she'd thought. That someday she might be able to use it? That, like Zach's perfect wave, another chance with Daniel might come along?

No, neither of those. Getting rid of it would have just been too final. The very last step in a long journey of painful steps.

She stopped near the top of the stairs and stared ahead, barely noticing when Daniel stopped beside her. A broad expanse of wooden floor stretched unbroken from wall to wall, golden underneath its heavy layer of dust. Again, the ceiling was high, at least eighteen feet, and chandeliers set in fancy plaster medallions hung overhead, nine of them evenly spaced. The windows were double-wide, tall and arched, four on each side of the building.

"It's a ballroom," Daniel said helpfully before taking hold of her elbow and guiding her up the last step.

"The floor's got a spring to it so dancing the night away isn't too tiring."

She let him pull her farther onto the floor, feeling the cushioning beneath the wood, still openmouthed while taking in the vastness of the space, the moldings and trims and the delicately patterned florals on the walls that were almost certainly hand-painted.

"Come on, you remember dancing," Daniel teased. "We used to do it a lot."

"Only when I bribed you."

"Not true. You only had to bribe me when the music was fast. I never missed the chance to slow dance with you." He released her arm and took her hand instead, drawing her closer, placing her free hand on his shoulder.

"This is a police station."

"There's no law against dancing in a police station."

"There's no music."

"No law against dancing without music, either."

Because neither of them had ever missed a chance to slow dance together, and because she wanted with every fiber of her being to get closer to him, she moved into his arms as she'd done so many times. The sensation that instantly washed over her was refreshing, peaceful, awe-invoking.

She was fifteen hundred miles from Los Angeles, fearful of her safety and Daniel's, restricted to rare moments sneaking out of her hotel, and none of that mattered one bit.

Because she was home.

Chapter 8

When Daniel was a kid, his fathers had insisted that every man should know how to dance. They hadn't gone so far as to put him in a ballroom dance class. That would have provided far too much ammunition to the bullies at school and would have exceeded his ability to cope with them. No, instead Archer had offered his receptionist a bonus for lessons at their house. Daniel had been thirteen and gawky. She'd been twenty-seven, a redhead, as graceful as any prima ballerina. Oh, and had he mentioned that she was the stuff thirteen-year-old boys' fantasies were made of?

For a long time, all his fantasies had revolved around the blonde in his arms, who'd just stepped on his toes for the second time. The last few years, when he'd congratulated himself on getting over her, on not wanting her anymore, he had been lying to himself. He hadn't stopped wanting her. He'd stopped wanting *anyone*. If he couldn't have her...

The thought brought stalker guy back to the forefront of his brain. *If I can't have you, no one can.*

No. Not now. There was no room in this ballroom, no room on this dance floor, for RememberMe. It was Daniel's time. Natasha's.

"What song are we dancing to?" Her voice was hushed, no more substantial than the air.

"Hmm...'Come Rain or Come Shine.'" It wasn't the first song they'd danced together, but it had been their favorite. It would have been their first dance at the wedding reception.

"Ella Fitzgerald's version or Ray Charles's?"

"B.B. King and Eric Clapton's."

"My favorite," she whispered.

"Any answer I'd given would have been your favorite except Frank Sinatra." It was the only flaw Jeffrey had found in her, that she didn't like Ol' Blue Eyes. Up till the time she broke his only son's heart.

Her only response was a mostly sweet, slightly smug smile that faded into dreaminess as her eyes drifted shut. He rested his cheek against her hair, silken and cool, and pulled her body a fraction closer. Her muscles beneath his hands were taut, and heat radiated from her, seeping into him, seeking out and thawing the last bits of cold and bitterness. This felt too good. It had been too right between them to go so horribly wrong.

She hummed a few bars then softly sang a few lines of "Come Rain or Come Shine."

Daniel's body went still, and after a moment, so did Natasha's, but he didn't release her. Wasn't that what a jilted fiancé should do? Let go and walk away?

After all, they weren't rekindling their old romance. She'd betrayed him. He was done. RememberMe was the only reason they were back in each other's lives. It was business.

But insanity—and honesty—triumphed over logic. Daniel was no more done with her than her stalker was. He'd claimed he was, and he'd even believed it, but he'd lied. He wasn't about to let go and walk away.

Was the song right? Could it be fine? Could a second time around ever be as fine as the first?

Slowly, she opened her eyes, and her fingers tightened briefly around his. She wore a dazed look, an apprehensive one. Her lips, colored in her favorite apricot shade—yeah, he remembered that—parted, but before she could offer what he was sure would be an apology, he bent his head and kissed her.

Some things never changed.

She pressed her body against his as if she couldn't get close enough, and his body responded as if he were still an inexperienced kid. His skin grew hot, and he swore he could feel the pounding of their hearts, not in sync, pounding, racing faster with each beat. It had been a lifetime since he'd held her, kissed her, touched her everywhere, and it felt like forever, or the blink of an eye. It was as natural, as good, as vital—

In the part of his brain that he never could turn off completely, he registered a sound from below, indistinct, almost certainly a summons for them to return to the conference room. Reluctantly, he broke the kiss and tried to catch his breath, his forehead resting against hers.

Her own breathing as ragged as his, she said, "I take it that was Ben who bellowed."

Opening his eyes, he found her wearing a hazy, lazy smile that was tinged with both satisfaction and regret. He understood because he was filled with both emotions himself, along with the desire to get a whole lot more of the one and to totally banish the other as soon as possible. "Dr. Armstrong must be here."

"Mustn't keep the good doctor waiting." But instead of pulling away from him, Natasha slyly shifted her hips against him. "Or maybe you must."

Ruefully he laid both hands on her shoulders and pushed her back a step, then another, so their bodies didn't touch. So the only contact between them was the palms of his hands on the fabric of her shirt. It didn't do a thing to ease the aching of his erection.

Who said shoulders and palms weren't erogenous zones?

At the moment, even breathing the same air she breathed was pretty damn erotic.

"Don't make me come up there," Lois called from downstairs, amusement in her voice.

"Keep in mind how long it takes a blue-hair to climb two flights of stairs and make yourselves decent," Ben added.

Daniel ran his hand through his hair. "Some cops work with professionals. Not me. I get the *Lois and Little Bear Show.*"

Natasha straightened his collar, her fingers lingering on his throat, making the nerves tingle. "I'll tell them you got a call."

"And you've got that rosy flush on your face because…?"

She grinned. "I just love hardwood."

Suppressing a grin, he shook his head then watched

her follow the trail of dusty footprints back to the stairs. He'd always appreciated watching her walk—toward him, beside him, away from him. The way her movements flowed so gracefully. The way her hips swayed, the muscles in her thighs and calves bunching, then releasing. The way it seemed so effortless and inviting and sexy and full of promise.

She had always been so full of promise.

Until she hadn't.

As she turned on the landing, then disappeared from sight, he pressed the heels of his hands to his eyes. Things were easier when she was in his arms, when he was wrapped up in that old familiar sensation of rightness. Now, standing there alone, things didn't seem so clear.

Could he risk trusting her again? He had just barely survived losing her the first time. Understanding, sort of, why it had happened helped, but it didn't guarantee it wouldn't happen again. But...

Every relationship had its good times and bad, but he and Natasha had never really had any bad. Sure, they'd argued sometimes. They'd even gone a week here, two weeks there, without speaking, but then he had called her, or she had called him, and they had worked things out and gone on.

Their first bad time had been when she'd dumped him.

One hell of a bad time.

He'd left. He'd built a new life without her. But he had never stopped loving her. Wasn't there a message in that fact that he should be listening to?

Wasn't there a message in the fact that he was in the

police station for a meeting on a case with the boss and was waiting for a hard-on to go away?

He wanted her. Had always wanted her. Was pretty sure he always would. When they had been happy. When they had been unhappy. Together. Half a country between them.

Always.

Joan Armstrong looked absolutely nothing like her daughter.

After excusing Daniel's absence—and noting smirks around the table—Natasha chose a chair at the end of the table and studied Morwenna and her mum. Where the daughter's style ran to the flamboyant, the mother's was classic. She wore a black jacket and matching trousers, a black-and-white striped button-down shirt and gorgeous pumps with a substantial heel. Her auburn hair was swept back in a chignon, her makeup subtle and perfect, and tortoiseshell glasses gave her sturdy face a serious air.

Seated next to Morwenna, she should have faded into the shadows cast by brilliant pinks and purples with a splash of lime green, but the doctor had too much presence to be so easily obscured.

"I imagine Daniel will join us in a minute," Sam said.

"Or three or five," Ben mumbled before his head jerked up and his gaze narrowed on Lois. If Natasha's memories of Friday morning were correct, the older woman had given Daniel a kick under the table at one point. Now Ben had gotten his own.

Daniel was right. It was the *Lois and Little Bear Show.*

"What did you think of our third-floor surprise, Natasha?" Lois asked innocently.

"It's incredible. The chandeliers, the dance floor, the Palladian windows... I never dreamed the police station would have a ballroom."

Lois extended her hand none too subtly to Ben, who very subtly gave her something that looked like money folded small. So Ben had bet they wouldn't make it beyond the second floor. Though Natasha would have happily kissed Daniel in any or all of those offices, she was glad he'd waited for the ballroom.

Daniel's voice sounded in the hallway and sent a shiver down her spine and, just for optimum contrast, heat into her face. She quickly lowered her head and rested her cheek in her hand to cover the blush.

He was talking in his professional voice. After she'd manufactured a phone call for him, had he really gotten one?

"I'm really sorry about that, ma'am. I'll do anything I can to help out." He came into the room as he put his cell away. He didn't avoid looking at her—that would have amused the others too much—but his gaze just skimmed across her face and everyone else's before settling on Sam's. "That was Mrs. Hilliard. My court case next week was her older son, Tommy. The two boys went out drinking, had an argument and got into a shoot-out."

"What's happened now?"

"Well, Tommy's been out on bail, awaiting trial—"

"Tommy's always out on bail, awaiting trial for something," Sam said darkly.

"He and Billy went to a friend's house in Muskogee

last night, got drunk and got in an argument, and Billy shot him. Killed him."

Stunned silence spread around the room, but it lasted longer for the civilians than the cops. "We've pretty much always known one of those Hilliard boys wasn't going to make it to thirty," Lois remarked grimly. "Hell, the first time I arrested Tommy, he was only twelve. Strong-arm robbery, and not one bit of remorse in him."

"Not when he shot Billy, either." Daniel sat down next to Natasha, the expression in his eyes dark and haunted. "Their dad's been a guest of the Department of Corrections the last twenty-five years. Their mom's a doper who's also done her time in the system. When she was locked up, they lived with their grandmother, who sent them out to steal so she wouldn't have to."

He took a deep breath and blew it out, and with it went that sad, powerful look. A moment's observation, regret and then on to the cases where the victims still lived, where he might be able to help. That, he'd told Natasha, was how he did his job. This was the first time, though, she'd actually seen any part of it.

After a moment, Sam began the meeting. "Dr. Armstrong, you're familiar with the usual crew. This is Natasha Spencer. She's Daniel's ex-fiancée, and she came here from California to tell Daniel that her stalker wants to kill him. The stalker was considerate enough to make the trip, as well, and he's been making his presence felt in both their lives. Since we get a little pissy when someone messes with one of our own, we thought it might be helpful if we knew something about the guy's personality, his motivation, his version of reality. Anything that might help us catch him."

Being so baldly identified as Daniel's ex made Natasha's smile waver, though hearing the chief refer to Daniel as one of their own made up for the discomfort. He liked it here. He belonged here, and though they might tease a lot, they thought so, too.

"I don't care about his version of reality," Daniel muttered. "I just want to know the magic words that will make him go away."

"The words are 'We find the defendant guilty,'" Ben said in a similar tone.

"How about 'justifiable homicide'?" Lois added.

Natasha ignored them, strengthened her smile and leaned forward to shake hands with Morwenna's mum. "I appreciate you taking the time to come in on a Sunday, Dr. Armstrong."

After the handshake, Dr. Armstrong angled her chair so she had a better view of Natasha. "You're a pretty girl. Your smile is lovely. Do you know how easy it is for total strangers to fixate on a pretty girl with a lovely smile? The stalker says you've met before, right? But you have no recollection of it?"

Natasha shook her head.

"It could have been anywhere. At a party. Chatting in line at the movie theater. Empathizing with a grocery checker who's just finished with a difficult customer. You might not have exchanged names with him. You might not have said anything of substance to him. But you caught his attention, and the impact on him was tremendous."

Natasha shivered and, next to her, Morwenna nudged her. "She gives me the heebie-jeebies all the time."

"All this could have come from something that meaningless?"

"It wasn't meaningless to him, Natasha. Most of these type of stalkers suffer from delusions. They live in a different reality from the rest of us. Take the store clerk scenario. You smile at people because you're a nice person. It's natural. But when you smile at our clerk, to him, it means that you like him, that you recognize he's special. You might brush his hand when you take your change, and he thinks this is his lucky day. You're *touching* him. You say, 'Have a good day,' and he hears, 'I'm so happy I met you and can't wait until we can be together.' You can't even remember what he looks like when you reach your car, but his whole life has changed because he's found you."

"Well, that's scary as all hell," Sam said.

Agreeing, Natasha sank a little deeper in her seat. When she and Stacia had spent all those hours trying to figure out who RememberMe was, they hadn't had a clue what a monumental task they were attempting. They'd been considering people she'd actually had some sort of real contact with. It had never occurred to them it could be a clerk at a convenience store, a guy who held a door open for her or someone she'd said hello to on an elevator.

RememberMe could be someone who, for practical purposes, didn't exist in her life.

"Sam let me read some of his messages," Dr. Armstrong went on. "There's one he sent about two months into the stalking. He signed it *RM*, as usual, but as part of his signature, there's a quote. 'When I saw you I fell in love, and you smiled because you knew.' He wrongly attributes it to Shakespeare—that's just not ol' Will's style—but it doesn't matter. That, in a nutshell, is what happened. He saw you. He identified you as his ideal woman. You smiled, and that sealed the deal. In his mind, you're a couple. He belongs to you, and you most certainly belong to him."

"So how do we get him out in the open?" Ben asked. "Should she tell him it's time to meet?"

"Part of the stalker's payoff is the control, particularly when the victim doesn't know who he is. He can give her peace by disappearing for a while. He can freak her out by letting her know he's seen her that very day. For example…" She pulled Sam's laptop from the center of the table and typed in a search phrase. "He sent this a month ago. 'You look so blond in black, but the shoes weren't your best choice for an art exhibit, were they?' That scared you, didn't it?"

Natasha smiled ruefully. "I tried to crawl into the back of Stacia's closet and never come out, but she and her boyfriend stopped me."

Her accent sounding more British the longer she talked, Dr. Armstrong went on. "He can take her mood from happy to hysterical in two seconds flat. He decides whether she sleeps peacefully or has nightmares. It's up to him whether she keeps a job, has a normal life, goes out for a meal—everything. That power is a big deal to him. He's not ready to relinquish it."

"Even though he knows the police are involved."

The doctor was shaking her head before Daniel's remark was finished. "This kind of guy sees barriers as challenges. He's put a lot of time and effort into stalking her. The only time this type is truly concerned about the authorities is when he's actually locked up. He sees his persistence in pursuing her despite the police as proof of just how much he loves her. He's showing that nothing can keep him away from her."

Daniel had told Natasha years ago that he would always love her, would always be there for her. His commitment had been sweet and perfect, exactly what she felt for him. It had made her feel loved. Worthy. Secure.

The same sentiments from—she couldn't help borrowing Stacia's nickname—crazy-pants stalker guy scared the crap out of her.

As if he knew what she was thinking, Daniel leaned closer and murmured, "Sanity counts for a lot, doesn't it?"

More than she'd realized. Now she knew her family might be unconventional, but they weren't crazy.

"As far as trying to lure him into the open… The only way to do that is using Natasha. The guy's clever, delusional and most likely has psychopathic tendencies. He knows how to cover his tracks. The tone of his messages has gotten harsher, threatening. Until now, he's been in control, but meeting her on her terms would require giving her control. That's not going to happen. Further, he's coming out of the obsessive-love stage. He's starting to find fault with her, which makes him potentially even more dangerous. That's when this personality type decides…" Dr. Armstrong trailed off, glancing around the table before apologetically settling her gaze on Natasha.

Maybe, because it was her life they were talking about, it was easier for Natasha to say the words out loud. Better for the others to not have to. "If he can't have me, no one else can."

After the meeting, the conference room cleared out pretty quickly. Sam and Ben walked out with Mor-

wenna and her mum, and Lois headed off for brunch
with her husband and the grandkids. Daniel and Natasha remained in their chairs. She had nowhere to go
but the hotel, and he had nothing to do but keep an
eye on her.

Her head was tilted back, her gaze on the fancy
crown molding. He settled his gaze on the beat-up desk
against the wall. Taped to one of its drawers was a
ragged internet meme someone had considered funny
enough in a sick way to share. *You say psycho like it's
a bad thing.*

It didn't seem amusing now.

Dr. Armstrong had said that psychopaths made up
an estimated 1 percent of the population. With about
twenty million people in the greater Los Angeles area,
that translated to... "Only you."

Natasha didn't lower her head, but her gaze shifted
his way. "Only me what?"

"Only two hundred thousand psychopaths in the
LA metropolitan area, and you found one of them."

"Without even looking." She straightened in her seat
and turned toward him. "The odds against my finding
you were even greater, and yet I did. Maybe I should
play the lottery."

Daniel wasn't a gambler. He'd always liked the sure
thing, always played it safe. Maybe it was time he did
take a chance.

"Am I going to be sneaked back into the hotel now?"

"Where would you rather go?"

She smiled wryly. "Anywhere."

His house was as secure as the hotel. Between his
weapons, the alarm system, the good-quality locks and
the fact that he had the only keys in existence, it was

even safer. RememberMe knew where it was, but he obviously knew even more about the hotel. A stranger skulking around a quiet neighborhood would stand out more than a stranger downtown.

Maybe it was time to take a chance…but with Natasha's safety?

Sam and Ben returned to the room while he dithered. "What now?" Sam asked. It was after eleven, and he needed to pick up his wife and her grandmother and head out to the weekly Sunday dinner with forty or more Douglases at the family farm.

In Daniel's family, it had been a Sunday supper, and there'd rarely been more than the three of them, plus, for too short a time, Natasha. He loved his very small family, but he'd always looked forward to the time when the table would include new little Harpers. Three would make a nice start, he'd teased her, and she'd made a face of mock horror.

Realizing they were waiting for him to respond, he pushed to his feet. "How about I take Natasha to my house?"

Ben and Sam exchanged looks, then Ben remarked, "It's only a minute from the station."

"Big yards. Hard to sneak around during the day," Sam added.

"Mrs. Jansen two doors down. Nosiest woman in town."

While they argued his case for him, Daniel turned to Natasha. She was still, but an air of taut expectancy shimmered around her. Or was it coming from him? Her face was expressionless, but her eyes held a memory of that kiss. The possibility of more. The desire for more.

"Have the dispatcher contact Liam," Sam instructed Ben. "Park him on the street, and put Simpson on the cross street."

Finally Daniel forced his attention back to the men. "Why don't we put out a big sign that says, 'Hey, both your targets are here'?"

"Morwenna's mum said he's determined but not reckless. Otherwise, he'd have been caught long before now." Sam picked up his Stetson from the table. "I'll be on the radio and the cell. Check in with me in an hour." His gaze flickered away slightly, not quite reaching Natasha, and he amended that. "Maybe two hours."

Ben was grinning when the chief left. Why not? It wasn't his potential for having sex today that they were hinting about. After making an effort to wipe away the smile, he gestured toward the door. "Come on. I'll take you home."

They left the same way they'd come, through the sally port, and pulled to the curb in front of his house a minute later. Ben and Natasha remained in the SUV while Daniel went inside and walked through the house. It was as still and unviolated as ever, bearing only one presence—his own. He wondered briefly what she would think of it, but then dismissed the question. It was where he lived. Nothing there would surprise her because nothing about him ever surprised her.

Except, in the beginning, how much he had really loved her.

Liam Bartlett was pulling his patrol car to the curb across the street when Daniel waved for Natasha and Ben to come in. He waved at the older officer, too, then subjected everything around them to a fierce glare.

Everything, because other than them, the streets, sidewalks, yards and porches were empty. Not even the fat cat was roaming.

He followed Natasha inside the door then faced Ben. "I've got a few hundred hours of video to go through, courtesy of my friend in LA. You mind coming over for dinner and helping?"

"Sure. I'll even bring food from Mom's. Give me an hour's notice." Ben's mouth twitched with the need to grin. "Before I leave, I'm going to check the perimeter, and I'll talk to Liam and Simpson. And like the chief said, cell and radio."

"Thanks." Daniel closed and locked the door, armed the security system and turned expecting to find Natasha a few feet away. She wasn't. He walked to the double door that led into the living room, where she was slowly making her away around the furniture, trailing her hand over the back of the leather couch, the gleaming wood of a family antique then the rougher aged surface of a primitive bench. She'd always been a tactile person, to the point that he'd had to hold her hands in museums to stop her from touching things.

She'd made him more of a tactile person, though the only surface he'd really been passionate about touching was her body.

His fingertips tingled just at the thought.

"I like this." Now she was rubbing the rough stone of the fireplace. "I see Jeffrey's touch a few places. And Archer's, too." She nodded to the exquisite inlaid coffee table.

"You know me and shopping," he said inanely.

"I know. You're very good at following people and, if need be, carrying their purchases. As long as you don't have to make any choices." She reached her starting point, smiled faintly at him then stepped back into the hall. To the right was the stairs and his office, to the left, the dining room, kitchen and powder room. She chose left, walking beneath a broad archway and turning into the dining room. "Wow."

His skin flushed, his nerves tingling, he moved after her. He found her where he expected: standing next to the simple rectangular dining table with its simple Shaker-style chairs, gently tracing over the seams of a very complicated compass rose inlay. "A hundred years from now, some young Harper is going to take this set to Antiques Roadshow and say, 'My great-grandfather made it for my grandfather, and it's been in the family ever since.'"

"I hope so." He shrugged. "My father loves to show off his talents."

"Yes, he does," she agreed, then added with a knowing smile, "Like his son."

She wandered into the kitchen, stuck her head into the mudroom then walked to the other end of the hall. After taking a quick look at the office, she stopped at the foot of the stairs. She didn't offer an invitation, didn't say anything at all. She just looked at him, and that sense of expectancy he'd seen in her earlier expanded until somehow it burst inside him. Did he want to take a chance?

Oh, hell, yeah.

He walked to her, not stopping until he was too close, and said in a raspy voice, "Do me a favor. Walk up those stairs in front of me."

Her smile came slowly, sweet and wicked and womanly. She knew how he liked watching her move, that he marveled how she could have the same equipment as all other women and yet she was the only one whose every movement he found enchanting and seductive and sexy and just pure pleasure. She turned her back, sashayed up the first few steps and then, with a giggle, she broke into a run, reaching the top before he'd thought to take even one step.

Seeing her smile like that, all the ugliness in her life pushed to the back of her mind, touched something in him. Humbled him. Made him weak.

But before he got too weak, he dashed up the stairs after her. Shrieking in a manner that would have done Stacia proud, she spun and ran down the hall, bypassing the first three doors as if instinct led her, racing into his bedroom at the end, darting around to the other side of the bed. There she peeled off the hoodie, dragging her shirt halfway up with it, exposing her flat, tanned middle and just a hint of a purple bra.

"Blinds closed, curtains closed. Don't want to shock the nosiest woman in town." Natasha tossed the hoodie at the chair in the corner and missed, then smoothed her T-shirt down. Fingers laced together, she swayed side to side. "This is…"

Daniel's throat tightened. "Second thoughts?"

"No. Oh, God, no. I just feel…bold."

The tension faded. "Men adore bold women. But if you'd feel more comfortable…" He crossed to the stereo, sorted through CDs there, then selected one and put it into the player.

"Ooh, an old-fashioned man. I like that."

"My fathers still have a turntable and all their old vinyl. At least I'm a few steps closer to catching up with technology." With the press of a button, Ella Fitzgerald's voice filled the air.

He offered Natasha his hand. "Dance with me?" She was a sucker for slow dances. So was he. If either of them was still coherent when the song finished, they weren't doing it right.

She laid her hand in his, and heat stirred deep in his belly. He drew her closer than he had in the ballroom, wrapped his arms around her, took a moment to enjoy the anticipation and greed and need. It had been five long years since he'd felt this way. Yes, he'd had sex since then, and he had enjoyed it, but it hadn't been…this.

Because it hadn't been Natasha.

And he'd still loved her even if he'd been too proud to admit it to himself.

Even though they'd already proven that love wasn't always enough.

They could dazzle on the dance floor if they wanted, but at this moment, they were hardly moving, just pretending, just enough to keep those sparks striking and flaring and burning. Just enough to kill him if they kept at it long enough.

Best female singer ever, she'd said of Ella. Her eyes were closed to better enjoy the song, and the dance, and the promise. Her hands felt small where they rested against him, burning even through the fabric of his shirt. The movement of her breasts and hips, tantalizingly brushing him, and the shallow sighs of her breath on his throat teased and aroused him, turning want to need to hunger to desperation to fierce satisfaction to humble gratitude.

Her first kiss was light, her lips feathering across his

neck, so insubstantial that he shouldn't even have felt it, but oh, yeah, he felt it. In every nerve, every muscle, every part of his body. Her second kiss landed on his jaw and started a quivering deep inside him, one he'd experienced every single time they'd made love. It sapped his energy and made him strong. It left him vulnerable and greedy, and it made him want everything. Anything.

No, everything.

God help him.

It had been dreamlike, dancing to music only in their heads in the dusty, unused ballroom, but here in the smaller space of the bedroom, with Ella crooning over the speakers, all of Natasha's womanly parts were so close to swooning. What little she'd noticed of the room was pretty—a deep chocolate wall, a super-thick geometric rug, a queen-size bed—but none of it mattered.

This, her and Daniel, touching, kissing, making love, making right... This was all that mattered.

Her next kiss went on his mouth, and his arms tightened around her, his hand sliding into her hair and tilting her head to the perfect angle for him to take control. He thrust his tongue between her lips, and she melted against him. The day they'd met, he had told her he was an expert kisser, and then he'd proven it when they said good-night. Her lungs had forgotten their function, her knees had gone weak and the only word her flustered brain had remembered was *more*.

She had told Stacia, "This is the one."

You always say that.

But this one really is.

You always say that, too.

But that time, she'd been right.

Just not smart enough or mature enough or whatever enough to realize it.

Though Ella had segued into another more up-tempo song, their rhythm didn't change. Natasha roused herself from the hazy stupor of indulgence and slid her hands to his middle. She had experience with removing his gun belt—when you dated a cop, you learned interesting things—but today she left it alone and tugged his shirt from the waistband of his pants. The nubby fabric was warm from his body heat and bunched softly over her hands as she pushed it up over his stomach, his pecs, reaching the barrier of their kissing.

He was loathe to let her go, she knew from the way he'd back off then come back for just one more stroke, one more nibble. Finally she was able to yank the shirt over his head and drop it, not caring where it landed. His skin was smooth, marked with only a few wisps of hair, his muscles lovingly defined, and he was responsive, so responsive to her every caress. Skin rippling, nipples hardening, gooseflesh rising.

And with a very impressive erection already risen.

Was it any wonder she liked to touch things when they were as beautiful as he was?

"Natasha."

He said her name in that strangled, you're-killing-me way that sent a thrill of feminine power through her. It never went to her head, though, because he had the same sweet power over her: to make her body hum, to deliver such satisfaction that she shattered, to put her back together even better than before.

Love. And lust. And trust. A heady combination.

She pressed hot, damp kisses to his chest while unfastening his gun belt. Since she couldn't just let it drop the way she had his shirt, he took it from her, laid it somewhere a few steps away, quickly balanced on first one foot then the other to unlace his boots and then came back to her. While she made agonizing work of unfastening his pants, drawing more than a few groans from him, he worked the boots off, kicking them to the side with soft thuds.

"Remember the time..." Her thoughts as well as her fingers got lost somewhere between undoing his zipper and sliding the pants off, finding instead that warm, solid, silken part of him.

"I got a concussion." His words were breathy, the look on his face strained and taut.

"Just a little one."

It had been early in their romance, when they couldn't get enough of each other quickly enough. Undone pants plus boots plus trying to move beyond the door where she'd grabbed him while he kissed her had equaled tangled feet, a fall, a lot of kissing to make it all better and, a few hours later, a trip to the urgent care clinic for a diagnosis of concussion.

"You didn't tell the doctor what we'd really been doing."

"I didn't need to tell him. One look at either of us, and people always knew."

Knew they had just been or soon would be intimate. Knew they were infatuated. Knew they were in love. Arguing with him had even been hard, because she still had that look in her eyes and he still had that tenderness. Sometimes when she was ranting, he had

looked at her—just looked—and everything inside her
had gone all soft and gooey, irritation forgotten.

He had been such a gift. She had been so honored.

Regret made a tiny break in the desire still bubbling
inside her, and she pushed it away. She rarely appreciated her mother's advice, but there was one piece she
was going to wholly embrace right now: *live in the moment.* Why would Natasha spend one minute in regret
when Daniel was standing there, half-naked, touching
her, hard for her?

One long swoop, and she removed his pants and
boxers. She stared at him, the whole picture, head
to foot. He was gorgeous fully dressed. He was gor-
geously impressive naked.

And for the next however-long, he was hers.

Vaguely aware of tugging, she blinked a few times
and realized he was undoing the buttons of her shirt.
The first time the back of his fingers touched her skin,
energy crackled, sharp and electric, and she dragged
in a pitiful breath. "It'd be faster if I do it."

All the buttons were loose except the top two. He
pushed the fabric to either side and slid both hands
over her middle, and then around to her bottom, lifting
her snug against him. "Who says I want to go faster?"

His mouth touched her jaw, her eyes fluttered shut
and her head tilted to the side so he could more easily
continue the kisses. She was hot and tingly, and her
muscles were quivering as if she'd just completed a
one-mile vertical hike. The air in the room had gone
thin, and pressure was building inside her, starting
low in her belly and working its way up and out. It had
been so long, and it was a fine line that separated want

from need, pleasure from pain, savoring from immediate gratification.

"Oh, my—"

He moved her back, onto the bed, his mouth taking hers as they fell. His body landed on hers without real force but with real, incredible, smoldering, leave-nothing-behind-but-ash heat. His fever spread, heightening her own, and when he thrust his hips against her, she damn near whimpered for relief.

He was naked. She was fully dressed. Something was wrong with this picture.

She pressed her pelvis into the mattress, making room to slide her hand between their bodies, to wrap her fingers around his penis, to stroke up and down, then lower, cupping his—

His entire body went rigid, and Daniel, for whom not swearing wasn't an option except in moments of great stress, gasped and blurted out a curse, an obscenity, a plea. Together they removed her clothes in a fraction of the time he would have taken, then he put on a condom and sank deep inside her with a groan that echoed her own.

Who said faster wasn't sometimes better?

When her brain became functional again, Natasha felt as if she'd completed a two-mile vertical hike. Making her own trail. In rain and heat and wind. Her body was heavy, her nipples tender, her skin raw and shocky. Her heart beat strongly, taking its sweet time returning to a normal rhythm, and her brain was still oxygen deprived, and her life-couldn't-be-better gauge was pinging over the top.

She was satisfied. At peace. Happy. Even—blissful.

Daniel lay facing her, arms around her. His eyes were closed, his hair damp with sweat, his breathing deep but slowing. During their whole lives, he had shown her nothing but love, loyalty, compassion and the calm she'd longed for, and she had loved him, oh, like no one had loved him. Hurt him like no one had hurt him.

It was beyond rational explanation that he lay there beside her, handsome, sweet, tender, passionate. Forgiving. She'd never thought him a forgiving man.

Or maybe she'd never thought she was worth forgiving.

Tears pricked, but when he opened his eyes, she blinked them away.

"What are you doing?" he whispered.

"Looking at you," she whispered back.

He released his hold around her middle and raised his hand to her face, wiping away a tear that had escaped despite her best efforts. "I never stopped loving you, Tash."

The admission was barely audible, but it rattled her universe. It overwhelmed her, caught her breath in her lungs and switched off everything in her brain but the emotions. The tears welled, filling her eyes and turning her world watery. "Oh, Daniel."

He caressed her cheek, along her jaw, down the curve of her neck. "Is that an 'Oh, Daniel, I wish you hadn't said that'? Or maybe an 'Oh, Daniel, couldn't you have waited?'"

A smile burst onto her face. "No, that's 'Oh, Daniel, you really are perfect.' I've been wondering if my memories are just heavily biased in your favor, if I was delusional myself, if I was forgetting the bad and playing up the good. But we didn't really have any bad, and all the good was totally you." She grew serious, laying her palm against his chest, feeling the steady thump-thump of his heart. "Daniel Harper, you're the best man I've ever had the honor of knowing and trusting and depending on and loving."

Before she could say anything even sappier, his phone chimed on the opposite bedtable. He was leaning toward her, as if he might kiss her, and after an instant's consideration for the incoming text, he went ahead with the kiss. Just a sweet one, gentle, a kind of claiming kiss. She was surprised because, between possible emergencies with his fathers and work, he never ignored the phone.

Then he released her and rolled across the bed to reach the cell. He returned to her side, snuggled her back into the warm spot next to him and checked the message. His muscles went taut, but nothing like a while ago, when she had kissed a meandering trail from his shoulder all the way down to his second erection. He'd been so rigid then, she'd thought he might break.

"'Message for Nat,'" he read aloud, his expression grim. "'Why did you go home with him? Do you think I can't reach you at his house just as easily as I can at the hotel? It seems, Nat, that you're deliberately trying to upset me. We've made vows to each other, till death do us part vows. Look at the ring you're wearing.'"

She and Daniel both looked at the small ring on her right middle finger. The stone was orange, an odd shape, inexpertly polished, and the silverwork was clumsy, but it was important to her because it was one of her mom's first pieces when Libby took up jewelry making. The jewelry-making hadn't lasted any longer than Libby's other hobbies, but Natasha had had the ring for ten years now.

After clearing his throat, Daniel read on. "'Are you sleeping with him, Nat? You know what will happen if you do. You will ruin everything I've done for you. You'll be no better than the whores on Olympic and Western. You'll be an embarrassment to me, and I won't have any choice but to punish you. I'll punish both of you.'"

Daniel tapped his index finger against the cell case, meaning he was paying special attention to some part of ScrewYou's message. She was curious about how crazy-man thought the vows had been made. Sometime when he'd followed her, had he projected promises of love and obedience into her brain from a block away and decided that turning left meant she accepted them, turning right meant no and going straight meant she needed more time to think about it? Had he broken into her apartment and done some ritual, imbuing her ring with magic that would bind her to him the next time she put it on?

Honestly, if the man could take a generic friendly smile and build a whole relationship out of it, who knew what else he was capable of creating in his head?

"'You'll be no better than the whores on Olympic and Western,'" Daniel muttered. "Olympic and Western…" He gave her a quizzical look. "Say you're back in LA. A friend comes from out of town to visit and says, 'I got a hundred fifty bucks. Where can I pick up a girl?' Where would you send him?"

"Back where he came from."

"You don't know where to find the working girls?"

This was definitely the first time in her life anyone

had asked if she knew where to find a prostitute. She replied with a shrug. "Sunset Boulevard, I guess. But that street's been walked since before we were born. It's a long-standing tradition. History."

"But RememberMe knows that Olympic and Western are good places, too."

"How do you know that?"

He mimicked her shrug. "I'm a cop. Cops always know where to find hookers."

"Where do you find them in Cedar Creek?" she asked curiously.

"Online or in Tulsa." He started tapping the cell case again. "Olympic and Western... There are plenty of other places in LA. I wonder why he picked those two."

"Maybe he lives in the area."

"Or works there himself. They're both in Olympic Division." His tone was thoughtful, and his gaze had gone distant. He might be lying beside her in bed, her naked body pressed against his, but his thoughts were half a country away. That made it a good time to fluff the pillow under her head and go back to indulging herself in studying every little detail about him.

"I should have asked Morwenna's mum if he would be the type to solicit prostitutes. Probably not, since he's so obsessed with you. If he does, I bet it's blue-eyed blondes. But then maybe he lives on the other side of town. You know, you don't play where you live. People are more likely to recognize you."

He was so serious, his voice pitched low, thoughtful, talking more to himself than to her. While he was lost in that world, she could do anything—get out of bed, take a shower, maybe even do an erotic little dance around the room in front of him—and he would be totally unaware. It was one of the things about him she found endearing.

Aw, hell, she found everything about him endearing. Everything.

Chapter 9

Daniel's muttering had trailed off, and he'd located five different patterns in the wood beams of the ceiling while his subconscious continued to wonder about the significance of those streets to RememberMe. Then he finally realized that Natasha had fallen asleep. She looked like an angel, kind of a sexy and sultry angel. If he had an ounce of artistic talent, she would be his only model, her every mood, clothed and nude, all her happiness, silliness, sexiness.

But his talent lay in police work. All he could do was keep her safe and find her stalker, and his email held hours' worth of work to help him do just that. Even though Ben was coming over later to help, it couldn't hurt to go ahead and get started.

Stay in bed or work? Peel himself away from Natasha, who was peaceful and resting and naked, and go downstairs to cuddle with his laptop instead?

Work could wait.

He forwarded RememberMe's text to the chief and Ben, told them he and Natasha were fine, then turned the cell to vibrate, laid it on the table and settled in close to her again.

The room was more shadowy when he awoke. Not dark, but the sun was definitely lower in the west. He yawned, wondered why he was asleep at four in the afternoon, felt a warm breath on his shoulder and remembered it all. Every incredible second of it.

Including admitting he still loved Natasha.

For half a second, he'd wondered if he should have kept that to himself, but why bother? It was true. And like he'd said, people looked at them and knew. Their connection had just been so…

She shifted behind him then slid her arm over his middle. "I'm starving. Are you starving?"

"Yeah, I am." His breakfast had been cookies from the vending machine at work, and they had missed lunch.

"Any chance Ben would want an early dinner?"

"I'll text him." He didn't right away, though. He was too comfortable lying there, all warm, her body pressed against his, a slight chance of falling back to sleep if he gave it a try, a better chance of having great sex again if he gave that a try. But Natasha let go of him, the mattress shifted and she rolled away. She sat then stood up. Scooped up clothes on her way around the bed. "Bathroom?"

"First door on the left." He admired the view as she walked out then finally reached for his phone.

It was about an hour later when Ben arrived with his laptop and three large brown bags. The smell was

incredible, though not all of it was for them. As soon
as he unpacked the food on the kitchen counter, he took
two smaller plastic bags and two drinks and headed
back outside. "Aw, he brought food for the other officers," Natasha said, sounding impressed. "He's a good
guy."

"He is," Daniel agreed. He'd worked with a lot of
cops who automatically considered themselves superior to small-town cops just because they worked in a
city. They assumed they were more sophisticated, more
worldly, and that was sometimes true on an individual
basis. But Ben and Sam would very easily hold their
own if they ever decided to move to the city. Smart and
capable had nothing to do with the size of the town
where they worked.

He set out plates, utensils and napkins, and when
Ben returned, they served themselves buffet-style before carrying their dinner into the dining room. His
computer was already set up there. Ben booted up his
own, and they sat down, plenty of food to eat and hours
of surveillance footage to go through.

Natasha didn't have anything to do but eat, so she
played hostess, refilling their plates or glasses when
needed, taking them away to the kitchen when they
were done. For a time, she stood behind Daniel's chair,
watching until she said the video made her eyes cross.
She found a book in the living room—Mila Douglas's
book, *The Unlucky Ones*—and brought it back to the
dining room. She didn't seem at all bored. Just…com-
fortable.

If she hadn't run away, this was how they would
have spent the last five years: sharing dinners and quiet
evenings at home. Hopefully, they would have had at

least one little Harper by now, maybe two. This being
a Sunday, the dinner would have been at his parents'
house, and Jeffrey and Archer would have spent the
entire time spoiling her and the kids. They did love
her a lot.

They could still have all that. Maybe not the weekly
Sunday suppers with his dads, but the rest of it. They
hadn't lost their chance. It had just been postponed for
a while. As long as there was breath in their bodies…

Which wouldn't be long if RememberMe had his
way.

After a few hours, Natasha made coffee, and they
ate slices of Mrs. Little Bear's excellent chocolate
meringue pie. Ben, who'd grown up eating her food,
wasn't overly impressed, but Daniel, whose parents
hadn't been available to cook regularly, and Natasha,
whose mother's creativity in the kitchen far exceeded
her skills, did everything but lick the plates when they
were done.

"I'd be fat and happy if I got to eat like this all the
time," Natasha said with a sigh.

His gaze back on the computer, Daniel said, "You
could. She runs a restaurant, you know. You'd just have
to move here." From the corner of his eye, he watched
her response. A slight raising of her brows. A moment's concentration as if she was trying to imagine
herself not in hiding but living here. Seeing the rest
of the town. Spending time with the Little Bears, the
Douglases and the Armstrongs on a regular basis. Living in this house with Daniel. Feeling safe and loved
and anchored, with no need to ever run away again.

Then a smile, just a little one, a curve of her lips

that was sweet and delicate and full of satisfaction. "I just might do that."

Could she leave her home and settle halfway across the country with him? Say goodbye to Stacia and everything familiar? Five years ago, marrying him hadn't been a complicated decision. She had planned to move in with him, eight miles from the apartment she shared with Stacia. They would have been within an hour's drive of her parents' place, and her job and friends were a crowded freeway's drive away. But here...

She would make—had already made—new friends. She could do video calls with Stacia and the others. As he'd told her earlier, planes flew that way.

He forced his attention back to the computer. When they were alone, he would simply ask her if she could live here. This time around, instead of assuming, they would talk like mature adults.

"Man, that brings back memories," Ben said, breaking the silence that had settled.

"What's that?"

Ben turned the computer to show him the paused video, a shot of an unassuming gray midsize sedan. "That was my first unmarked unit. The department got a good deal on them because they were all crap. Mine had no radio, no siren and no heat in the winter. I hated it."

"LAPD must have got a good deal on them, too, because that was my only unmarked unit out there. At least mine had a radio and a siren." Daniel had been so happy at his promotion that he hadn't cared he was driving a crappy vehicle also driven by a large percentage of the county's residents. He'd worked with officers who had no desire to get out of uniform and into detective ranks, but from day one, he'd wanted to move up. That was what had attracted him to the job. It was what he was good at.

When his cell phone buzzed, Daniel glanced at the time—coming up on 9:00 p.m.—and rubbed his eyes wearily before he picked it up. He was having trouble focusing, both his vision and his mind. He might have seen enough of cars whizzing past silently for one day.

Apprehension washed over Natasha, seated at his right, feet drawn onto the chair. She closed the book, marking her spot with her finger and looked at him with a fear that cut right through him.

"'Message for Nat,'" he read aloud. "'What the hell are you still doing there? You need to go back to the hotel. Now. Don't make me tell you again.'"

Five minutes later, the phone buzzed again. "'You're pissing me off, Nat, and trust me, you do not want to do that.'"

Three minutes later: "'Get out of there, Nat.'"

Two minutes after that came one more. Daniel didn't read it aloud, but he grimly handed the phone to Ben. He looked grim, too, when he handed it back.

"What does it say?" Natasha demanded.

"It's for me."

"From him?"

"Yeah. It's just the usual threat, Tash. Nothing new." Okay, maybe the wording was more obscene and more graphic, but in the end, the message was the same: RememberMe wanted Daniel dead.

She wavered between wanting to read it for herself and not wanting to know what had made him and Ben both grimace. After a moment, she shuddered and got to her feet. "Can I take a shower?"

"Sure. The jersey's in the bottom dresser drawer." It was a relic from his high school baseball days, pinstriped and well-worn once it had become her favorite of all his clothes.

Smiling wanly, she touched his shoulder on her way out of the room.

When the shower came on upstairs, Ben leaned back and stretched his arms above his head. "I wonder why our crazy guy wants to do anything else once he's already ripped your effing head off. You'd think it would be more satisfying to desecrate a live person than a dead body."

"You'd think," Daniel agreed sardonically. "Too bad RememberMe isn't thinking clearly. Gee, while we're at it, why don't we wish he was sane?"

"Yeah, if he was sane, you'd be going to sleep all alone in a cold bed tonight." Ben grinned as he began shutting down his computer. "We can start again tomorrow, but right now, I find myself forgetting that I'm watching this stuff for a reason. I need a break. What's the plan for tomorrow? You staying here or is she coming in with you?"

Daniel stood and stretched, too. "I'll let you know when I know."

He walked to the door with Ben, locked up behind him then watched through the peephole to see he made it safely to his vehicle. Feeling an odd combination of fatigue and energy, he shut off the lights, except for one in the kitchen and another in the living room, and slowly climbed the stairs. The running water became louder with each step, and musky floral scents drifted on the air. Natasha had left the bathroom door open, a silent invitation they'd used way back.

He stepped inside the large square room, looked at the pile of clothing on the black-and-white tile floor, felt the sweet warm air damp against his skin and, finally, shifted his gaze to the shower, where Natasha was peering out from behind the curtain. Her blond hair was plastered to her head, giving her a sleek look—like a seal, he'd say, but she might not be amused—and her mouth was curved in a sweet, inviting smile that he found more seductive than any deliberately sexy smile could be.

"Come on in," she said, her voice husky and vibrating through him. "The water's steamy."

"What a coincidence," he replied as he began undressing. "So am I."

The cell phone buzzed a few more times over the next hour, until Daniel had finally left the bed and taken it downstairs. He still had a landline, he'd said, and if Sam or Ben needed anything important, they could radio the officers on surveillance to bang on the door.

Natasha wasn't sure which surprised her more: that he had a landline or that he would ignore the cell. He felt such an obligation to responsibility and duty. She knew from his face that ScrewYou was saying some ugly stuff to him, but she didn't see any worry in his reaction. Irritation, annoyance, frustration, but no worry.

It was too early for bed, and she thought maybe they were both too tired to make love again. That last time had been lazy, easy, kind of like an aftershock to a powerful earthquake. That kind of sex was her favorite because you had to be pretty much a part of each other for it to really work.

But she didn't want to get out of the warm bed, didn't want to go back to reading the scary-sad-hopeful book she'd started, didn't want to be out of sight of Daniel for longer than it took to pee. So she combed her fingers through a first-class case of bedhead and wriggled into the baseball jersey. Then she slid under the covers and turned on her right side to look at him. "I take it I'm spending the night here."

"Unless you'd prefer us both to spend the night with the iron birds."

"If we do that, instead of Morwenna telling humiliating stories about her sister-in-law's encounter with the birds, she'll be telling about ours. And we'd be sure to have one."

"Those birds... What were they thinking?"

The question was familiar. She'd heard it plenty of times when she'd dragged him through various art exhibits. He appreciated art, he'd insisted, but paint splattered haphazardly on canvas? Rusty pieces of trash welded together? Blobs of shapeless clay? What were the artists thinking when they did the pieces, and what were the museum people thinking when they called them art? Hearing him say it now gave her a sense of comfort. She scooted as close to him as she could get and whispered, "God, I've missed you."

His gaze locked with hers, and his fingers brushed her jaw. "These last years have been like someone ripped out a part of me, Tash. Everything healed over, but life was never the same. I was never the same."

"I'm so—"

His fingers touched her mouth. "Don't apologize. You never have to apologize to me again. I'm just saying that's what it was like, and I don't ever want to feel that way again."

Her chest tightened mid-breath. When he'd said he still loved her, she'd thought… Oh, God, she'd jumped immediately to dreams of second chances and happily-ever-after. Had he simply been stating a fact? *I still love you, and I want to keep you safe and protect you from your stalker, but I don't want to be with you*?

It happened. Her mom said it was that way with her father: they loved each other, but they were a lot happier apart than together. Could she love Daniel if they were apart? The last five years were proof. Could she bear it if he didn't want her in his life?

Apparently unaware of the panic racing around in her brain, he went on in a ragged, emotion-thickened voice. "Of course, everyone feels that way at some point in their lives. The only way you can *not* get your heart broken is if you never love anyone, and that's no way to live. I just want to know, Tash, that you'll do your best to not do it again. That you'll talk to me. Trust me. Understand that you're a part of me, and I have a stake in what's going on with you. When you're afraid or unsure or unhappy, I need a chance to help make things right. I need to know you won't run away again. I need to know you'll stay."

Her relief was so complete that, if she'd been standing, she would have sagged onto the nearest piece of furniture. Her bones dissolved, her muscles went weak and her nerves quivered. She wanted to blurt out promises. Of course she would stay with him, never leave him, never break his heart again.

But it was a big promise coming from the bride who'd run away four times. In fact, she'd made that promise to him once before. *You won't abandon me like Kyle and Eric?* They'd just fallen in love, just gotten engaged. Their faith in their love and each other had been 100 percent. Unshakeable. *Never*, she'd answered, and he'd pulled her close. *I know.*

She pressed a kiss to the palm of his hand. "I'll do my absolute best. I'll stay forever. Till death do us part."

That last part made her shiver just a little. Happiness could be fleeting. Everyone knew of a love story where happily-ever-after had been cut tragically short. RememberMe could kill her or Daniel tomorrow. This day, this night, could be all they got.

Of course, she could get hit by a car the next time she was out. He could be tracked down by an ex-convict with a grudge. An airplane could crash into the house or a tornado could blow them away. No one got promises on how long they would live.

RememberMe just made their expectations a little iffier than most people's.

"Till death do us part when we're creaky old people surrounded by all kinds of Harpers," he corrected her. "Big ones, little ones, young ones, old ones, pregnant ones, funny ones, smart-ass ones..."

"Those will be the ones who take after my side of the family." Talking of having babies gave her warm and fuzzy feelings that she wanted to hug to her chest and bask in as long as she could. But it also stirred uneasiness deep inside her.

RememberMe was coming out of the obsessive-love stage, Dr. Armstrong had said, making him even more dangerous. His plan to kill Daniel in some sick effort to advance his nonexistent relationship with Natasha had failed spectacularly, pushing her and Daniel together instead, pushing her even more out of his psychotic reach. His jealousy had grown; based on his texts this evening, his control was giving way to rage.

He'd reached the if-I-can't-have-you-I'll-kill-you stage. Tomorrow, maybe the next day…

Either she would live or die. Daniel would live or die. Their future was out of their hands. If RememberMe succeeded, all these sweet, lovely things she and Daniel had discussed would be meaningless. There would be no marriage, no little Harpers, no anything in her future but an early grave.

She'd never wished harm on anyone, not seriously. Okay, there'd been a few times when she'd told Stacia to drop dead, when she'd shrieked at Nick that she wished he'd never been born. But tonight she was going to pray for death for RememberMe, whoever he was. She wanted the fear gone. She wanted to put an end to the runaway-bride legend. She wanted to marry Daniel and have his children and die an old, satisfied, well-loved woman.

She wanted to live, and dear God, most of all, she wanted Daniel to live.

Monday morning might have been the best morning of Daniel's life. He'd spent the last three hours watching more dull and boring video, drinking too much coffee that was sitting heavy in his stomach, eating sugary snacks and nothing of substance, but he'd awakened with Natasha curled beside him, all sleepy and beautiful, and that made up for everything else.

"How many texts have you gotten from this guy?" Sam asked as he rubbed the kinks from his neck. He'd been reading the messages RememberMe had sent in order from the beginning.

"Twenty-nine," Ben replied for Daniel. He'd taken possession of Daniel's cell this morning, setting it on vibrate and making a point of being subtle when he read each incoming message. They'd bothered Natasha from the beginning and had set Daniel's nerves on edge a couple of hours after starting. If he had to read each one as it came in, he'd have a stroke by five.

"And the IT guys still have nothing on his location."

"He's better at hiding his tracks than they are at finding them."

"He could use a class on accepting rejection," Sam muttered. "Hell, he could teach a class on it."

From outside the conference room came the sound of feminine laughter. Daniel couldn't help looking that way, even though he couldn't see into the dispatcher shack, where Morwenna was entertaining Natasha between calls.

"Gotta admire a woman who can still laugh when things have gone to hell around her," Sam remarked.

"Like Mila?" Daniel had been pretty amazed by Mila's resiliency back when it had been her life they were trying to protect. He'd thought she was the strongest woman he'd ever known. Still did, but Natasha was coming in a close second.

"Mila didn't have much to laugh about before things went to hell." Sam gathered his stuff and walked to the door then looked back and grinned. "But she's learned."

Being raised by parents who were serial killers, who used her to lure their victims and abused her in between their kills, would have done irreparable harm to a lesser person. But no one would guess her history by watching or talking to her. She'd done a lot of healing in the years after her grandmother rescued her and a lot more since falling in love with Sam.

Daniel gave a moment's thanks that Natasha's biggest problem with her parents was that they loved not too little but too many. They'd welcomed everyone into their home and their family, and while Natasha and her siblings had a few issues resulting from their upbringing, abuse was never a part of it.

He turned his attention back to the computer screen. The footage he was currently viewing came from a traffic camera at the intersection where her apartment complex was located. She'd shown him last night just the glimpse of her balcony, all that was visible from this view. It was the second of the three apartments where she'd lived since acquiring the stalker, and at some time during regular business hours on the day this was recorded, someone had left a small bouquet of orchids and a card at her door. It could have been someone hired by someone else who was hired by someone else, or it could have been RememberMe.

"Huh," Daniel murmured, stopping the video. He shrank the screen, opened another of Flea's files and scanned through before stopping it, too. "That gray sedan you mentioned last night... I know the tag wasn't visible, but did it have any identifiable marks?"

Ben's gaze narrowed in thought. Despite his notorious list-making, he had better recall than anyone Daniel knew. *Pay attention to details* was his golden rule, and he did it well. "Yeah, a sticker on the rear window, lower left side. Most of it had been scraped off, but there was adhesive and a little strip of blue on the bottom."

"Where was the video taken?"

"Stoplight near her first apartment. You have the same car?"

"Yeah. Once outside the second apartment, once outside her work."

"How many gray sedans do you think are in Los Angeles?"

"A lot." Daniel blew out his breath. "This guy could live and work in the same neighborhoods she does. It wouldn't be unusual." Was he grasping at straws? Probably. It was frustrating to be so completely in the dark about a suspect, especially one who wanted him dead. But prisons were full of people convicted because of a lucky break on the cops' part, because coincidence or maybe the grace of God saying take a closer look at *this*.

They went back to working in silence. Natasha and Morwenna's occasional laughter made the job less tedious, but that wasn't saying much. By noon, Daniel needed a break, but first he wanted to watch one more video: the traffic cam at the entrance to Kyle's neighborhood. He'd seen it three times now, but clicked start yet again. The street was the only way in; anyone who'd gone to Kyle's house the day of his accident either climbed a ten-foot wall or drove down this street.

And there it was. The view from the front showed the gray sedan completing the turn into the neighborhood just as the light turned red. The driver's face wasn't visible—he was pretty sure it was a man, though—and the front tag looked as if someone had smeared a handful of thick mud over it. The only thing he could say was that it was a California tag.

He fast-forwarded through the next sixty-seven minutes then watched at regular speed before stopping once again on the car. "This is him."

Ben looked up, his usual placid expression replaced with sharp anticipation. He came around the table and bent over Daniel's shoulder, his gaze fixing on the car. "Can't see his damn face," he muttered.

"This is the camera closest to Kyle's house. He went in, stayed a little more than an hour, then came out. Kyle was discovered by his girlfriend twenty minutes after this was recorded." Frustration vibrated through him. If RememberMe had gone back the same way he came, they could have gotten a look at the rear license tag, though it was probably obscured as well. "I'll call Flea and see if they can track his movements through other cameras on that street."

He was reaching for his phone when Ben said, "Hang on a minute. I want to bounce something off you. He sent this to Natasha last Tuesday, after she'd left LA." He circled back to his chair to read from the computer. "'Are you too sick to answer your phone? Should I ask Dispatch for a welfare check?'"

Daniel leaned back, relaxing muscles that resented too many hours hunched in front of a computer. "We do welfare checks on a pretty regular basis."

"Yeah, we do, but most people don't say I'm gonna call Dispatch. They call the police. And they don't usually say, 'Will you do a welfare check on my grandmother?' They say, 'Granny's been sick and she isn't answering the phone and we're three hours away. Could you send someone by to check on her?'"

A knot formed in Daniel's gut. Too much coffee, he wanted to think. A very bad feeling, he knew. "LAPD has a lot of those cars for unmarked units."

Ben shrugged. "A cop can find out information. He knows what kind of inquiries will lead back to him and how to avoid them."

"And it's easier to stay two steps ahead of the investigation when you know what the next move will be." Daniel pinched the bridge of his nose. He'd rather not believe that RememberMe was one of their own. He knew a lot of people in the Los Angeles Police Department, and even the ones he didn't know, the job itself was a bond. They'd all been through the academy, made it through their probationary periods, done the patrols and put up with the crap. They'd all worked for too little pay and too little gratitude. No matter what colors their uniforms were, they were the thin blue line. The brothers in blue.

They were—geez, now he was teetering on hokey—*family.* Family didn't do this to each other.

Another thought occurred to him, choking out a bitter laugh. "All this time Natasha's been feeling guilty because she brought the stalker into my life. If this guy is a cop, there's a fair chance that *I* was the one who brought him into *her* life."

Wasn't that a kick in the teeth?

Natasha looked at Daniel blankly. Of all the questions he could have asked her, this was one she hadn't expected. "Cops in LA?"

"Do you know any?"

She shrugged and continued to pass out bags from the deli with names written on them. Hers, she'd been

informed, was the bag marked "Sam 2." She slid the
sandwich out of the bag and reached for a pile of napkins at the center of the conference table. "There's
Flea—Detective Martin, of course. I met dozens of
them when we were together, at dinners, parties, cook-
outs, but I...no. I still see some of them around, and
we say hello, but I wouldn't say I actually know any of
them." Nausea curled in her stomach. "Do you think
RememberMe is a cop?"

Daniel avoided answering, which was, of course,
an answer. The possibility angered more than it frightened her. She'd already been afraid of crazy-man, but
it pissed her off that a cop, the person who was supposed to protect and defend people, could be the biggest danger of all.

He took a bite of his sandwich before going on. "His
first message—he sent a picture of a sunset. Said it reminded you of the day you two met. Said you probably
didn't remember because you had been surrounded
by admirers. There were always a lot of guys hanging
around at department functions. They all wanted to
meet you, talk to you, figure out how solid we were,
whether they had a chance. And you probably don't
remember most of their faces or any of their names."

He was right. There had been a beach party where
she'd been introduced to fifty people or more in one
afternoon. A barbecue with close to forty. A Halloween party with so many guests that she'd become practically claustrophobic in the crush. Stacia and family
had dominated her and Daniel's social life, but they'd
spent a good number of evenings with small groups
of officers and their significant others, even if it was

just a drink at a bar at the end of their shift. So many people she wouldn't know today.

"What about dates?" Morwenna asked. She pointed her index finger at Daniel when he frowned her way. "You said everyone wanted to meet her, to figure out whether they had a chance. Did any of them ask you out?"

"Yeah, a couple did. One, while I was still with Daniel. A nice kid, just out of the academy, very young and brash, but it couldn't be him."

"Why not?"

Natasha looked at Daniel, who wore the same sorrowful look she was sure was on her face. Under the table, he stretched out his leg and bumped hers, the action reassuring, then answered for her. "A month into his probationary period, he stopped a car on traffic, walked up to the driver's door and the driver shot and killed him. Shot his training officer, too, but the FTO survived."

"Oh." Morwenna was silent a moment before asking, "Anyone else? Especially after you did a runner on Daniel?"

The runner phrase made Natasha wince inside, but it was nothing less than the truth. "There was the guy whose career path included being the youngest chief of detectives in LAPD history. Remember him, Daniel? Always bragging about his connections to the chief and the mayor?"

He grimaced. "We figured if he stuck around long enough, one of our own people would shoot him. How'd he take it when you said no?"

"It rolled right off him. It was like an odd thought popped into his head, he asked and he blew it off.

Didn't do a lot for my ego, I'll tell you, though the next one was a little more insulting. Cop was working traffic at a concert. He asked me out, and I said no, thanks. So he turned to Stacia, standing right beside me, and asked her. She said no, and he asked her friend, right in front of us. She agreed to meet him when he got off. That was four years ago, and they're still together."

"See why I'm still single? Who wants to be someone's third choice when there are only three to start?" Morwenna shuddered. "I would've shoved his baton someplace special."

"See why she's still single?" Ben said in an aside to Daniel.

Morwenna stuck her tongue out at him. "So that's all of your police officer date candidates?"

"The last one's a financial crimes detective. I met her through a friend of Stacia's, though, not Daniel. And she didn't want a date so much as a hookup." Natasha picked up her sandwich, spilling ingredients on the wrap, then set it down again. "A cop. Damn." Aside from the fact that it was just ugly to think about, it offended her that her tax money might have gone to give RememberMe some of the training he was now using against her. "What makes you think so?"

"This car keeps showing up." Daniel turned the laptop so she could see the sedan. "We're thinking it might be an unmarked car."

Natasha stared at the image, a side view: midsize, four doors, adequate transportation without any hint of style. She wished some insignificant little memory would pop up from the shadows of her subconscious mind, connecting it to anyone in her life, but nothing popped. It was just a gray car.

After wiping her hands on a napkin, Morwenna turned the computer slightly to get a better look. "Of course it's an unmarked car. Look at that."

She jabbed her finger at the screen, at a spot somewhere around the rear passenger window. Natasha looked and saw nothing out of the ordinary. Maybe a bit of a bump on the roof, or maybe it was just blurry from the movement of the car.

Daniel leaned across Natasha to look, and Ben got up from his chair. She wheeled her own chair back, giving them room, and saw the look they exchanged a moment later. Ben was smiling, relief in his dark eyes, but Daniel looked absolutely radiant, if that were a word he would bear without grimacing. He grabbed Morwenna in a hug, smacked a kiss on her cheek then jumped to his feet. On his way around the table, he snatched up his cell phone. "I'm going to call Flea."

"I'll tell Sam Morwenna deserves a raise," Ben replied.

In the abrupt stillness that followed, Natasha slid forward again, squinting at the picture. All she saw was that the car looked inconspicuous, which unmarked units should be, and the city needed a better quality camera. "Okay, I give. What do you see that I don't?"

"See this little round thing here, looks like a hockey puck?" Morwenna pointed to the maybe-a-bump. "It's an antenna. There'll be one on the other side, too. All our unmarked units have them. All the departments in our area use them or the stubby little cylindrical kind, but hockey pucks are more popular."

Natasha studied it, leaning close for a better view. Hmm. Maybe she just needed to see it from a different angle, because it still looked like a bump. But she was deeply grateful for Morwenna's help and said so. "Thank you." She squeezed the other woman's shoulder.

Morwenna patted her hand reassuringly. "Oh, the guys would've seen it sooner or later. They're just tired from looking at so many cars."

Finally Natasha picked up her sandwich again and took a bite. So RememberMe was apparently a police officer. She was grateful he hadn't come out of the obsessive-love stage back home. In the areas she frequented, a police officer could have picked her up, even when he wasn't in uniform, even when he was driving an unmarked car, and no one would have paid attention. People noticed when something was obviously wrong, and in that case, all they would see was a police officer taking a criminal, probably a shoplifter, into custody.

And then RememberMe would have been free to do whatever he wanted with her.

She should have asked Dr. Armstrong what his initial intent had been. Had he thought she would be delighted that he had come for her, that now they could share their love and their lives in the way they both wanted? Would he have been so enraged to discover that she didn't love him, that she'd led him astray, that he would have just killed her and been done with it? Or would he have locked her up, chained her down and done whatever was necessary to try to instill his delusions in her?

Every possibility led to the same conclusion: death for her. And soon enough, some other poor woman would smile at him or shake hands with him or say something that his twisted mind would turn into an invitation.

"Have you ever been stalked?" Natasha asked. She needed distraction, but her mind was a little too narrowly focused.

"No. My friends seem to think that I'd come down on the wrong side of that equation. You write 'Morwenna and Henry forever' in one patch of freshly poured concrete, right on the busiest corner in town, and no one ever lets you forget it."

Natasha laughed. "Did you really?"

"My best friend dared me. She said I needed to show my love for Henry in a really big way, and his family lived above the shop at the corner, so… And he didn't even appreciate it. There was a bunch of us coming home from school, and my friend said, 'Look what Morwenna did.' I've never seen a guy look so mortified, like he was going to be sick right there. He said, 'Oh, God,' in a really disgusted, how-can-you-be-so-stupid way, and he ran off. I was horrified, all the kids laughed and I promptly fell out of love with Henry Braithwaite." She heaved a sigh as if telling the story had drained her.

"Wait a minute. Henry Braithwaite the fabulously sexy and sought-after actor?"

"The very one. But unless he's changed an awful lot, he's still a prat." She gathered the wrapper from her sandwich and stood, then grinned. "I was twelve at the time. Never let it be said that Morwenna Armstrong doesn't know how to hold a grudge."

Natasha responded to her wave as she headed back to work, then took another bite of her sandwich. Daniel had to be pleased that they'd narrowed the suspect pool from the entire population of California to the much smaller number of law enforcement officers in Los Angeles County who were given unmarked cars.

But he must also feel an extra measure of disdain that RememberMe was likely a cop. She was sorry for that, but she wasn't going to add it to her guilt. In fact, since yesterday morning's talk with Dr. Armstrong, her guilt had been slowly shrinking. She hadn't done anything wrong. Though she hated the word, hated the way it made her feel, she was a *victim* in this whole mess, just like Kyle and Daniel. She couldn't—wouldn't—accept responsibility for RememberMe's actions.

She finished her lunch, threw away the trash and circled the room a time or two before the computer drew her. The screen had gone to sleep but woke when she swiped her finger across it, bringing up the picture of the car. It was impossible to tell from the background on which street it had been captured. There was a convenience store with a ridiculous number of gas pumps, a pharmacy, a business she couldn't make out and three fast-food restaurants. It had been sunny, hazy, a business-as-usual day for everyone in the area.

Could anyone have suspected that business as usual for the guy in the unassuming gray car was stalking a woman he didn't know?

Daniel returned, and she straightened. When he came around the table, she stepped into his embrace and sighed. His heartbeat was steady and strong. He was warm and calm and wore her favorite scent in the whole world—eau de him. He was her rock.

After a moment, he pushed her back so he could see her face. "You okay?"

She nodded. "How about you?"

"I won't be satisfied as long as this guy's out there, but we're getting closer."

She shifted against him, rubbing side to side. "Is that a challenge?"

His laugh surprised him, she could see in his eyes, but it was exactly what she needed to hear. "You know what I mean, Tash."

She did, and this was his workplace where someone could walk in at any minute. She promised herself she would behave and even get serious again. "I hope it's no one you know."

"So do I. Flea's going to try to get us a picture of him—follow his direction of travel and hopefully find an angle that shows his—" His cell phone buzzed, and he scowled, glanced at the screen then set the phone on the table. "His face. She's also looking to see if anyone in the department has been checking you out—DMV, traffic, utilities, that kind of thing. Everything digital leaves a trail."

Natasha glanced at the silent phone then swallowed down the lump in her throat. "Unless you're good enough to hide it."

"Everyone screws up sometime."

"Aw, when have you ever screwed up?"

He snugged her close again and kissed her jaw. "When I let you go without a fight." Before he kissed her mouth, he murmured a promise, and she believed him.

"I'm not going to lose you again."

Chapter 10

They were in the middle of that kiss when Ben cleared his throat behind them. Daniel finished it—no, broke it off; he wouldn't have been finished for a long time—and rolled his eyes. "His timing sucks."

Natasha's smile was sweet and teasing. "It'll give us something to look forward to later."

Oh, he had a lot to look forward to. So much that he was going to need a whole life to see it all.

Ben came on in and sat down. He pulled the computer over and busied himself with it before raising his gaze to them. The grim look was back in his eyes. Not good news.

Daniel pulled out a chair for Natasha then sat beside her. "What is it?"

"Seattle PD called. Someone took a shot at fiancé number two about an hour ago. He's okay—just a couple of cuts from broken glass. The only description he could give was a white guy, average height, dark hair."

Beside him, Natasha went stiff, her breath catching in a gasp. Daniel took her hand, squeezing it tightly, but his own muscles relaxed enough that he could sink back in his chair. "That's good news."

Ben's gaze narrowed. "How do you figure that?"

"If RememberMe's in Seattle, shooting at Eric, then he can't be here tracking us." He would come back, no doubt about that, but it gave them a few hours of breathing space.

Ben echoed his thoughts. "He'll come back."

"Yeah, but he's not here right now. We can move Natasha someplace safe. If she doesn't have her electronics and isn't using her credit card, he'll have no way to track her, while we're finally on our way to identifying him." Just the idea of her being totally safe sent an overwhelming sense of relief through him. She would still be in hiding, but she wouldn't be in danger. It would give them time.

Five years ago, he knew she would have protested the notion of being stashed away somewhere for her own good. Today, she merely clasped his hand in both of hers. "You'll go with me."

"No. I want to take this guy down. I need to—"

"Sounds like an excellent idea to me." Sam walked in the door, stopping at the end of the table. "I told you, Detective, I'd hate to lose you. You're officially one of the victims that needs protection in this case. My uncle Dave has a cabin at Keystone Lake, about twenty-five miles from here. It's quiet, out in the woods, no neighbors nearby. Leave your cell phone—Ben would hate to miss any of the guy's charming texts—and take your radio so we can stay in touch. Okay?"

Three gazes turned on Daniel, making him frown. It wasn't okay. He didn't want to be off in the wilderness when psycho guy was arrested. It was personal. He needed to see the case through, to be there when they put handcuffs on him, to outsmart the guy who claimed he was smarter than them all.

Then he inhaled deeply and caught a whiff of Natasha's perfume, and his common sense kicked in. Time alone together in the wilderness? A cabin, the lake and all the privacy and intimacy they could want? He'd have to be as crazy as the psycho to turn that down.

Besides, she was still RememberMe's obsession. If by some strange quirk of fate, he found her again...

"Okay," he said, and those three gazes all registered some measure of surprise. "Okay, we'll go. We'll have to stop at the hotel to pick up her stuff, then go by my house. Should I get anything special? Linens, dishes?"

"No. The cabin gets all the family's castoffs. Nothing matches, but you'll have everything you need. I'll take you out there, then pick up some groceries." Sam shifted gears. "What about the photo?"

"I haven't shown it to them yet." Ben passed the laptop across the table.

"You guys really should get a tablet for this part of a job," Natasha commented, her tone light but stressed underneath. Was she more afraid of looking at the picture and knowing RememberMe or looking at it and still seeing a total stranger?

That was how Daniel felt. He didn't want to see the face of one of his buddies looking back, but at least he could identify a buddy. They would have a name and a driver's license or an official police department photo. They would have coworkers and family to interview, a home to search, a car to look out for.

Actually looking was kind of anticlimactic to the buildup. It was a shot taken as the car sailed through an intersection, giving a profile of the driver. A white guy, looked to be about average height, with dark hair. Someone who knew him might be able to identify him from that photo, but Daniel didn't have a clue. He was both relieved and disappointed.

"Detective Martin says that's the best they've found so far, but she's still looking," Ben said. "Natasha, does it remind you even remotely of anyone you know? Anyone you've had contact with?"

She shook her head. "It's like those pictures they have on the news when there's a bank robbery. Only their mothers would recognize them."

"Print some copies anyway," Sam said. "Show them around. Have someone locate Ozzie and see if it's the same guy he saw."

"Already printed." Ben stood, picked up the folder he'd brought in and tapped it. "Let's get your stuff and head to the lake."

They were about to turn down the stairs to the basement, to leave by the sally port, when Natasha spoke again. "Can we just walk to the hotel? I've been inside way too long, and if he's in Washington..."

Daniel and Ben exchanged looks and shrugs, and they went out the main entrance instead. The afternoon was sunny, warm enough to not need a jacket but with just enough bite in the breeze to remind them that winter was on its way. In another week or two, the trees would hit their peak color. Natasha would be suitably impressed by the amazing colors of the maple near the gazebo. Once she actually got to see and know the town, she would love it. Daniel would make sure of it.

The three of them crossed the square, ignored the sign about jaywalking and jogged across the street in the middle of the block. The hotel lobby was empty when they went inside, but Claire called a greeting from the counter.

"Why don't you get started packing?" Daniel suggested. "I'll be up in a minute." He watched until she reached the top of the stairs and turned right—never missing a chance to watch her walk upstairs—then joined Ben at the counter.

"…quiet," Claire was saying. "Everyone's checked out except Natasha and the wine ladies. They're leaving this afternoon. But it's like that. We have a guest or two during the week, fill up for the weekends, then are blessedly empty on Mondays. It gives me a chance to recharge."

"We don't get time to recharge," Ben replied. "Our customers are full-time criminals. Weekday, weekend, holiday, football season…nothing keeps them from their work."

"Which is why we have our work," Daniel reminded him. "If everyone started obeying the law, you and I would have to… I don't know. Go wash dishes in your mom's kitchen?"

"I've washed my share of dishes at the restaurant. Didn't get paid for it, either." Ben pulled out a copy of the photograph. "Claire, can you take a look at this? Does he look familiar?"

She took the picture, tilted her head to one side and studied it, lips pursed. A moment passed then another, and her forehead wrinkled. "I hate to say because it's just kind of a feeling, and I assume this person is wanted for some reason if you're showing his picture around, but…" She expelled a breath. "It kind of looks like Rob."

Daniel's mind went blank for a moment, but then he remembered: the guest Natasha had been talking to when he and Morwenna arrived to take her to dinner on Friday. Oh, hell. Had RememberMe been sleeping right here in the same building with Natasha all this time?

If so, the bastard hadn't been bragging. He really was smarter than them.

But somebody in the department had looked into this Rob guy, had verified that he was from San Francisco, that he was here on business. Claire herself had said he'd come at the same time every month for three months. He'd been here before Natasha had even arrived in the state.

"You said he's checked out?" Ben asked.

"Yes, he left this morning about eight. I can give you the information I have on file for him." Without waiting for a response, she called up her guest files on the computer.

Daniel restlessly tapped his fingers on the counter. *Kind of looks like* wasn't the kind of eyewitness identification that made a cop or a prosecutor happy. And if RememberMe had taken a shot at Eric in Seattle a couple hours ago, he couldn't possibly have been here at the hotel to check out at eight this morning. The number of men just here in Cedar Creek who matched the poor description Eric had given was probably in the thousands.

It couldn't be.

But he was getting a very bad feeling.

Claire came back with a page torn from a notepad. The full name was Rob Miller, along with his address and phone number, as well as the make, model and license tag of his rental car.

"Rob Miller." Ben placed his thumb on the page, blocking out the *o* and the *b*. *RM*. "Coincidence?" he murmured.

Before Daniel could process that, sound came from upstairs: a thud, a grunt then a piercing shriek that stopped his heart cold.

It was Natasha, and she was screaming his name.

Filling her lungs in a panicked gasp, Natasha gave voice to the kind of chilling scream Stacia was so good at. *"Daniel, help!"* She'd been standing beside the bed, packing neat piles of clothing into her suitcase, when strong arms had grabbed her from behind. In the first instant, she'd thought it was Daniel, but then she'd realized that the scent was wrong, and under the circumstances, Daniel would never sneak up on her like that.

Then the man had spoken. *Hello, Nat. Remember me?*

He was pulling hard, but she'd wrapped her hands around the footrail of the bed. One gripped smooth steel; the other was clutching one of the damn birds. She kicked back, screamed again then went limp and forced him to support her weight fully.

But he was damn strong. He held her, one arm cutting into her middle, and peeled her hand from the rail, one finger at a time. When she lost that hold, he yanked, and her other hand was jerked loose from the bird, its wings and beak slicing her palm.

With nothing for her to grab, he easily yanked her across the room. When she lunged for the doorjamb, he wrapped both arms around her, trapping her arms at her sides, expelling the air from her lungs, and pulled her along the corridor. Below, Daniel yelled her name, and steps thudded on the lobby's wood floor, but before she could find breath for another scream, her stalker was dragging her like a bag of grain up the smaller, less-ornate stairs to the third floor. On the landing, she managed to hook her foot around the baluster, but it didn't slow him even a bit. He gave an extra heave and continued down the hall to a door at the back of the building.

Once through that doorway, he shoved her, lungs heaving, against the wall, holding her there with one steely hand pressing too tightly around her throat, and used his free hand to close and lock the door. They were in another stairwell, this one dusty and dark. No windows let in the sun, and if there was a bulb, he didn't bother turning it on. He didn't seem to need it, as he began hauling her up the stairs.

They were going to the roof. Oh, God, that couldn't possibly be good. Did he think he could force her down a fire escape quicker than Daniel or Ben could run out the back door? Was his plan to go across the roof to the next building?

Or did he intend to throw her off, onto the street below?

Her heart pounded so hard that Daniel must surely hear it, and her breath was little more than ineffectual wheezes. As he fumbled with the doorknob at the top of the stairs, she scratched the hand that held her, digging her nails in deep, making him swear, but his grip didn't loosen. He opened the door into fresh air and brilliant sunlight, shoved her outside, locked that door, too, then let go of her.

Run! Tasha screamed, but as if he heard the voice himself, he slapped her. The force of the blow knocked her to the floor—the roof—whatever the hell it was called—and sent pain ricocheting from her cheekbone all the way down to her toes. The deck surface was coated with tar and gritty with dirt, dead leaves and windblown debris, bits of it pressing into the unharmed side of her face.

Before her brain could give her throbbing muscles the command to *move*, a shadow fell over her, and she saw her tormentor for the first time. Bewilderment flashed through her. "Rob?" *He* was her stalker? A computer guy from San Francisco? She'd visited the city, of course, but not since she was in middle school. How could she possibly have come to his attention?

He smiled, his face handsome even though she knew what lay behind those blue eyes, that chiseled jaw, that straight nose. Shouldn't evil *look* evil?

"You do remember me. I knew you did."

Remember you from where? No matter how hard she stared, she couldn't find anything the least bit familiar about him. Their meeting, if it had even happened, had been so inconsequential that it wasn't even a flutter in the most faded of her memories.

Slowly, she sat up, testing various parts of her body. The entire left side of her face throbbed, and her right hand stung from the cuts. Those damn birds really ought to be set free before they seriously harmed someone.

But she didn't have to worry about birds. She had her very own psychopath looming over her.

She also had Daniel coming after her. The locked doors might slow him down, but he would come. He would save her.

Still cautious, she stood up, swayed a bit then got her balance back. The roof was the same footprint as the hotel—not very big—and there was nothing on it. No place to run to. Nowhere to hide. Climbing over to the next building to escape was out of the question; the building on the west side was one story taller, and the alley ran on the east side. The fire escape must have stopped at the third floor. It was just one big open space, with a full ten feet of stone on one side and a low brick edge on the others. The edge, she knew from all the old buildings she'd toured, was strictly aesthetic, not protective.

RememberMe—Rob—wasn't kidnapping her. He wasn't taking her to some isolated spot where they could live happily together. He wasn't coming out of the obsessive-love phase. He was so far past it that he probably wouldn't remember ever loving her once he killed her.

Hesitantly she backed away a step, another, a few more. She didn't want to be any closer to the edges than she had to—she'd always thought falling was a horrible way to die—but she didn't want him facing the door, either, when Daniel came out. He hadn't shown a weapon yet, but she was certain he had one.

He turned to watch her but didn't follow. "I knew you remembered me. That you were just playing when you pretended you didn't."

"Th-there were a lot of p-people around when we

met." Her voice quavered, but that was okay. Inside she was shaking so hard, she was surprised she could even talk. What did a person say to a psychopath? What might set him off? What might appeal to his twisted sense of reason?

"There were always a lot of people around you."

Always? Did that mean they'd met on more than one occasion? Or was it just something he'd noticed while stalking her?

"I-I thought you were in Seattle."

He made a dismissive gesture. "I'm a cop. Do you know how easy it is to find someone who will shoot someone else for a price?"

A lump rose in her throat. "And it made us think you were gone." It made them let down their guard and gave him his chance.

"I told you I was smarter than them." When he smiled, she saw the first hint of ugliness in his smug expression, in his disdainful look. "Harper's never been half the cop I am. He couldn't cut it in LA, so he came here, a crap little town where nothing ever happens. He's an idiot."

A blur of movement behind him distracted her for an instant: the door to the stairs opening an inch. Hastily she spoke louder than necessary to cover any noise Daniel might make. "He knows you're a cop, too."

Rob shrugged. "It's too late." He raised his voice, too, as he began walking toward her. "I'm here. You're here. He's stuck on those stairs, knowing that if he bursts out here, trying to be the hero, I'll blow his damn head off."

Natasha glanced at the stairs for an instant. When she turned her gaze back to Rob, he was less than ten feet away and holding a pistol. She backed up, and he lunged and grabbed her arm, pulling her around in front of him, tight against his body.

"I told you you were mine," he whispered, turning so they faced the stairs. "I told you you would always be mine. We made vows, Nat. You can't break vows."

He drew a deep breath then went utterly still. "You smell just the way I remember. You've worn that same perfume all this time. Just for me. Everything you do—the way you dress, the way you laugh, the way you smell, the way you move—for me. I've always known it. You've always known it, too. Now you can quit pretending, Nat."

Then he called, "Come on out, Harper."

Frantically she ran through every possible scenario in her mind and couldn't find a single one with a good outcome. He'd moved them too close to the roofline. Two steps back, and there was nothing to save them from a forty- or fifty-foot fall. She could try going limp again, but the value of the action was in the surprise, and with his arm so tight around her waist, it wouldn't require much more effort to hold her in place, even if she refused to cooperate. The running shoes she was wearing hadn't made any impact when she'd kicked him, and her arms were pinned at her side, her fingers starting to go numb from decreased circulation.

She couldn't do anything, and so she prayed. She thought about Stacia and Nick, their parents and Archer and Jeffrey. She said a silent *I love you* to Daniel.

And then he stepped through the doorway.

"Alex Robin Miller."

Rob laughed. "Ooh, my full name. I guess I'm in trouble now."

Daniel's pistol was comfortable in his hand, though he hoped to God he didn't have to use it. He had no qualms about shooting Miller, but it would take every ounce of desperation in him to do it while the bastard was using Natasha as a shield.

His gaze locked on her, moving swiftly from head to toe and back up, relief rushing through him. Her face was white, her eyes huge and distressed and, even from this distance, he could see the shudders that racked her. There was blood on her hand, one side of her face burned red, and judging by the bangs and thuds as he'd dragged her up the stairs, she must have plenty of aches. But she was okay. Thank God, she was okay.

Daniel moved away from the door, sidestepping to the right. Ben was positioning himself on the roof of the building next to the courthouse, directly across the street from this one, and Lois was delivering a sniper rifle to him. Sam and a couple of uniforms were in the stairwell, awaiting the signal, and every other officer in town was setting up in the vicinity; there would be no escape for Miller.

But that sick tangle deep in his gut told him Miller didn't plan to escape. He was making his stand, and he was taking Natasha with him.

No damn way.

Keeping his pistol trained on Miller, Daniel stalled. He'd had no time to grab a radio or earpiece, so he had no way to communicate with his fellow officers. When Ben was ready, he'd said grimly, Daniel would know.

"Remind me where you met Natasha."

"She remembers. She said so. Tell him, Nat." He yanked her, made her grunt as she lost her balance.

Daniel added that to the list of RememberMe's sins.

"She hates being called Nat," he said casually.

"She hates anyone else calling her that. It's my special name for her. I'm the only one allowed to use it."

"So where'd you meet? Or is that another of your fantasies?" Daniel could imagine Sam shaking his head at that last bit. *Don't upset the crazy psycho guy holding a gun on the hostage.*

But Miller didn't take offense. He did, however, take the bait and answer the question. "The cookout for Captain Franklin's retirement. Nat can give you the exact date if it'll help jog your memory."

Natasha's eyes widened, and she gave a tiny shrug. She was still as clueless about their introduction as Daniel was. Sure, he remembered the cookout. Mostly he remembered that there had been a couple hundred people there, that after a half hour, he'd stopped even listening to the names of people they were introduced to. Miller had definitely come around after that half hour.

"No, I remember. It was a long time ago. We broke up a couple months later. Why did you wait so long?"

Miller's face contorted into a smile. "Broke up? She dumped you. She didn't even care enough to do it face-to-face. She sent her sister to humiliate you in front of everyone."

A breeze sent an advertising flyer skipping across the roof and stirred the leaves there. Daniel watched as they crackled back down, making a deliberate effort not to look at the rooftop across the street. He couldn't betray Ben's intentions with even a glance. "Yeah. She dumped me. Broke my heart. Maybe she even did it for you. But you didn't make a move on her then. Why not?"

Miller awkwardly caressed Natasha's hair with his gun hand. She stiffened but didn't flinch. Daniel flinched, hating every second of this on her behalf. Having to face her stalker, to endure his touch and bear his aggression... It would take a long time to erase the ugliness of the past few minutes from her mind.

Daniel intended to be by her side for a very long time.

"I had to wait for the right time. She wasn't ready to settle down. I didn't have to worry about someone taking her away because she loved *me*. She was mine. So I gave her space. I didn't abandon her. I stayed in touch, and I waited for the perfect time."

I stayed in touch. He must have been the most patient man in the world, watching from afar, keeping tabs on her. That kind of obsession freaked out Daniel—would freak out any sane person. Why hadn't he just asked her out, like any other guy, as soon as he found out the wedding was off?

Because he wasn't like any other guy. He was a psychopath whose delusions controlled his life.

Miller's smile returned. "Are you through stalling, Detective? Do you think I'm unaware of your plan? You've got a sniper in one of these buildings, most likely the one across the street." He shook his head in dismay. "People give you credit for being a much better cop than you actually are. You and your big partner, you do everything by the book. Even a common criminal can predict your every move—and trust me, Harper, I'm far more clever than the common criminal. Now, if you don't mind—or even if you do mind—Nat and I have a vow to keep."

His arm tightened around her, her pained gasp slicing through Daniel like a dagger, and he raised his pistol so it was pointed at her chest, center-mass. The weapon was a .40 caliber Glock, no doubt carrying a very hot load. He meant to kill them both with one shot.

"No!" Daniel shouted, taking half a step forward.

"We promised. Together forever. In life and in—"

Ben's shot boomed, cutting off Miller's words, slicing into the right side of his chest, spinning both him and Natasha to their left. Her scream echoed off the stone wall as panic burst through her. She freed one arm and twisted, shoved and scratched in a frantic effort to get away as Miller landed, but the upper half of his body pinned her to the roof deck, the lower half dangling in air over the roof edge.

"Daniel!" she screamed, scrabbling and kicking at Miller, but he had a death grip—*please, God, let him be dying*—on her arm.

Horror propelled Daniel forward, closing the distance in seconds, as she was pulled over the low brick edging. Miller wasn't trying to pull himself back onto the roof. He was dragging Natasha off with him.

Daniel dived, skidding across the rough surface, and grabbed her around the waist just as Miller succeeded in heaving her body over the edge. Her scream vibrated in his ears, churned in his gut, her free arm flailing before she grabbed hold of Daniel's gun belt.

"Oh, God, Daniel…" Looking down, she kicked at Miller. "Let go, you crazy bastard! Let me go!"

He laughed. Miller actually laughed, though it was weak. "Never, Nat. Together…forever…"

"I've got you, Tash," Daniel said, forcing as much calm as he could fake into his voice. The bricks must be tearing up the tender skin on her stomach, but she was probably too scared to feel the pain. He wished Ben would shoot the son of a bitch again, but it was a risk. Miller might lose his grip, or he might clamp on even tighter. Natasha was already battered. She couldn't hold on much longer.

But Daniel would never let go.

"Hang on, babe. You promised to stay forever, remember?"

Her gaze locked with his even as her body slipped through his tightest grasp, falling another two inches. Tears welled in her eyes, and a whimper escaped that broke his heart. "I love you, Daniel."

"I know."

Heavy boots thudded, then Sam dropped to his knees next to Daniel. Cullen Simpson took the other side. Both men leaned over the wall, grabbing whatever part of her they could reach. It wasn't much—shirts tore, fabric didn't allow a good grip, skin got slick—but it eased a bit of the strain on Daniel's muscles.

"You guys have her?" Sam asked.

"I've got two belt loops," Simpson answered.

"I'm not letting go," Daniel said.

Grimly Sam released his hold and drew his pistol from its holster. Natasha's gaze was still on Daniel. He murmured, "It's going to be loud," and she darted a look at Sam. Panic flared anew in her face, but after a moment, it vanished. She looked down at RememberMe and said in a quiet voice, "I forgot you the moment I met you."

Sam took the shot.

Chapter 11

Nearly four weeks had passed since that day on the roof—painful because Natasha had had injuries that needed healing; quiet because everyone had given her and Daniel the privacy they'd needed; and happy because…well, everyone had given her and Daniel privacy.

Stacia had been elated that RememberMe was out of their lives, doing a little dance in the middle of the street she'd been crossing when Natasha called her that Monday night. *I won't be sorry*, she'd declared. *He tried to hurt you. He tried to throw you off a building! He was crazy. He was mean. And I'm going to celebrate his death.*

Natasha intended to celebrate the freedom his death had given her. No more fear, no more hiding, no more guilt.

She climbed the last couple of stairs, her hand trailing along the railing that gleamed like moonlight. At the top, she stood at the edge of the dance floor, comparing the dusty room she'd seen a month ago to this sweet-scented fairy-tale wonderland. Everything that could glisten or sparkle did, including her, she was sure, if she could find her reflection anywhere.

Her bruises had faded, the deep scrapes across her ribcage had healed and she no longer needed layers of makeup to cover the spectrum of colors the blow from Rob Miller had left her with. She was beautiful, Daniel had told her this morning. But he'd told her the same thing in the emergency room that day, and the next morning when she'd looked like an extra from one of Stacia's horror films. He was biased.

But she felt beautiful, and when she came up here tomorrow morning, she was going to feel incredibly beautiful.

They'd learned a lot about Rob Miller. He'd been an average cop, skillful with computers, not with people. He was egocentric, patronizing and never missed a chance to let his coworkers know he was superior to them in every way. The LA Police Department hadn't come across anyone willing to claim friendship with him. It didn't seem, when they'd searched his condo, that he'd had time for anything but work and stalking. It hadn't been a shrine, Flea said, so much as a repository: the life of Natasha Spencer in photos, notes and, yes, as Daniel had once suggested, discarded items. His dedication to his obsession had taken away Flea's breath.

Of course, his neighbors had said he was a quiet guy, rarely home but kept to himself when he was.

He'd also had a family who loved him. Who had

thought he was just odd; weren't most really smart people? Who had never imagined in their wildest dreams that he could stalk a stranger or had the capacity for violence. Who were grieving their son and brother as surely as Natasha's own family would have grieved her if Miller's plan had succeeded.

She felt sorry for them. Sorry that her side was relieved by his death while his side was bewildered and lost. Sorry that his twisted delusions had created a situation where the only way she could live was if he died.

He had set the rules, she reminded herself, and he had lost.

Quiet steps came up the stairs. She'd ventured out onto the ballroom floor without noticing, and when the footsteps stopped, she swirled around a few times to the music in her head. The third swirl ended with her facing Daniel. He wore his usual work clothes: gray suit, burgundy tie, white button-down. His coat was pushed back, his hands in his pockets as he looked at her.

He'd been her rock this past month. The first few days, her mood swings had been dangerous. She'd hated that Ben had been forced to shoot Miller without putting her at risk instead of killing him outright, and that Sam had then had to look the man in the face and kill him. She'd hated that the choked sob escaping her when she saw Miller's broken body covered on the sidewalk had been one of joy. She'd hated the dreams that plagued her the first few nights, the irrational fears that popped up from nowhere, the paralyzing thought that it could happen again.

Through it all, Daniel was there, strong, tender,

compassionate, understanding, loving. *I'm gonna love you like nobody's loved you.* And he had. He would.

He finally broke the stillness, strolling toward her. "They're gathering downstairs."

"Everyone?"

"Ben and Sam. Stacia and Nick. Jeffrey and Archer." He broke off, a grin forming. "Your mom and dad. Libby's having a hard time grasping that a daughter of hers would voluntarily walk into a police station, much less get married there, but your dad's keeping her calm."

She smiled, loving her parents less critically than she had in a long time. They'd been great role models for loving passionately and poor ones for keeping a commitment, but that was who they were. Natasha was okay with it now, because she'd found an incredible role model for both loving and committing in Daniel.

He reached her and slid his arms around her. When she nestled against him, she felt again that overwhelming sense of *home*.

He began humming and moving her ever so slightly around the dance floor. He was a beautiful dancer, but sometimes, Stacia used to tease, they weren't dancing, just engaging in foreplay. This was one of those times. Heat curled through her as his body pressed against hers, her breasts tingling, her knees going weak. If their families weren't downstairs, ready to come up as soon as Sam's minister arrived, they might be doing a whole lot more in the police station than rehearsing for the wedding.

Finally he spoke again. "Your mom and Stacia want you to spend the night at the hotel with them."

"Do they have plans to put me under guard to make sure I don't do another runner?"

It was a credit to Daniel that his immediate response was a sweet, confident smile. "If we thought that would happen, we'd put you in a cell downstairs. Though, if you stay with me instead, we could have a tutorial on Fun with Handcuffs 101. That would accomplish the same thing."

She rubbed provocatively against him. "That sounds tempting."

They swayed a few more inches, then he murmured, "It's okay if you want to stay with them."

She considered it for a moment. Most brides she knew spent their last single night in their own place or with family. But none of them had almost died a few weeks before. "I'm not sure I'm ready to walk into the hotel again," she finally confessed. It was a beautiful place, but the memories were too recent, the screams still echoing. It would take some time before she could climb those stairs again. Live the trauma again. Face those damn metal birds again.

"And I *know* I'm not ready to spend a night away from you."

He kissed her, long and slow and lazy, and she melted into him. Some dazed part of her mind realized they'd stopped their pretense of dancing, and another wondered if they really needed a rehearsal and a dinner catered by Mrs. Little Bear, and a third part wished they could just disappear into their own little blissful world.

But a truly blissful world needed far more than two people, no matter how much in love they were. It needed family and friends, and judging from the noise, theirs were gathering at the top of the stairs, full of warmth and love and happiness for them, at least until the kiss went on longer than they wanted to wait.

The pastor cleared his throat and wryly suggested, "You might want to let her breathe now." When Daniel finally did so, leaving Natasha light-headed in a way that had nothing to do with lack of oxygen, the man went on. "Are you ready?"

Daniel stepped back, smoothed his tie and took her hand. "For better or worse."

Her smile was automatic. "Good or bad."

He oh, so gently touched her face, his voice lowering to a husky rumble. "Come rain…"

Tears welled in her eyes, and pure happiness bloomed inside her. She wouldn't do a runner. This was right. Perfect. Exactly where she belonged. Resting her head on his shoulder, she finished the line for him. "Or come shine."

* * * * *

Don't miss out on any other suspenseful stories from Marilyn Pappano:

Killer Secrets
Detective Defender
Nights with a Thief
Bayou Hero

Available now from Harlequin Romantic Suspense!

She wasn't accustomed to sharing a bed with anyone.

Irritated, she flopped onto her back, trying to find a comfortable position.

"Are you going to do that all night?" Xander asked.

"Sorry. I'm not used to having company in my bed," she groused. "And you take up more than your share."

"I promise I don't have cooties."

"I know that."

He chuckled. "Then relax."

"It's not that…" She risked a glance toward him. "It's because…there's history between us."

"One time does not history make," Xander said. "Or so I'm told."

She wasn't going to argue the point. Exhaling, she deliberately closed her eyes and rolled to her side, plumping up her pillow and settling once again.

A long beat of silence followed until Xander said, "Do you really regret that much what happened between us?"

That was a loaded question—one she didn't want to answer. She regretted being messed up in the head, which made it impossible to trust, which in turn made her a nightmare to be in a relationship with. Not that she wanted anything real with Xander.

Or anyone.

Her silence seemed an answer in itself. "I guess so," Xander replied with a sigh. "That's an ego-buster."

Scarlett turned to glare at him. "Did you ever think maybe it has nothing to do with you?" she said, unable to just let him think whatever he liked. For some reason, it mattered with Xander. "Look, aside from the fact that I'm your boss…I'm just not the type to form unnecessary attachments. Trust me, it's better that way. For everyone involved."

Every time she ignored her instincts and allowed something to happen, it ended badly.

"I'm not cut out for relationships."

"Me, either."

His simple agreement coaxed a reluctant chuckle out of her. "Yeah? Two peas in a pod, I guess."

"Or two broken people with too many sharp edges to be allowed around normal people."

"Ain't that the truth," she agreed, the tension lifting a little. She turned to face him, tucking her arm under her head. "Maybe that's why we're so good at what we do… We can compartmentalize like world-class athletes without blinking an eye."

"Mental boxes for everything," Xander returned with a half grin. They were joking but only sort of. That was the sad reality that they both recognized. "I know why I'm broken, but what's your story, Rhodes?"

This was around the time she usually shut down. But that feeling of safety had returned and she found herself sharing, even when she didn't want to.

Don't miss
Soldier for Hire *by Kimberly Van Meter,*
available December 2018 wherever
Harlequin® Romantic Suspense books
and ebooks are sold.

www.Harlequin.com

Need an adrenaline rush from nail-biting tales
(and irresistible males)?

Check out **Harlequin Intrigue®**
and **Harlequin® Romantic Suspense** books!

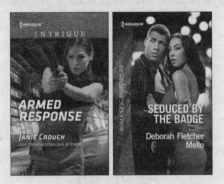

New books available every month!

CONNECT WITH US AT:

Facebook.com/groups/HarlequinConnection

 Facebook.com/HarlequinBooks

Twitter.com/HarlequinBooks

Instagram.com/HarlequinBooks

 Pinterest.com/HarlequinBooks

ReaderService.com

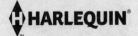

**ROMANCE WHEN
YOU NEED IT**

Love Harlequin romance?

DISCOVER.

Be the first to find out about promotions,
news and exclusive content!

Facebook.com/HarlequinBooks

Twitter.com/HarlequinBooks

Instagram.com/HarlequinBooks

Pinterest.com/HarlequinBooks

ReaderService.com

EXPLORE.

Sign up for the Harlequin e-newsletter and
download a free book from any series at
TryHarlequin.com.

CONNECT.

Join our Harlequin community to share
your thoughts and connect with other
romance readers!
Facebook.com/groups/HarlequinConnection

**ROMANCE WHEN
YOU NEED IT**

HSOCIAL2018

Earn points on your purchase of new Harlequin
books from participating retailers.

Turn your points into **FREE BOOKS**
of your choice!

Join for FREE today at
www.HarlequinMyRewards.com.

Harlequin My Rewards is a free program (no fees)
without any commitments or obligations.

MYR18

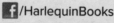